THE UNINVITED

Egg Dancing
Ark Baby
The Paper Eater
War Crimes for the Home
The Ninth Life of Louis Drax
My Dirty Little Book of Stolen Time
The Rapture

THE UNINVITED

A NOVEL

LIZ JENSEN

BLOOMSBURY

NEW YORK · LONDON · NEW DELHI · SYDNEY

Published by Bloomsbury USA, New York

All papers used by Bloomsbury USA are natural, recyclable products made from wood grown in well-managed forests. The manufacturing processes conform to the environmental regulations of the country of origin.

LIBRARY OF CONGRESS CATALOGING-IN-PUBLICATION DATA HAS BEEN APPLIED FOR.

ISBN: 978-1-60819-992-1

First U.S. Edition 2013

1 3 5 7 9 10 8 6 4 2

Typeset by Hewer Text UK Ltd, Edinburgh
Printed in the U.S.A.

For Clare Blatchford Rees
An inspiration

Our birth is but a sleep and a forgetting
The soul that rises with us, our life's star
Hath had elsewhere its setting
And cometh from afar . . .
Hence in a season of calm weather
Though inland far we be
Our souls have sight of that immortal sea
Which brought us hither
Can in a moment travel thither
And see the children sport upon the shore
And hear the mighty waters rolling evermore.

William Wordsworth, *Ode: Intimations of*
Immortality from Recollections of Early Childhood

There is always a moment in childhood when the door opens and lets the future in.

Graham Greene, *The Power and the Glory*

PROLOGUE

MASS HYSTERICAL OUTBREAKS rarely have identifiable inceptions, but the date I recall most vividly is Sunday 16th September, when a young child in butterfly pyjamas slaughtered her grandmother with a nail-gun to the neck. The attack took place in a family living-room in a leafy Harrogate cul-de-sac, the kind where no one drops litter and you can still hear birdsong.

Three shots. Three half-inch bolts of steel. The jugular didn't stand a chance.

No reason, no warning.

The little girl's father was the first on the scene. Hearing a blunt vocal noise – the woman had tried to scream – he rushed in to find her haemorrhaging on the sofa, while the kid sat staring at the wall in a trance that resembled open-eyed sleep. When the others joined him and saw the blood, they all had the same thought: a terrible accident.

But it was a mistake to think that, because a few seconds later the child jolted awake and grabbed the tool again. Before anyone realised her intention, she'd put it to her father's face and fired.

Eyes are delicate, so no chance there either. He was fortunate it wasn't worse.

A lightweight pump-action Black & Decker. One murder, one blinding. Two minutes. No accident.

She can't have been the first. But I'll call her Child One.

At the time of the assault, she had just turned seven.

Is violence contagious? By what mechanism does a series of apparently random events start cohering into a narrative of cause and effect? Can there be such a thing as psychic occupation?

For me, these became pressing questions.

The day the news broke, I'd just flown in from Taiwan. In the car park of Glasgow airport I blinked in the sunshine. After the pressurised heat of downtown Taipei, the air shuddered with freshness. While my plane was touching down, the little girl was preparing her weapon. By the time I'd cleared customs, she'd executed the attack. And as I drove towards the coast and the ferry, skirting the sprawling edges of grey Scottish towns, two police officers were contemplating a crime scene which they later described as 'the most distressing and perverted' of their careers.

I lived, at the time, on the island of Arran, in a landscape that flitted unpredictably between light and dark: shafts of sunlight, charcoal clouds, sudden rainbows, the pale featherings of fog on scrub, the pewter glint of the Atlantic. I'd rented a stone cottage on the eastern coast straight after my split with Kaitlin: ideal for someone who cherishes his solitude and needs only appear at Head Office on the rare occasion. It was dark and low-ceilinged. The front door opened on to a flank of scrubland a short walk from the shore: in the middle distance lay the rhomboid outline of a black granite rock and a cluster of hawthorns, side-swiped by wind. I could watch the rotating blades of the wind turbines on the horizon for hours. At the back of the cottage, by an abandoned vegetable patch, lay some rusted tractor parts and an enamel bathtub on brick supports which a previous tenant had turned into a crude pond. When I cleared away the chickweed, I found a pale goldfish. Once in a while I'd empty the toaster and feed it crumbs.

'Here, Mr Fish, Mr Fish, Mr Fish!' I'd say. Strange to hear a human voice, in that empty place.

There are certain fixtures in my life which constitute a kind of home. The antique optometrist's charts in Cyrillic, Hindi, Chinese and Arabic that Professor Whybray bequeathed me when he retired; my paint catalogues, foreign-language dictionaries and folk-tale compendiums; some of the mathematical diagrams and origami models I've constructed across the years, and a cardboard dinosaur Freddy made at primary school. Good shelving is important. I have that too. I'm a creature of habit. After three days in Taiwan working flat out on the sabotage case, it was comforting to be surrounded by what I cherish. Fortress Hesketh, Kaitlin used to call me. Entry forbidden. If she had a point – and yes, the general consensus was that she had – then my self-containment wasn't something I had a mind to fix.

★　　★　　★

I had one day to write up the Taipei investigation, and explain the anomaly of Sunny Chen. That's what was preoccupying me as I unpacked my suitcase. Five identical shirts, ditto boxer shorts, two pairs of trousers, wash-bag, Chinese dictionary, electronics. I put on a wash, then flipped on the TV to catch the midday news. *Growth figures up for the third consecutive season; the UN warns of 'catastrophe within a generation' if birth rates fail to drop; severe weather alert as Hurricane Veronica heads for the West coast.* But it was the domestic atrocity that snared me. My exhaustion lent the report the drifting, sub-oceanic quality of a nightmare.

The little girl's grandparents were on their regular weekly visit to her home. The distraught family insisted that nobody had done anything to antagonise the child. Neither on that Sunday or any other day. When she woke that morning, she was in good spirits, according to her mother. She had even recounted a dream about 'walking around in a beautiful white desert that sparkled'. It looked like Heaven, she said.

The TV showed a semi-detached house in a Harrogate suburb. The reporter demonstrating how a small hand might clasp and operate a nail-gun of this type. A psychologist struggling to hypothesise why such a young child would turn on people she loved. An elderly neighbour declaring the family to be 'perfectly ordinary' and giving the detail about the pyjamas. Her own granddaughter had a similar pair. From Marks and Spencer, she said. 'With blue butterflies on.'

Strange, what makes people cry.

I wondered what kind of blue. Celestial, Frosted Steel Aquamarine, Inky Pool, Luna? I could name you thirty-eight off the top of my head.

As a boy, I read everything I could lay my hands on, regardless of its function: dishwasher instruction manuals, TV schedules, the works of Dostoyevsky, lists of cereal ingredients, my mother's *Cosmopolitan*, fishing magazines, porn. But mostly I devoured comics featuring a panoply of onomatopoeic words deployed to render specific sounds. A blow to the jaw would be *BAM,* while an arrow loosed from a bow might be *ZOOOSHHH.* A regular gun would typically go *BANG.* But a nail-gun's sound is shallower, and features a distinctive click. I would spell it *SCHTUUKH.*

Plato suggested that the realm we inhabit after death is the same territory we lived in before birth: a fusion of time and space that encompasses both pre- and post-existence. Ever since the High Energy Research Organisation in Japan confirmed the results of CERN's experiments in which neutrinos travelled faster than light, it has struck me that Plato was closer to the mark than anyone could have imagined. Not least Einstein, whose notion of special relativity had been violated. The fact that a unified theory of physics had come within our grasp for the first time in human history was something I came to reflect on much later, in relation to Child One's attack and the others that followed. But perception is personal. In the early days, some saw the atrocity as a symptom of a spoiled generation's 'pathological' craving for attention in a world in which the future of mankind, through its own mismanagement, appeared blasted. I'd seen no evidence of this myself, in my observations of Freddy and his entourage. On a point of style, I also considered the interpretation to be unduly masochistic. As an anthropologist I read the phenomenon more as a sick fairy tale, a parable of dysfunctional times. None of us got it right. The message was written in letters too big to read, letters that could only be deciphered from a vast distance or an unusual angle. We were as good as blind. This, by the way, is a figurative expression. Unlike many on the spectrum, I can deploy those.

The nail-gun murder struck me with particular force because Child One was Freddy's age: seven. Having made the association, I couldn't help picturing my stepson aiming his catapult at another human being and letting fly.

Who is Freddy's chosen target, in this image?

It doesn't put me in a good light, but I'll say it anyway, because it's the truth: his mother, Kaitlin.

I see Freddy, with his curly black hair and pixie face, take aim and fire at her heart – *ZOOOSHHH* – and I hear her cry of shock.

One of my chief coping mechanisms, in mental emergencies, involves origami: I carry an imaginary sheaf of delicate rice paper in my head, in a range of shades, to fold into classical shapes. When the image of Freddy shooting Kaitlin first reared up I swiftly folded eleven of the Japanese cranes known as *ozuru,* but I couldn't banish it. Kaitlin used to call me, affectionately, an 'incurable materialist'. Later, this changed to 'a robot made of meat'. This is unfair. I'm not a machine. I feel things. I just register them differently. The story of the pyjama-clad killer and the unwelcome images it inspired rocked my equilibrium.

After she confessed to her affair, and its excruciating nature, and the lies ('white lies', she insisted) that she'd told to cover it, Kaitlin and I stuck it out for a while, at her insistence. This involved a form of mental torture known as relationship counselling.

What do you most admire about Kaitlin, Hesketh?

Kaitlin, can you identify what attracted you to Hesketh when you first met?

As well as being irrelevant to the issue in hand, it was purposeless. There are certain things I am not cut out to do. Fieldwork, my mentor Professor Whybray always told me, was 'very probably' one of them. Sharing my life with a woman, I'd long suspected, was another. The fact that my first and only attempt had ended in failure confirmed it definitively. I would not be trying again. I moved away from London and the home Kaitlin still shared with Freddy. I have always been fascinated by islands, both linguistically and because of the social-Darwinian speculations they invite, so Arran suited me perfectly. That said, I saw few people: the cottage stood alone, five miles from the nearest village, in a landscape of sea and heather, boulders and sheep. Here, with the capital far behind me, I took strategic command of myself by developing a ritualised schedule of work and half-hour walks, began work on an ambitious origami mollusc project, and trained myself to think of Kaitlin in the past tense. But nothing could fill the vacuum left by the boy.

'Look at me properly. In the eye,' Kaitlin used to say, at the climax of a fight, or sex.

It was a kind of taunt. She knew I couldn't. That I'd simply turn my face away or shut my eyes tighter.

When she got me, she got the things I was, including the elements of my personality she deemed defective. She got the package called Hesketh Lock and all that it contained. Where was the logic in wanting me to be someone other than myself?

Freddy never did that. He'd never heard of Asperger's syndrome. And if he had, he wouldn't have cared. He accepted me from the start. To him I was Hesketh.

Just Hesketh.

Anthropology is a science which requires you to observe your fellow men and women, their traditions and their beliefs, as you would members of another species. The impulse to fabulate is a natural response to a confusing and contradictory world. Grasping this helped me to unlock the thought systems of my fellow men, and move on from the state of frustrated bafflement that dogged my childhood and teenage years. I grew adept at sketching mental flow charts to track the repercussions of real events as well as hypothetical scenarios. Tracing narrative patterns through the overlapping circles of Venn diagrams – still my tool of choice – revealed to me the endless interconnectedness of human imagination and memory. Armed with these templates, I worked on adapting my behaviour. Under Professor Whybray's tutelage, I learned to mimic and then assimilate some of the behaviours I observed. I was not the first: others had exploited their apparent disadvantage with great success, he told me – most notably an internationally celebrated Professor of Behavioural Psychology. But apparently I still lack some of the 'normal social graces'. Men like Ashok, my boss at Phipps & Wexman, tend to take me as they find me. Women are different. They see a tall, dark, well-built man with strongly delineated features, and this classic combination triggers something at cellular level: a biological imperative. When they discover my personality is at odds with what they wishfully intuit from my 'handsomeness', their disappointment is boundless. It's often accompanied by a disturbing rage.

Ashok once said to me, 'We're all liars, bud. It's human nature.'

No, I thought. He's wrong. Through a quirk of DNA, I am not part of that 'we'. I can get obsessive about things. Or sidetracked. I can appear brutal too, I'm told.

But I know right from wrong. And I revere the truth.

So you will at least find in me an honest narrator.

In the days that followed the Harrogate attack, the little girl in blue butterfly pyjamas still refused to speak.

GIRL WHO DREAMED OF HEAVEN –
AND MADE HELL
SICK CHERUB'S SHOTS OF HATE

What happened next to the child whose dream about a sparkling white desert gave birth to such lurid headlines? Speculating on the possibilities and their variables, I pictured the family moving to another part of the country, or even abroad, to start a new life. The child would accompany them, if the father could still bear to be around her. If not, they'd install her in a secure home. I'll admit that I considered the case to be as unique as it was isolated: a thing of its own and of itself. I am a natural joiner of dots, and I saw no dots to join.

And then came the distressing phone call about Sunny Chen, which sent my thoughts hurtling back to Taiwan. And because of the drastic nature of what followed, Child One was relegated to the back of my mind.

CHAPTER 1

THE PHENOMENON KNOWN as the fairy ring is caused by fungal spore pods spreading outwards like a water ripple around a biologically dead zone. In European legend, they represent the gateway to the fairy world, a parallel universe with its own laws and time-scales. The rings are evidence of dark forces: demons, shooting stars, lightning strikes.

Jump into one and bad luck will befall you.

From the air, Taipei is like a fairy ring: a city built in a crater encircled by mountains.

It was early morning when my plane touched down, but the day's heat was already rising. I'd spent the flight from Manchester to Taipei listening to audio lessons on headphones to brush up on my Mandarin. When the last one came to an end, I pressed play and started again from the beginning. I once attended an intensive language course in Shanghai, hoping to refine elements of my PhD. Linguistically, I am more of a reader than a speaker, so inevitably it was the ideograms that excited me most. I'd copy pages of Chinese characters and use the dictionary to make translations.

The effort on the plane paid off. My taxi driver understood me when I gave him directions. The air shimmered invigoratingly, reminding me of TV static.

I dislike change of any kind. But paradoxically, something in me – a kind of information-hunger – seeks and requires it. If sharks stop moving, they die. Kaitlin once said my brain was like that. We drove past suburban tower blocks stacked like grubby sugar cubes; flat-screen billboards and rotating hoardings that advertised toothpaste, nappies, kung-fu movies, mobile phones. All this alongside glimpses of an older order: street hawkers selling tofu, lychees, starfruit, sweets, caged chickens and cigarettes beneath tattered frangipanis and jacarandas. Violet bougainvillea frothed over fences, and potted orchids swayed in the breeze. Even with sunglasses on, the intense light drilled into my retinas. Here and there, on street corners or in doorways and temple entrances, thin trails of incense smoke drifted up from offerings to the dead: fruit, sweets, paper money. For the Chinese, September is Ghost Month. The spirits of the dead pour out from Hell, demanding food and appeasement, and wreaking havoc.

I inhaled the foreignness.

Fraud is a business like any other. Anthropologically speaking, it involves the meeting, co-operation and communication of tribes. The space between sharp practice and corporate fraud is the delicate territory Phipps & Wexman regularly treads. As Ashok tells clients in his presentations: 'After a catastrophic PR shock, our job is to ensure nothing like that ever happens again anywhere on your global team, because it won't need to. Phipps & Wexman has the best investigative brains in the business. And we have the success stories to prove it. Sanwell, the Go Corporation, Quattro, GTTL, Klein and Mason: all companies whose reputations have been definitively recast by our profile makeovers.' I have heard this speech eighteen and a quarter times. I even feature in it. ('Hesketh Lock, our cross-culture specialist, who has analysed sabotage patterns from Indonesia to Iceland.') Ashok has that easy American way with audiences. 'Nobody at Phipps & Wexman claims to be saving the world,' he continues, 'but we're sure as hell pouring oil on its troubled waters.' It always stimulates the clients, this notion that we're healers. Shamans, even. It was the brainchild of Stephanie Mulligan, a behavioural psychologist with whom I have an excruciating history.

They clap and clap.

Hardwood trees are slow to grow, and prices have skyrocketed in recent years. There were logging restrictions, even before the weak anti-deforestation protocols. But where there's a will, there's a loophole. And a panoply of crooks. The fraudulent trading of hardwoods culled from protected forestland is a global business lucrative enough to have spawned countless millionaires. Jenwai Timber's bosses and their suppliers and shippers among them.

The week before my visit to Taiwan, an anonymous source had sent the Taipei branch of the police's Fraud Investigation Office a set of documentation relating to the purchase of hardwood for Jenwai's timber factory from a Malaysian supplier. These impressively produced forgeries had served to whitewash a raft of illegal transactions concerning wood sourced in Laos and marked, for good measure, with apparently legitimate stamps. The paperchase that followed the first police raid triggered further investigations, and within a matter of days, the entire Laos–Taiwan element of an extensive international logging scandal was exposed. Detectives, environmental campaigners and the media were already busy writing up their reports. But my own assessment would be of a very different nature.

As investigators affiliated to a multi-national legal firm, we'd been hired by Ganjong Inc., the parent organisation under which Jenwai Timber traded. At Jenwai Timber, the main players consisted of corrupt NGO staff, Laotian traffickers, Thai middlemen and Chinese factory managers. And one employee with a conscience. My mission was to find him.

In most organisations, whistle-blowing is seen as a form of sabotage. But it's impolitic to say this publicly. Phipps & Wexman's brochures delicately classify the phenomenon as 'a sub-story in a wider David and Goliath narrative of workplace unrest'. Officially, I was in Taiwan to identify the whistle-blower, pronounce him a hero and award him a generous financial package or 'golden thank you' for alerting Ganjong Inc., via the police, to the corruption it had – unwittingly, it stressed – presided over. In reality, I was there to do a situation autopsy, as a part of a wider damage-limitation exercise.

★   ★   ★

The Taipei branch of the national Fraud Investigation Office, a modest low-rise to the south of the city, had the feel of a huge walk-in fridge. Here, over the course of several hours, kept awake by coffee, I heard several theories about the whistle-blower's identity from the police and a sharp-featured young journalist who had covered the case for his newspaper. Although they were curious about his identity, their main concern was the crime itself, and the domino effect of its exposure. They seemed puzzled that Ganjong should have called in a Western personnel specialist.

'It's known as the Outsider Impartiality Effect,' I tell them. 'My presence here is Ganjong's message that it rewards honesty and condemns corruption. Standard strategy.'

The sharp-featured journalist made a face I interpreted as 'wry' and said, 'Cover your ass, right?' And they all laughed. He went on to speculate that the mystery man was in fact female, and the wife of a Jenwai manager who had been having an affair with a bar-girl. This prompted further theories: a shop-floor grudge, a power tussle between senior managers, a rival company's attempt to bring Jenwai down, infiltration by eco-campaigners. I spent the rest of the day probing deeper, only to find the actual evidence was either thin or non-existent. It's often the case, at the beginning of an investigation, that you spend eight hours in an over-air-conditioned office, learning what seems barely one level up from rumour. It's only later that you might spot a stray detail that's part of a bigger pattern, and things fall into place. Over 80 per cent of the time, that doesn't happen.

★　　★　　★

The next morning I was at the timber plant on the outskirts of Taipei by 8.25 for my meeting with Mr Yeh, the only Jenwai manager untouched by the scandal: at the time of the illegal wood-trafficking transactions, he'd been on sick leave with colon cancer. The air was humid, and pulsed with the heavy, electric heat that heralds thunder. Undulating lines of *altocumulus castellanus* and *altocumulus floccus* patterned the sky.

The plant itself was a functional warehouse building in a high-fenced compound. In the office section near the front gates, the skeletal Mr Yeh welcomed me with a dry handshake and we exchanged business cards. I accepted his with both hands according to custom. The skin of his scalp, which was the distinctive yellow-grey of Dulux's 1997 River Pearl, looked alarmingly thin and desiccated.

'I am pleased to meet you Mr Lock. You are very tall,' he said. Then he laughed. In Chinese culture, amusement display can mask embarrassment.

'One metre and ninety-eight centimetres,' I told him, pre-emptively. 'But I've stopped growing, I promise.' This is a joke I have learned to deploy to 'break the ice', but Yeh didn't laugh, as Westerners tend to, so I inclined my head and told him in Chinese that I was honoured to meet him. This worked better: he broke into a cadaverous smile and complimented me on my facility. I told him languages were a hobby of mine, though my Chinese was unfortunately rudimentary.

'Call me Martin.' His English was assured and American-accented.

'If you'll call me Hesketh.'

'Hesketh. Unusual name.'

'Originally Norse. It means horse-racetrack.'

'Horse-racetrack?' He laughed. 'And Lock is a Chinese name. But spelled L-O-K. In Cantonese it means happiness. Joy. Good name. Lucky name. Lucky-Lok.' He paused. 'So if you should bet on horses, you win. Ha ha.' Then his face changed. 'As soon as the current orders are completed the factory will close. It is a terrible situation, Mr Lock. Hesketh. It pains me.' He touched his chest, as if to show me precisely where it hurt. In the cottage, five to the left on Shelf Three, I have a book of da Vinci's anatomical drawings. The valves, aortas and arteries of an ox heart are on page eighteen. 'By the way. I am sorry for the way I look. I know it is shocking.'

'No, I'm interested. I like seeing new things.'

There was quite a long pause which I did not know how to fill. Then he nodded towards the door and said, 'Well, Hesketh. You didn't come here to talk about death.'

In his office, we settled on either side of a desk littered with wood samples labelled in both Chinese and English. It took half an hour to get through my list of questions. He answered diligently, checking dates and figures on his computer. It all added up, and he appeared clean. As for the four female administrative staff, they had already been eliminated by the police: none of them had access to the relevant files.

'I'd like to see round the factory,' I told him.

'Of course. Our operations manager will be happy to show you.'

He made a call and within minutes, a slight man he introduced as Sun-kiu 'Sunny' Chen appeared in a hard hat. I'd been curious to meet Sunny Chen, not least because one of the fraud officers had referred to him as 'an oddball', a term which always piques my interest. He hadn't gone into details, but just tapped the side of his head in the international gesture denoting madness, and said I'd see for myself. The others had grinned.

Sunny Chen's movements were jerky and puppet-like. I couldn't tell his age. Mid-forties perhaps. He was diminutive, with much darker skin than Martin Yeh (Monsoon River) and a hectic look. The two men conversed briefly: I missed most of what they said, but their body language told me there was respect between them. Sunny Chen and I shook hands. We began in Chinese, but I found myself struggling, so after two and a half sentences we switched.

'You know, my father worked here, until he retired. My grand-father too, and four uncles. Jenwai was a good company. Moral. Trustworthy.' Sunny Chen wiped his brow, which bore a sheen of sweat.

Martin Yeh sighed. 'If I had been here . . .' He didn't finish his sentence, but shrugged and began a new one. This was about need-ing to go home and rest. I responded that this seemed wise, given his health status. After I'd seen the factory, he said, Sunny would take me to lunch on his behalf. The two of them had a swift exchange in Chinese, about the name and location of the restaurant. Then we said goodbye and I followed Sunny Chen outside.

The courtyard faced the factory entrance, which was festooned with warning signs and surveillance cameras. In the shade of its concrete flank, Sunny Chen offered me a cigarette which I declined. He lit one for himself and inhaled deeply. His fingers were stained with nicotine. He jerked his head towards the building. You could hear the machinery inside working at full tilt.

'So what do you make of the whistle-blower?' I asked.

'He deserves to die,' said Sunny Chen. 'In fact, I would like to kill him myself.' Then he laughed. His teeth were an ivory colour – somewhere between Silver Birch and Musk Keg.

'Why?'

'He has brought us shame.' This remark indicated he was more bothered by corporate loss of face than by the company's intrinsic rottenness. Did this make him a traditionalist? I made a mental note.

'Have you any idea who he is?'

His head gave an abrupt twitch. 'The police asked me the same thing. And I said yes. But they didn't listen. Please come in. I will show you inside.'

In an antechamber near the entrance, we put on fibre face masks and overalls. Mine were far too small. Sunny Chen gave me a hard hat like his own with built-in ear mufflers. I like wearing headgear. The skull feels pleasingly cushioned.

'We will have to shout in there,' he said, waving me in.

In the vegetable world there's no real time of death. In the right conditions, flowers can last a week, irradiated strawberries a month, apples or onions a year. Technically, a tree is killed when it is chopped down. But its aroma – of bark, of sap, of dense, massed fibre – lingers for decades afterwards. It is a smell that attracts me in the same way as certain colours, shades of violet and green in particular. Inside the factory, the trunks that were being processed were freshly felled, so it was overwhelming: thick and heady and mixed with machine oil. Parallel rows of conveyor belts fed huge tree trunks into mechanical saws which sliced them as effortlessly as a knife cutting through cheese, then dropped them on to another belt system which bore them to the far end of the warehouse, where they were sorted according to width and mechanically stacked. It was a cleverly constructed system that required minimal manpower. The fifteen workmen I saw ticked off checklists, swept bark and sawdust from the floor, drove forklifts and righted skewed planks on the conveyors. The loading of the trunks and the shifting and transportation of the cut wood, Chen told me, was done outside. Like all manifestations of mechanical efficiency, the process was mesmerising to watch, despite the searing noise. And even that had its merits: it was regular, and it meant something. Everything was powdered in a layer of fine, dark wood dust. Standing there in my comfortable helmet, I felt very content. I was Lucky Lok.

'Pencil cedar,' shouted Sunny Chen in English over the racket, pointing. 'From Indonesia. Over there is Malaysian kauri and teak.'

He indicated another section of the shop floor, where wide planks of a darker wood were being sliced to the narrower width typically used for decking and garden furniture. The offcuts and shavings from the closest sawing machine fell on to a conveyor belt, which transported them to the overhead funnel of the machine in front of us, which stood about four metres high. Sunny mouthed something I couldn't hear, and directed me to the wide service ladder. By the time we reached the top rung I was sweating and high on the atmosphere. Peering over the metal rim that curved downward like a hanging lip, we gazed far down into the dark whirring hole of its innards.

'Long way to fall!' Sunny Chen shouted, pointing down. The pulping mechanism worked like a giant food processor, accepting whatever it was fed and chomping it into a coarse mash of wood-chips. 'Turn you into hamburger!' His face mask hid his features. I'm not good at second-guessing people's emotions but his eyes didn't seem to be smiling. The flayed wood was collected in a vast skip below. 'We use this to manufacture chipboard,' he yelled. 'The sawdust is re-used also, so nothing's wasted, all recycled.'

I stared at the jostling blur. Repetitive movements snare me. As a child, I would happily watch the washing machine for an entire cycle.

'So you said you knew who exposed the corruption?' I yelled at him when we had climbed back down to the bottom.

He didn't answer directly. 'I showed the police something important here, but they didn't take it seriously.' His brow was beaded with sweat. He pulled off his mask and wiped it with his hand, leaving a smear of wood powder. 'Messy place.' Still no smile. 'Come with me.'

I followed him round the base of the machine to the side nearest the wall, where he pointed to what appeared to be a small, blurred hand-print low down on one side of its steel flank. You had to bend down to see it properly. 'Evidence.'

'Of what?' I asked. But he just shook his head and fiddled with his piece of wood. Perhaps I had misheard him. 'Mr Chen, Mr Chen, Mr Chen! What are you saying?' I shouted.

'It means they come here to wreck things. They hate us! They hate everything we do!' He seemed agitated.

'Who do you mean?' My throat was drying up from the wood dust.

'The ones that made this mark. The ones you are looking for!'

'Campaigners?'

'No! Not campaigners. Just very desperate and naïve people.'

This was making no sense to me. 'What did the police say?' I yelled.

'They say it's nothing. Just a hand-mark. Can't get finger-prints.'

This didn't surprise me: I could picture the detective dismissing it, and see why he called Sunny Chen an 'oddball' and made the international madness gesture. What Sunny showed me was nothing more than a crude smear with a bit of wood dust on it, as if someone had slammed a dirty hand against the machine's steel side.

'They say the CCTV doesn't show who made it.' He pointed to the overhead security camera. This didn't surprise me either. It might have been there for weeks, and those images are typically on a three-day recycling loop. 'But it is important, Mr Lock!'

Everything has an explanation. It's just a question of identifying and deploying the right analytical template. The frustration I felt was with myself.

'Is it a message?'

'Maybe. Yes. Yes, a message.'

'So what's it saying, this message?'

He shook his head and said, 'I don't know. You just need to note this down for doing your job right, OK? I say the same thing to police.'

'But what do *you* think it means?' I persisted.

He shook his head. 'It's bad. Like a warning. Like a stop sign. I am telling you, it's evidence!'

I don't know much about unbalanced minds, but I do know the importance of meticulousness. I hadn't travelled all this way to miss something. If Sunny Chen said it was evidence then I'd treat it accordingly. I took out my camera and photographed the little smear of filth on the wall. Since it was only three feet or so from floor level, I had to crouch down to get a decent angle on it. If it was a hand-mark, whoever had made it was very short, or had assumed an odd posture.

'I'll take a sample too,' I called to him, and he nodded vigorously. I scraped some of it off and folded it into some origami paper for analysis. It was crystalline and coarse. A brown close to Cinnamon Stick with a few darker grains. It looked like mud and salt, with traces of fibre. I sniffed it and noted a faint vegetable smell with a touch of iron to it.

When we'd disposed of our protective gear and come outside, the sky was darkening and grumbling with thunder. We walked to the main road where Sunny Chen flagged down a taxi. As we drove, flashes of sheet lightning began to scald the sky. The restaurant was in a square at the edge of a public park: we reached it just as the rain began to fall. Huge, swollen drops, silted with fine grit, hammering the formal flowerbeds. Picnickers, roller-bladers and children with kites rushed in all directions across the concrete prairie. I like to be in countries where everyone has black hair. The running people resembled matches being scattered by a giant hand.

Sunny Chen whipped out an umbrella and beneath its shelter we sprinted towards the nearby park and up some steps into a garish, soy-smelling place with Funfair Crimson tablecloths and matching napkins. The wind coming in from the open balconies set the lanterns overhead gyrating: I had to tear my eyes away from their spin. Sunny ordered for both of us and we sat contemplating the antics of the sky outside, lavishly lit one moment, and dark the next, the deluge lending everything a neon brashness. The greens of the foliage seemed to vibrate.

As we waited for the food, Sunny Chen's mood shifted. His eyes roamed the restaurant, as though he was expecting someone to appear. At one point he reached for the salt dish, took a pinch of crystals and put it on the end of his tongue. This struck me as strange, and I speculated it was due to a residual nervousness. To reconnect to him, I asked him a few questions in Mandarin which he answered patiently, using simple phrases I could understand. I learned that he had a wife who was a teacher, and three daughters, two still at school and one at university. When he asked about my own domestic arrangement, I told him I had recently split up with Kaitlin (for simplicity's sake I called her 'my wife') and I now lived alone. I told him about Freddy, that I collected foreign-language dictionaries and paint-colour charts (here I used the translation app on my phone) and made origami. At this latter news his eyebrows shot up. People have trouble believing someone big can do something delicate.

Small dishes of spicy Szechuan food arrived: squid in black-bean sauce, chicken and chilli, wonton soup, jasmine rice, green tea. He explained them to me in both languages and I memorised the new vocabulary. Then we filled our soy dishes and began to eat. We both got lost in the food for a while. It was excellent.

'Would you say that the mark you showed me is a hand-print?' I asked after four minutes.

'Yes,' he said, putting down his chopsticks. 'It appeared after Ghost Day. You know Ghost Day?'

'Yes. It falls on the fifteenth day of the seventh moon of the lunar calendar.' His eyes narrowed. I'd aroused curiosity. 'I have a good memory for anything I've seen written down,' I explained. 'Especially facts involving numbers.'

I hadn't mentioned my PhD in the anthropology of belief systems: as far as Sunny Chen was concerned, I was just a corporate troubleshooter.

'Well you know then, that's the day we honour the hungry ghosts, in the month when the gates of Hell are opened.' I nodded. The term Hungry Ghosts was also used to describe the starving victims of the famine caused by Mao's Great Leap Forward. 'The spirits wander the earth. They are restless. They need help. They expect us to give it. They scare us. So we do what they want.' As he spoke, he refilled his soy bowl with sauce, the liquid shooting from the bottle in tiny dark spurts. Like the gyrating lanterns above us, the movement was mesmerising. At one point he picked the little bowl up and tipped its contents directly on to his rice. This seemed to me very un-Chinese: more something a Westerner might do. Soy is very salty, so I wondered about his blood pressure. 'They can be family members. But they don't have to be. They need to say something, or they need you to do something for them. Then they appear in your sleep. That's called *tong-mong*. You know this?'

I nodded. '*Through dreams.*'

There is no Heaven in Chinese tradition. Just different levels of Hell. The spirits that come out around Ghost Month are from the lowest levels of the underworld. Sunny Chen was looking at me intently, as though he had said something momentous which would lead me to a specific conclusion. It didn't. I can't play the game where you must guess and guess. I put my chopsticks down and set my small digital recorder on the table between us. The detective at the Fraud Office was right: Sunny Chen's theory, if I'd read between the lines correctly, certainly fitted with the description *oddball*. But the anthropologist in me was stirred, and I have learned that when people have something important to say, they often spiral their way into it. I pressed Record.

'Please, carry on.'

He took a deep breath. 'The spirits don't always want the best thing for us,' Sunny Chen began. 'If we don't show them enough respect they need to be . . .' Here Sunny Chen couldn't find the word, and set aside his chopsticks to key it into his mobile translation app. 'Appeased.' I waited for more. He grabbed the salt dish and sprinkled a blizzard of coarse crystals into his bowl. 'That's why we visit their graves and burn Hell notes. Pay them off. Very different from the West.'

I said: 'Beliefs are more global than most people realise. Every society has its ways of trying to calm the spirits. Or whatever you want to call them. The Catholics have favours. They're a down-payment on sins not yet committed.'

'But do they get punished, if they do wrong? If they . . . wait. I must find the word.' He keyed in another Chinese character, and held the little screen out for me to read.

Commit a sin/ Transgress.

'Yes. But they can confess and seek atonement. Mr Chen, did someone at Jenwai commit a sin slash *transgress?*'

He didn't answer directly. 'You please one and then you offend another. It's like being torn into small pieces, you understand?' I didn't. Professor Whybray always advised: *when in doubt, say nothing.* So for a while we ate in silence. Sunny Chen continued to add more salt to every mouthful he took. In between he sipped green tea. 'I think we make a big mistake about ghosts,' he said suddenly. 'We think they are from the past. We think they are all dead. But they are alive. And some of them are not even born yet. They are travellers.'

'Travellers?'

'Yes! They move about.' His voice caught in a strange choke. 'They go wherever they like. They enter your body and make you do things.'

I'm not proud of my reaction, which was to register his welling tears and look away.

Through the window, forked lightning cleaved a blinding white slash across the sky's deep grey, chased by the cymbal-crash of thunder. A tourist coach drove past, headed for the National Museum: I recognised the ideograms on its destination plate. Chen's raw emotion was very desperate. And for me, awkward to contemplate. A behavioural psychologist such as Stephanie Mulligan would have known what to do or say. I did not. So I reached in my briefcase for the lime-green praying mantis I'd pre-creased on Arran and started constructing at Manchester airport. While Sunny Chen recovered himself and paid the bill, I did the last twenty-eight folds and presented the paper insect to him with both hands and a small bow of the head.

'A gift.'

It seemed to cheer him. 'I want to take you somewhere,' he said. 'I will show you what I mean about the spirits.'

Outside, we caught another taxi: he had a brief conversation with the driver and we drove through dense Taipei traffic. The rain stopped and the sky cleared. Chen seemed absorbed in his own thoughts. He didn't say where we were going. The hotels and department stores of downtown gave way to suburbs, then a netherland of factories, silos, warehouses and repair workshops. Finally, after twenty-three minutes and fifteen seconds, we took a fork to the right and began to climb upwards into the mountains that ringed the city, heading west towards the district of Yang Ming Shan. Six and a half minutes later the taxi driver asked Sunny Chen a question about the precise location of our destination and he answered distractedly, pointing. The storm had cleared completely, replaced by piercing sunshine. Rocky outcrops and feathered trees and small rubbish dumps exhaling coils of smoke dotted the roadside. Eventually, the taxi took a left turn down a narrow side road flanked with high bamboo. After three minutes and five seconds we slowed and entered a gateway into a concrete car park with weeds pushing through the cracks. The rainwater was evaporating in the sunshine: you could see the rising vapour. The driver parked under a tree with coarsely corrugated fan-shaped leaves and Sunny Chen told him to wait for us. I was pleased by how much Chinese I could understand.

The shrines hugged the earth, so it took me a while to register what we had entered. There must have been a hundred or so monuments in marble, granite and cement, scattered across the hillside overlooking the city. Up here, we were right on the edge of the fairy ring. Distant enough from the sprawl of humanity to see the scale and enterprise of it. Around us, the sunlight danced on the puddles left by the storm.

'Good feng shui,' said Sunny Chen, spreading his arm wide to indicate the view. It was spectacular. Beneath a blue sky streaked with wisps of cloud squatted the great urban crater: a centrifuge of money, metal, glass and cement, of malls and sports centres and arterial roads dotted with the pinpricks of cars, emanating a faint hum. A heat haze scrolled over the glittering ceramic rooftops of the outer suburbs. You couldn't see any human life from here, but you could do a mental X-ray and sense how the cityscape seethed with it. Taipei is home to four million and counting. I wondered: why has Sunny Chen chosen to take me to a place where the vivid living and the unforgotten dead converge? Far below, black birds whirled above the skyscrapers like coarse flakes of ash. After a few moments we turned and wandered among the family shrines: low, squat constructions with wide thresholds. Some lay crumbling and neglected, while others were lavishly tended ancestral showcases. The higher surrounding walls featured alcoves containing urns. Stray cats sunned themselves on the cracked slabs, or nudged at the remains of food offerings. After the air-conditioned taxi the air was sweltering. A hot breeze came from the west like the blast of a hairdryer, shaking the black-stemmed bamboos and rustling half-burned paper models attached to shrines. Small mounted black-and-white photographs of the dead glinted in the sun, dotted with rainwater. You could see the legacy of Qing Ming, the April tomb-sweeping festival in the form of soggy, charred incense sticks, plastic and silk flowers and the remains of burnt offerings. Streams of red ants transported ancient food crumbs amid faded and rain-damaged cardboard or paper replicas of coveted objects: miniature houses, yachts, cars and mobile phones, all fitting, I supposed, into the cultural category known as popular kitsch. The artistic standard was not high.

'Is this where your ancestors are?' I asked.

'Over there.' He pointed to a shrine, studded with photographs, only two of which were in colour. Most of the faces were stern, though one woman wore a half-smile. The men were jacketed, and the women wore cheongsams. None of them resembled Sunny Chen. 'You don't expect them to be dressed in rags, do you?' he blurted angrily. He waved his hand at the photographs. 'You think they will look like in the photos. Normal size. Wearing smart clothes. You don't imagine they smell bad. You don't expect them to eat insects.'

I waited for an explanation for this bizarre outburst, but none came. His face flickered in an agitated way. Then he reached in his inner pocket and brought out a wad of scarlet paper, ornamented with gold. Hell notes. Each leaf of the pretend currency was covered in Chinese characters. I recognised a few of the simpler ones, such as 'heavenly' and 'respect'. BANK OF HELL was stamped across the bottom of each in English.

He handed me a note.

'Can you please make me one small man?' he asked. I couldn't read the expression on his face. 'Let us sit there.' He pointed to a shrine shaded by a feathery-leafed tree with candelabras of furred buds.

On its low surrounding wall I laid the Hell note flat, folded a line and ripped it to a square. He sat next to me and watched as I folded. The wall was dry, but these were still not ideal conditions. I had no proper work top and the cheap paper dye left red stains on my fingertips. When I'd finished, I handed him the squat figure — boxy limbs, triangular head — and he accepted it with both hands and a jerky nod. The little man glinted red and gold in his palm.

I hadn't done a very good job. It was clear he thought so too, because he reached for a plastic lighter, which had the Chinese character for 'good fortune' engraved on it, and angled it beneath the man. I was glad he was going to burn it. It's exactly what I do myself, to poor specimens. It's what you might call a cathartic ritual.

But he was hesitating.

'Who is he?' I asked.

He laughed. 'Who do you think?' he said, igniting the pointed end of the man's leg. I would have bent it to form a foot, but in these conditions it was too fiddly. A bluish flame crept up the paper limb.

'I don't know.'

I feared he would burn his skin but he dropped the flaming paper just in time. Together we watched the little effigy blaze, shrivel to a crisp and waft sideways, disintegrating as it went.

'But you do know, Hesketh. Because you are a clever man.' He spoke urgently. I noted, in my brief connection with his eyes, that they were so dark that pupil and iris merged into one. When people like you their irises grow big. When they hate you they get small. The degree of light must be factored in, but dappled shade is tricky to calibrate. I felt very distinctly that this was a test. No: more than a test. A challenge. More games. More things not said straight. But I've studied the tendencies and the rules. 'He's the whistle-blower,' I said. 'The Jenwai saboteur. The man you want to kill.'

He didn't say anything. His jaw was working oddly. Then I realised why. Once again he was in tears. Then it dawned on me, what he was saying, and why it was so painful to him. Of course. Stephanie Mulligan would have spotted it long ago. How do you address a man who has just symbolically set himself alight? We stood there for a long time, watching the ashes of the tiny paper Sunny Chen drift across through the coarse weeds.

Finally I cleared my throat.

'Do you think your ancestors are angry with you?'

The laugh came again. 'Sure, I will have to take the blame.' I blinked and wiped my brow. An intense, laser-like heat can follow thunder in this latitude. I wished Stephanie Mulligan had not entered my head. But now here she was, judging me and finding me wanting. And behind her, somewhere, was Kaitlin. Different women, both making the same assessment. 'But it wasn't my choice. Something can get inside you.' He was becoming animated. 'Sometimes it's asleep. But when it wakes up, it's in charge. You can't make the decisions any more. You are a clever man Hesketh, but I am sorry, I don't think you are the kind of person who can understand what is going on here. How they make you do things.

You are –' he whipped out his mobile and looked up a word. 'Too *rational.'*

He'd made a confession. He'd come to seek atonement. And I was his witness.

But capitalism employs me, via Phipps & Wexman. Not God.

I am not sure what 'too' rational might mean. But Sunny Chen was right; I have a respect for facts, and the logic systems that connect them. Which is why what he said was immediately unsatisfactory. While whistle-blowers tend to have an inflated view of their own importance, Sunny Chen's ego was virtually non-existent. I admired him for standing up for the rules. But he didn't match the profile.

'I'm going to record this,' I say. 'For my report.'

He shrugged. I pulled out my device, settled it on the marble slab between us and pressed the button. 'This is very bad for me,' he said.

'It's not bad at all,' I countered quickly. I was on safe ground here: this was something I had rehearsed, though not, I'd thought, for him. 'You'll get a reward. A generous one. That's why I'm here. You'll be a hero.'

'The last thing I want,' he said in a flat voice.

When I computed this statement it made a kind of sense. He'd brought down his company. Inevitably he felt torn. Publicly, he'd receive a financial reward as a face-saver for Ganjong, and be hailed as an eco-warrior, a crime-fighter, a corruption-buster, a champion of honesty. But in reality, small, insecure, tormented Sun-kiu 'Sunny' Chen was none of these things.

'So why did you do it?'

He looked uncomfortable and fiddled with a Hell note. 'I didn't want to. I can't explain. Even to myself. I was not in charge.'

'You respect the tradition of ancestor-worship. Do you have any other beliefs?'

He shook his head absentmindedly and took a drag of his cigarette. 'No.'

'How does your respect for your ancestors relate to your exposing corruption at Jenwai?'

'I can't explain.'

'Try.'

'I can't. Just ask me another question.'

'The mark you showed me at the timber plant. Who made it and why do you think it's relevant?'

'I made it,' he said. 'That's why I wanted the police to take fingerprints. Evidence. But they refuse.'

'You mean those are your own fingerprints?'

'I am not sure. I would like to know.'

'But you just said the hand-print was yours.'

'They make you do things. From the inside.' He touched his chest.

'Who?'

'Them. They're our blood, but they hate us. They blame us. I can't explain.'

I decided to try another tack. 'Do you consider yourself a moral person?'

'Not really.'

'Do you have views on deforestation? Or the environment?'

'No views,' he said, gazing into the middle distance. He took another deep drag on his cigarette and shook his head as though to get rid of a fly. 'I'm just an ordinary person.'

'Ordinary people can have views.'

He blew out a stream of smoke. When smoke mixes with air it obeys mathematical rules. 'So as an ordinary person I don't especially care about the environment.'

'So why did you do it?'

'Pressure.'

'What kind of pressure? Who from?'

'I told you! The spirits! Them!'

He shook his head, stubbed out his cigarette and lit another one. We sat there for a while. Two metres away, a tabby cat with a kinked tail was nursing a litter of black, white and tortoiseshell kittens.

'Do you fear that there will be a reprisal of some kind?' I asked after a moment. 'That the Jenwai staff who were exposed might attack you in revenge?'

He made a noise with his mouth, as if he were stifling more choking. 'It's not their business. It is nothing to do with them. You see, it was not me that did this thing. They come in. I don't know how. Maybe you eat the wrong thing and they get in your blood. Like a parasite. And they make the body disobey the mind. Do you understand?'

'Not yet. But I'm here to try. That's my job. So I can write my report.'

He reached for my recorder and turned it off. 'No. Sorry Hesketh. We finish this now.' He blew out a thin stream of smoke. 'I can't. I don't understand it myself. I'm not in charge of anything, you see. I am just a . . .' he trailed off.

'Just a what?'

He flicked some ash off his sleeve. 'Just a little man made of paper.'

Then he stood up. I did too, and made to follow him, but he signalled for me to stay where I was. So I sat down again and watched as he walked stiffly back to the family shrine where he took a wad of red Hell notes from his pocket, knelt to place it on the stone, fanned it out and set fire to it with the plastic lighter. Then he fished in his briefcase for some incense sticks, bowed three times, then placed the incense in a small jar and lit it. His shoulders were shaking.

The smoke drifted towards me: I smelled sandalwood. I recognised it instantly. Last Christmas when Kaitlin and I rented a cottage in Devon, Freddy insisted on lighting sandalwood joss sticks in every room. Kaitlin's moods tended to be capricious, but on this occasion the atmosphere was positive. She had drunk four glasses of wine and there was a sheen to her skin that made me want her urgently. My body has a mind of its own and I have learned that when it comes to sex one need not fight this because sex has its own rules. That night she was very receptive and for once she shut her eyes too. But I misunderstood why. I thought she was giving me something, finding a way to join me in what she called the Fortress. But it wasn't that. The truth was, she'd already begun her affair.

I was actually present when they met. It was a Phipps & Wexman reception. They talked all evening. I saw that they stimulated each other. One minute they'd be serious. The next they'd be laughing. Ideas were bouncing around. It was the kind of exchange I struggle to participate in. It was classic courtship behaviour, but I failed to identify it as such. Later Kaitlin told me this was because I'd been 'complacent'. I had 'made assumptions', and 'failed to appreciate' her sexual appetites. I had taken her for granted. I should have been jealous and I wasn't.

I asked her: 'Are you saying I'm to blame for your having an affair?'

'Don't twist what I'm saying.'

'My intention is to understand the logic. Not just of what you did, but why you hid it from me. I need to know why.'

'Look. Not everything can be explained by some damned behavioural flow chart, OK? And not everyone shares your rule book.'

'It's not a rule book. It's just morality.'

'People change, OK? They evolve over time, they want to explore who they might be, as well as who they are!'

'They should just be who and what they say they are.'

'Well one of us failed to do that, OK? One of us committed the apparently unforgivable crime of *changing*.'

Her body language and facial configuration told me to leave it there.

A flock of green birds flew overhead, squawking, then disappeared into the smog coiling around the mountainside. Parakeets. I went and joined Sunny and we watched the glowing tips of the incense sticks.

He said, 'Thank you for making me the man. And the insect. What is its name?'

'A praying mantis. It's called that because it rocks to and fro like someone praying.'

I like to rock too. It soothes me.

'Ha. A holy insect.'

'Not really. The females devour the males after they've mated.'

He shifts a little, and glances at me sideways. 'Not my business, Hesketh. But your wife—'

'Girlfriend. Ex. Met someone else.' I might as well learn to say it aloud.

He studied his hands. 'Very sorry. I should not ask.'

'Later she regretted it and wanted us to carry on like before.'

He looked up and smiled. 'So the best man won!' he exclaimed, play-punching me on the arm, American-buddy style. But he might as well have shot me. He meant well of course. He wasn't to know the appalling nature of what happened. 'You're the best man,' he continued. 'She saw that, so she wanted you back.'

'But I couldn't trust her any more. That's why I live alone.'

'Man of principle. Good.' I knew he was looking at me. 'But you miss your son.'

'Stepson. Freddy's hers. From before we met. He doesn't know his real father.'

'He still needs you. You know, Hesketh, families are with us all the time.' He gestured at the shrines. 'Dead and alive. The ones from the past and the present and the future too. They're living in us. We can't escape them even if we want to. They send us signals. This is what holds us together. Blood. DNA, Hesketh. It's very strong.'

'Freddy and I don't share DNA.'

'Then you are lucky. DNA is cruel. It makes demands.' He leaned down and stubbed out his cigarette in a dried pomegranate shell. 'Hesketh, I am glad it was you they sent.'

His eyes were glittering again. I looked across and met them for a second. I couldn't manage any longer. But perhaps there was an exchange of sorts.

I said, 'Yes.' Then in Chinese: 'Me too.' I meant it.

'We will say goodbye now. I have told you all I can. Go and do your job. I will stay here. Take the taxi back to the hotel.' I started to object, but he stopped me. He had his mobile, he said. He would order another car when he was ready to leave. 'I want to be here for a little longer. To work out what I must do now. But be careful, Hesketh. The spirits are becoming very active.'

'What do you mean?'

'They are angry and starving. They live in bad conditions. You like the truth. So I will be honest with you. This is not something Phipps & Wexman or any other organisation can resolve. The spirits will do what they came to do. They won't give up. They are fighting for their survival.' He sighed, then held out his hand. We shook, then exchanged a small head-bow. 'It was good to meet you Hesketh. Have a safe journey. Please go now.'

He called out to the taxi driver, who snapped awake and started the engine. We shook hands and I got in the car and Sunny waved me off. I looked back at him, but he'd already turned away to face the city. Hands in his pockets, shoulders high. On the way back to the hotel, I used my BlackBerry to let Phipps & Wexman know I had identified the whistle-blower. Ashok's instant reply: *You're the man.*

The best man, according to Sunny Chen.

The man who won.

He wasn't to know.

As the taxi drove off, I looked back and saw the small figure of Sunny Chen standing like a hunched sentinel at the shrine of his forefathers, near the blown ashes of his little origami self.

CHAPTER 2

HURRICANE VERONICA STRUCK during the night, devastating towns on Ireland's western shore before strafing its way up the Scottish coast. I woke to its dying howls. When dawn broke I saw that one of the hawthorns had been blown down, its branches scattered across the moor. My roof had lost a few tiles, and a dead sheep lay on the beach. Otherwise, there was little sign of the weather's passing, save for the sparkle of salt borne by the wind: coarse crystals winking on the slate roof of my cottage and on the granite boulder.

My living-room smells of damp wool and wood smoke. I've put logs on the fire, and from time to time air pockets in the bark detonate like gunshot. It's already autumn up here: spider season. Because of this year's wet spring they are numerous and huge, with long legs and bloated abdomens. The structure of each cobweb is the same, but every spider has its own style, like handwriting.

Sometimes I sit and watch them at work, single-minded and fanatical. I have to tear myself away.

The lunchtime news was full of the hurricane damage and the scientific row over whether the freshly replicated CERN results 'disprove' Einstein's theory of relativity. At the end, there's a small update on yesterday's 'pyjama killer': the girl's father is still in hospital, while the remaining family is undergoing counselling.

I've been trying to summarise the results of my Taiwan investigation, but my notes amount to little more than a list of Chen's agitated remarks about the spirit world. I can't quote this kind of thing in my report. Clients don't want superstition and uncertainty: they want closure and a three-point plan. I do too. I throw more wood on the fire and watch the sparks. I enjoy starting these miniature contained blazes. I use crumpled newspaper and failed origami figures. I am harsh on my own craftsmanship: a bad fold, the wrong kind of kink, or a small paper tear, and it's sacrificed. I think of Sunny Chen, burning himself in effigy. The body can disobey the mind, he said. How can that happen? Is it like my nocturnal bouts of Restless Leg Syndrome, where the brain craves shut-down, but the lower limbs enforce their own meaningless, agitated agenda? *They are in your blood*, he said. *Like parasites.* But what do they eat, the hungry inner creatures he conjured as his tormentors? I look it up. Rice, says one source. Fruit. Soup. Sweets. Meat. Anything they can lay their spirit hands on, and stuff into their spirit mouths and absorb into their spirit bloodstreams.

★　　★　　★

Sometimes a feeling of physical constriction overwhelms me: to use an analogy, it's as if I'm trapped inside an egg and must burst free. At three o'clock I give in to it and close the Chen file. Shucking on my anorak, I grab my umbrella and push out into open air. I have my routines. Five and a half minutes to the gate. Nine minutes along the sheep-path. A thirty-second pause at the sheer-sided black boulder, then down past the bluff where a row of trees cringe from the wind, and down to the shore. Most of the island is rocky and dry, but in this particular region the bog-land absorbs the liquid with the capacity of a sponge. It exhales methane. The fossil gas streams to the surface in tiny bubbles like champagne, then ignites and dances with flickering blue tendrils of light. You can see it now, through the massing late-afternoon dark. In the old days they called it will-o'-the-wisp and conjured goblins to explain it. Other native beliefs: wild fairy children once roamed here. Sometimes they swapped places with humans and lived as changelings.

According to Japanese lore, if you fold a thousand *ozuru*, you'll achieve your heart's desire. Like most origami aficionados, I've folded many more than that, but I'm no closer to knowing what my heart's desire might be.

Once, it was simply peace: to be left to myself, as I am now, walking on a moor, with a case to puzzle over.

The boy changed all that.

When we lived as a family, Kaitlin would wake him and then leave for work. By the time he was dressed, I'd have Freddy's breakfast ready on the table. Every schoolday for two years I prepared him a bowl of yoghurt with eleven raisins on top and a four-minute boiled egg. While he ate the yoghurt I put the egg in boiling water and pressed the button on the timer and we'd play 'the Egg Game': I'd throw a tea cloth over the timer and we'd each make a ping when we guessed the four minutes was up. If you missed the real ping, you lost completely. The skill lay in being an accurate judge of time. By the time I decided to leave, we had both become extremely good at the Egg Game.

'I know your mum has already talked to you about this,' I said, after he'd won again, three seconds short of the real ping. But he must have been anticipating the conversation because he slapped his hands over his ears. I continued anyway. 'We've decided not to live together any more.' It had to be stated. By me as well as Kaitlin. 'But we'll still see each other I hope.' I put the egg in his eggcup and set it in front of him. 'Mum will pick you up from school today. I won't see you tonight. But I'll come by whenever I can. Freddy K?'

He didn't answer.

We had our rituals. One of them was that when I gave him his egg he'd say '*Foonk-you-fonk-you-fank-you,*' in the deep distorted voice he uses for the archaeopteryx, and then – here was the educational part – I'd say 'You're welcome' or its equivalent in a foreign language, some basic phrases of which I'd looked up earlier. We'd covered over a hundred countries. Then we'd talk about the culture and traditions of the day's country, and I'd tell him one of its folk tales while he ate. When Kaitlin came home he'd try out that morning's language on her, or a story. He especially loved Russian, and the story of Baba Yaga Bony-legs, the witch who lived in a house that stood on chickens' legs. Often he said *nyet* for no, and *da* for yes.

But now he didn't even say that.

He just threw his egg on the floor. It broke open and lay there steaming. He refused to speak to me. I didn't know what to do. So I cleaned it up. A few minutes later Kaitlin phoned to ask how it had gone. When I told her, she said she was coming home.

'It's best you don't see him for a while,' she said when she returned. 'It only upsets him.'

I went out and rinsed the mop under the outdoor tap.

It's getting darker now, the sky rinsed by the dregs of the hurricane. The scent of wet gorse is vital and crude. I can recognise several bird species now. Black guillemot, cormorant, eider. I've seen peregrine falcons too. Here's what I'd tell Freddy, about birds. I saw some green parakeets in Taiwan, flying over shrines to the dead. In cities, some bird species have begun to imitate electronic devices such as car alarms and doorbells, and even incorporate them into their song patterns. When it comes to ringtones, they favour Nokia. Then I'd ask him: but what if they start to copy a ringtone that is itself a bird-call? Then you might get blackbirds posing as toucans and marsh waders pretending to be mynah birds. Which in turn would copy something else.

The boy would like that. He'd laugh and you'd see his little teeth. There's usually a gap somewhere, with a new one pushing through. He doesn't like brushing them, so to cajole him into it, I used to stand next to him in the bathroom and we'd do it together, trying to hit a kind of synchrony. We'd end up pulling grotesque faces, gurning at the mirror and spitting toothpaste.

Sometimes we pretended we had rabies.

★   ★   ★

My phone vibrates. I pull it out of my pocket and press answer without looking, expecting it will be Kaitlin. I'm hoping that when she's finished demanding that I fetch the rest of my stuff – something I refuse to do unless she lets me see Freddy – I'll get to talk to him. As I'm not officially Freddy's stepfather, Kaitlin is aware of the power she wields.

But it's not Kaitlin.

'How's it hanging, Maestro?' Ashok Sharma.

Odd. Normally Phipps & Wexman don't call me on my mobile: they have a face-to-face policy, and favour Skype.

'It's hanging well, thank you, Ashok,' I tell him. I assume the 'it' referent is penis-related, in origin. I picture him the way I so often see him on the screen, shirtsleeves rolled up, feet on the desk, slightly pixellated and time-lagged. He once described his skin colour as Starbucks latte, but when I put a colour chart to his wrist he was forced to agree that Sanderson's Burnt Umber, from the 2003 range, was more accurate. His mother's family was originally from Mumbai and his father is Kashmiri, but Ashok, whose name means 'without sadness', was born in Florida and calls himself *Yankee to the boner.* This is a pun.

'Er. Reason I'm calling is the guy you investigated on your Far East trip. The Taiwan whistle-blower?'

Sunny Chen. I quicken my pace.

I say, 'You'll have my report by late tomorrow.'

Ashok says, 'About that.'

I once overheard a colleague referring to Ashok as 'an irritating jerk'. But I like him. I like his leather and aftershave smell and his playful if somewhat childish nature, and I don't mind that he calls me Maestro or Spock. When I'm in London, we'll sometimes go for a drink together by the Thames, where he introduces me as the Pussy Magnet and himself as the Pussy Magnet's Horny Sidekick, and in between buying drinks for women he wants to have sex with, he tells me about his latest losses on the stock exchange, which he seems to find amusing, like a spectacle he's not involved in. He sees it as a challenge to make me laugh, and when he succeeds, he punches the air with his fist and shouts, 'I win!' and demands that I make him an *ozuru* as a 'humour tax'. I've worked with Phipps & Wexman for five years and he now has thirteen of them on a shelf next to his family portrait: a set of parents and a big-eyed sister with her husband and four kids. He likes to amuse visitors by pretending to feed the origami birds confetti collected from hole-punchers.

'We'll have to do some rethinking,' says Ashok. 'I'm sorry to lay this on you, but Sunny Chen's dead.' I mentally select a sheet of origami paper. I make a frog base. This I double-sink fold, then blintz. 'You still there bud? You hear what I said? Sunny Chen. Your factory-manager guy. He's eaten it. I didn't know how to tell you, so I just thought hey, what can I do. I'll just come right out with it.'

I can hear my boss chewing rapidly. So he is *eating it* too. But Ashok and Sunny Chen aren't eating the same thing. The thing Sunny is eating is dust, as in 'biting the dust'. Whereas Ashok has been psychologically dependent on chewing gum since he gave up smoking: 'eating' in his case involves spearmint and a gelatine-based product derived from pigs' trotters. But Sunny Chen is dead. I can be slow to absorb things. Something like this could take a long time to sink in.

I ask, 'When?'

'Today. Our morning, his afternoon. At the timber plant. I'm sending his folks flowers on your behalf. It'll be appreciated, since you hung out with him.'

I fold some more paper mentally, at high speed. I must be extremely upset. If Kaitlin could see me now, she wouldn't call me 'a robot made of meat'. But she might call me an unusually fast walker. Sunny Chen in overalls and a white hard hat showing me round the factory. Sunny Chen in the restaurant, piling on the salt and using the soy bottle like a little watering can. Sunny Chen at the shrines, burning the effigy I made him from the Hell note and talking about badly dressed ancestors eating insects. Sunny Chen's eyes with tears in them. How I looked at a yellow and blue coach instead, and then folded a praying mantis. I do not know how to behave or what I feel. Perhaps I don't feel anything.

But I do feel something, of course. The usual suspects: confusion and overload.

It was Martin Yeh who was supposed to be dying. Of cancer. Not Sunny Chen, of – what? A heart attack. Of course. I see the da Vinci diagrams. An artery blocking, a ventricle in spasm.

'How did it happen?'

I'm aware of Ashok taking a deep breath. 'Sorry to lay this on you too – but the guy killed himself.' He pauses. 'As in, suicide.' I must have made a noise of some sort – a sigh or sob or groan or something. 'You OK there?' says Ashok.

'No.'

'Jeez. Like I say, I'm sorry. Take your time, my friend.'

'Yes.' We are not actually friends. More colleagues.

I stop walking and start to rock. My heartbeat changes. I rock more urgently. I can get overwhelmed.

'How do you know it was suicide?'

'Seems there were witnesses. And CCTV footage. Plus he left a note for his wife. Jeez, man. I'm sorry to break it to you this way. Wish I was there to, I don't know. Buy you a beer or something. Offer my condolences.' I turn my face to the wind and breathe in wet air. 'So what's your gut feeling here?'

I don't have gut feelings: I have often told Ashok this. He calls me pedantic. He also refers to me as 'the in-house Martian' though he always stresses that he means it 'with love, my friend'. But I do have instincts. These are different from gut feelings: they are a component of the deductive process; a form of recognition on the subconscious level, of something the conscious has not yet processed. A trick of the mind. But a useful one. That Sunny Chen was an unhappy man I don't doubt. If there's CCTV footage, does that mean he killed himself in public view, deliberately? If so, did he intend it as another 'grand gesture', despite his discomfort in the role of hero? Most suicides are private. Unless they're political. The bombers. The self-immolators. The cries for help that go wrong. I need to know how he did it. I met the man and watched him agonise about his ancestors and pour soy sauce directly into his rice bowl in a very un-Chinese way. I told him about Kaitlin and Freddy. This doesn't mean nothing. This means something, even if I don't know the word for what it means. His cigarette lighter with 'good fortune' printed on it. The black-stemmed bamboos, the feral cats, him saying, 'I am glad it was you they sent' and me saying I was too, in Chinese, because it was true.

'How did he do it?'

He lets out air from his mouth. 'Look. Are you quite sure you want to know the gory details, Maestro?' I straighten my back to spread the weight that's settled on my shoulders.

'Yes.'

'I mean, it's not something you'd want to dwell on and analyse too much and stuff. You're all on your lonesome up there in your Scottish croft, right?'

'Ashok. Just tell me.'

'Er, Jeez. Well. You've been to the timber plant, right? Seems there was a health-and-safety issue with access to one of the machines . . . Hey, you still there?'

We peered down into the metallic roil of blades. *Long way to fall,* he said. *Turn you into hamburger . . . It's like being torn into small pieces.* When he showed me the pulper, did he really want me to picture what would happen if he threw himself in?

'Yes. Still here.'

'The question is why. D'you have any kind of answer?'

I think. 'Normally suicide is connected to some variant of depression.'

But that's inadequate. Sunny Chen's mental pain was a highly focused and particular form of derangement. He had a conviction that he was unable or unwilling to fully convey: a story about hungry spirits that for whatever reason he found untellable. The cargo on my shoulders shifts, then resettles in a new way. Did my investigation trigger his suicide?

'Anyway, bud, you'll need to incorporate something on his death in your report. Stephanie Mulligan can give you some input, if you want the psychological angle.'

'No thanks.' I say it too quickly and with too much force.

Stephanie Mulligan has been with Phipps & Wexman for four years. She is a competent and extremely ambitious operative who will probably be running the Psych Department within a few years. She is generally considered to be extremely attractive despite her bra size being probably no more than 34A. I try to avoid her. Whenever I think about her no amount of mental origami can counter the damage she inflicts on my nervous system. My attitude towards her is complex for reasons I don't enjoy going into.

'She's done some work on work-related suicide. Could be of help to you.'

'If I need it, I'll look it up.' Too fast, again.

He sighs. 'Whatever. But turn it around quick.' I trudge along the muddy path, my anorak brushing against wet swatches of broom, wishing Ashok hadn't mentioned Stephanie Mulligan. I thought I'd relegated her to the past. 'So how are you doing otherwise, Maestro?'

'Fine,' I say. 'I've been enjoying nature. And I have a goldfish.'

'Good. Sounds like a start. So. Clear your head, then finish that report and call me when you're done. It's a tough call I know. Don't think I'm unsympathetic. But I'm counting on you to deliver.'

He knows I will. When Professor Whybray recommended me to Phipps & Wexman it was Ashok Sharma who spotted my talent for identifying and tracking patterns, 'like one of those French pigs that root for truffles in the forests of *la* Wherever-the-Fuck', as he put it. It was he who took me on.

After we've said goodbye I switch off my phone and breathe in deep lungfuls of dark, saturated air. Sheep are scattered here and there, white blobs in a murk of collapsed bracken and heather. I turn and head back for the black granite boulder that marks the turn of the sheep-path. Seagulls wheel overhead.

'Sunny Chen is dead. Sunny Chen is dead. Sunny Chen is dead.'

If I say a thing aloud it can sound like someone official speaking, and then I can begin to believe it. I walk faster, visualising the pulping machine, and the heap of woodchips and sawdust in the skip below, stained red from Sunny Chen's blood. Sunny Chen mashed to hamburger. I have to go through the whole process with him. I don't know why. Not just once, but again and again, with his heart and his da Vinci aortas and ventricles sliced through by the whirring blades, and the crimson blood splattering against the stainless steel walls of the machine.

When I first asked Sunny Chen how he felt about the whistle-blower he'd said, *I would like to kill him.* Later, when he burned himself in effigy, he was showing me he planned to do just that.

I missed it. But someone else might not have.

In the absence of anything you could call a body, the police would have had to scoop up the pulped sawdust to verify Sunny Chen's DNA. They'd probably have used an ordinary shovel. Then they'd have put the material into a Ziploc plastic bag for analysis.

A company can lose millions of pounds through an act of sabotage or through bad publicity generated by a disgruntled worker. It will need a complete rebranding, and may have to relocate. Profit is an end product of a motivated workforce. It would be absurd to expect all employees to be happy all day long. But when the seed of discontent is sown, it can spread like contagion. With Sunny Chen's suicide, the negative PR impact has been amplified.

In my dealings with him, he didn't strike me as a brave man so much as a desperate one.

Yet it was Sunny Chen who blew the whistle and became an international – what?

A star, some will say. But he's gone. So technically, a more accurate analogy would be 'comet'.

Phipps & Wexman protocol defines him as a saboteur.

While to the police, he's now some red-pink mush in a bag which will be stored in a refrigerator unit along with similar bags containing parts of other Chinese people, all clearly labelled using a standardised numerical code linking each specimen to a police case file. Every discipline has its own methodology, but this at least is what I imagine happening to Sunny Chen's pulped remains, which will later make their way into a traditional Chinese coffin.

They make the body disobey the mind, he'd said. The spirits had got inside him and made him act against his will. *They're our blood, but they hate us.*

The French term *un acte manqué* describes a form of self-sabotage whereby the unconscious sets about wrecking – for whatever reason – what the conscious has built. Could it be that one version of Sunny Chen sabotaged Jenwai while another turned a blind eye? And that when he'd returned to normal and seen what 'they' had done, he'd panicked and felt such remorse that his only recourse was suicide?

Mental breakdown explains both Chen's suicide and the uncharacteristic behaviour that preceded it. That's the slant I'll use in my report, to explain his arrival in the Ziploc bag. For now, it's the closest I'll get to the true answer.

But if the Sunny Chen case were a piece of origami I would flatten out the creases, work out where I went wrong, and start again.

Outside, the moon is a thin, luminous scrape and the stars throb weakly above the sea. I switch off my computer and swivel my chair from side to side in rhythmic arcs. I can hear the gulls screech.

Is human hamburger a foodstuff that a hungry ghost might crave?

CHAPTER 3

SOMETIME AT THE end of the twentieth century there was a break-through in the world of origami. Before then, it was considered impossible to fabricate an animal or other form that had a large body and thin appendages from a single sheet of paper. This limited your range of designs. Anything like an insect with feelers, for example, was out of the question. But then, thanks to mathematical computer models pioneered by the physicist and origamist Robert J. Lang, which involve dividing the original piece of paper into circles and then sub-dividing the circles into creases, you can make just about anything with protrusions. A millipede. Mating locusts. A spiked sea urchin. Or Lang's famous hermit crab, which I am tackling now. The back-coated kozo paper I have chosen is tough, but thin: Indian Violet with a black dot pattern. I began it when I moved here and it is now one-third complete. It's a job requiring both paper clips and tweezers.

★   ★   ★

On balance, I'm glad I have to recast the Taiwan report. Chen's suicide means that some of his more cryptic behaviours – the dark references to 'the pressure', the preoccupation with the muddy smear, the ancestor-talk – can be seen as symptoms of his break-down. But my own culpability is another matter. I've never previously known anyone who committed suicide. Will it take the rest of my life to process what has happened? I don't know.

If Freddy were here, he would say, 'Yet', as per the rules of a playful accord we have concerning unacquired knowledge, whereby if one of us said they didn't know something, the other had to say 'Yet'. And then the other one – usually me – would provide the missing information, or we'd look it up, or just speculate.

But it is untested ground.

It's Tuesday 18th September. My laptop tells me the forecast is for more rain, and highs of twelve degrees. After two hours' work on the hermit crab with Dvořák on the speakers I'm interrupted by Skype ringing.

Caller: Ashok Sharma, Phipps & Wexman. Time: 08.18.

That's early, for Ashok. I'm tempted to reject it, but I can't. Working from home was a right I campaigned for after things deteriorated with Kaitlin. Ashok agreed in the end, on condition that I stay contactable at all times. I turn down Dvořák and press answer. Ashok's looking tired and dishevelled and a shade paler. I focus on the door handle which is visible behind his left ear. I don't do eye contact, but I have ways of hiding it.

'You there bud?'

'Yes. Working on the hermit crab.' I hold it up to show him.

'Cool, man. Look, things are turning weird on us. It's happened again.'

'What has?'

'Just had another case like Chen's. Sabotage followed by self-harm, take two. The world of finance this time. Employee of Sverige Banken, the Swedish bank. They're the client.'

I settle the hermit crab back on the desk. 'Go on.'

'Guy called Jonas Svensson.'

'Ashok, Ashok, Ashok. Scandinavian languages have a soft J. So it's pronounced *Yonas*.'

'Whatever. The good news is, our friend *Yonas* is still alive. But only just. They pumped his stomach and induced a coma. When he wakes up – we're talking tomorrow or the day after – you need to talk to him.'

'What did he do?'

'Deliberately screwed up some coffee futures deal. Lost the bank millions. Didn't deny it. Wouldn't explain. Or couldn't. I've mailed you the details.' Ashok's PA, Belinda Yates, appears with a steaming cup which she places on the desk next to him. 'Thanks babe.' He posts a piece of nicotine gum into his mouth then points at me. 'OK. Your wish is my command. What'll make you happy?'

Freddy, I think. Freddy here, with me. But I don't say that as it's inappropriate to the matter in hand, so I say, 'I want to see Sunny Chen's suicide note.'

Ashok says, 'Cops in Taiwan say it doesn't make sense.' I see the white blob in his mouth as he speaks. 'Turns out it's not a note. Much weirder. Some little drawings and a hand-print. Chen's wife says he can't have done it. She's very insistent. But she found it next to a shrine thing they have in the kitchen, where they left each other messages. So sounds like wishful thinking to me. Didn't know the Chinese had shrines in their kitchens. Something new every day, right?'

Sunny Chen said he'd made the hand-mark in the timber factory himself. But at the same time he'd wanted the police to take finger-prints. Why?

'I need to see the note. Have they taken fingerprints of it?' I reach for my Swedish dictionary, and flip through it. I have a habit of underlining words that appeal to me. *Utveckling. Olika. Näktergal. Talartid.*

'Doubt it. But I'll check. By the way, got something to cheer you up. Whybray's in town.'

'Professor Whybray? You're sure?' I close the dictionary. The professor retired after Mrs Whybray died. He moved to Toronto. He called it *a city after my own heart*. 'What brought him back?'

'The Home Office.' I have known the professor for fourteen years and seven months. But it's three years and two months since I saw him in the flesh. Not a week has gone by when I have not remembered something he taught me, and applied it. Last Christmas he sent a card. *To the young and bright from the old and wise*. I could hear him saying those words aloud. *I follow your work with interest*. His voice is high and reedy and always sounds a little hoarse. *Congratulations on solving the Hungarian conundrum. With affection, Victor*. I never called him Victor. He used to tease me about my inability to drop the formality of his title. I'm excited. I can feel chemical changes in my brain.

'What's the project?' It must be something big to have brought him back. Something to 'get his teeth into'. That's how he'd put it. He could never resist challenges.

'It's hush-hush. But he asked after you and hinted at a contract for us. Wanted to know if you're still Venning. So I said what's Venning. And he said get Hesketh to educate you.'

'He was referring to Venn diagrams. They're a very effective device for analysing patterns of unity and differentiation. Named after the mathematician John Venn, who incorporated them into set theory in the 1880s. If you're looking for a speedy categorisation tool that's highly visual and comprehensible at a glance, and flexible enough to accommodate an infinite number of new factors, you can't do much better. They consist of overlapping or interlocking circles. You can incorporate U-shapes too. And the S-form. Depending on complexity.'

'Get out of there! So when I see you doodling a bunch of amoeba fucking, that's what you're up to?'

'Yes.'

'And there was I thinking, ask not the reason why. Hesketh is Hesketh.'

'Who else would I be?'

'No one. And they only made one of you. Which is why you're packing for Sweden.'

'I want to go by train.' I like trains.

'I anticipated that, bud. Belinda says it's do-able if you can get to Edinburgh tonight. Svensson should be out of his coma by the time you arrive. Find me the pattern. Love you, my friend. Bye.'

He gives his signature dismissal – head down, a fist-clench high in the air, like a sportsman – and then he's gone.

When Ashok says 'love you, my friend', he doesn't mean it. It's a florid form of expression, of the type Kaitlin once classified for me as 'the vernacular of dick-swinging'. When I say to someone that I love them, however, I mean it. For someone aged thirty-six I have not said it very often. Three times in two years, to the same woman. And when I stop loving them, I say: 'Kaitlin, I don't love you any more and I can never love you again.'

She confessed to her affair on Saturday 5th May. By tacit agreement, my workroom was my territory and she and Freddy never came in. I don't know how long she'd been standing in the doorway watching me work.

She said, 'Hesketh. I made a mistake. You and I can go back to normal. It's over.'

I was doing a tricky blintz fold at the time, on a moth. It demanded all my concentration.

'What's over?'

But she didn't reply. When I finished the next fold to my satisfaction and looked up, I saw her staring at me urgently, as if expecting a response. As if I were telepathic: as if I, of all people, should have guessed that she had been leading another secret life, in parallel to the one that was on show. I have no radar for lies. Why would I suspect that her yoga lessons were not real yoga lessons, or that her 'late conference meetings' masked another type of rendezvous?

I said, 'Whatever it is, you're going to have to explain.'

And so she did explain. And then I understood.

She'd had an affair. It had lasted eight weeks. And now it was over. That's what she meant when she said we could 'go back to normal'.

But we couldn't.

Two species of bird feature in the glossary of cuckoldry. First, the cuckoo, which lays its solo egg in another bird's nest, leaving others to do the nurturing. In this reading, the 'cuckold' is the cuckoo's victim: the non-biological father of another man's offspring. The second bird is the cockerel, which echoes 'cuckold' linguistically. Some accounts claim that the origin of the 'horned cuckold' dates back to a time when cockerels were castrated, and their spurs sliced off and stuck through their combs where they were said to implant themselves and grow, giving the impression of horns. As the cockerel had been castrated, the 'horns' became an obvious symbol of the bird's impotence. From a physiological point of view, the implantation seems unlikely. Meanwhile, the whole notion of horns representing men who have been sexually betrayed is also puzzling, because horns, being of a phallic shape, prominent on males, and often used for fighting, are generally associated with potency.

These were some of the things that passed through my mind when Kaitlin was telling me the story of her liaison, the fact of which eventually led to our parting of ways. When she had finished, she declared that it was my 'impenetrability' which made her seek comfort in a lover. That's when she called me 'a robot made of meat'.

But I am not a robot made of meat.

In that moment, though, I wished I was.

★　　★　　★

The early part of the train journey to Stockholm is long and pleasantly uneventful, through the dusty post-harvest landscapes of Belgium and Germany. I spend the first few hours reading the complex financial documents Ashok has sent. The day after his sabotage was revealed, Jonas Svensson swallowed more than a hundred aspirin. If his teenage son Erik had not come home from school early and found him, he'd have died. There's a ferry to the Danish island of Zealand, then another train to the Central Station in Copenhagen, where I change trains. The next part of the journey involves crossing a long and elegant bridge with a view of wind turbines. I like wind turbines, both from an engineering and an aesthetic standpoint. In Sweden itself, the geography is monotonous and rain-washed, with oceans of fir forest. It's a centralised nation with a largely urban population: now I'm seeing for myself how this translates visually. There are few towns and vast tracts of land which, save for the railway line itself and a few isolated farms, are unmarked by any human presence. I have brought my Swedish dictionary. Suicide is *självmord*, meaning self-murder. Sabotage is *sabotage*, just as it is in many European languages, deriving from the French word 'sabot': in the eighteenth century protesting workers would fling their wooden clogs – *sabots* – into a factory's machinery to wreck the production process. I know that in Sweden they have advanced public services and a solid welfare system. Crime is low, but modern Swedes are preoccupied with its genesis, a preoccupation which has spawned much popular fiction. The theory is that if someone breaks the law, their actions are seen to represent a wider societal dysfunction. Like the parents of wayward children asking themselves how they failed their offspring, the focus is not on what the criminal did wrong, but on how Swedish society could have prevented it happening.

The morning after my arrival in Stockholm I discover that Jonas Svensson's boss Lars Axel is in this sense a classic Swede. He wants, urgently and desperately, to know the explanation for Svensson's inexplicable act, and the distress which led to it. The Svensson and the Axel families were friends. They cross-country skied together. His office overlooks a large and elegant square. The interior walls are white and the furniture is black apart from a lamp whose metal shade I identify as Weathershield's 2011 Autumn Mustard.

'We are relaxed in this organisation. And open,' he tells me, leaning back in his chair and scraping the hair off his forehead to reveal the shape of his skull, which is strong and majestic, in contrast to the smaller and more delicate features of his face. 'If Jonas had a problem with coffee futures, or anything else, why didn't he tell me?'

'He may not have known how to articulate it.'

He shrugs. 'Well he certainly wasn't himself. To commit sabotage on this scale, and for absolutely no reason, after all the hard work he has done, and then try to kill himself . . .' He trails off, as though exhausted, and inspects his hands. I think again of Sunny Chen's *acte manqué*. A single oddity is a one-off. Two is the beginning of a Venn. 'He wouldn't talk to me after he'd done it. He was avoiding me. I didn't know what was happening at that point, of course. But when it came out, I think he felt ashamed. Or at least very confused.'

'Is there no explanation?'

'None that makes sense.'

'Tell me anyway.'

'Annika, that's his wife, she says he claimed he was bullied into it. I said to her, who would bully him? Nobody here at work, we are all like a family, it's very informal.' His voice is cracking. 'She said it was kids. *Kids!* He must have been having a breakdown.' He gulps and shifts in his chair, offering me a three-quarter view of his features. They're struggling, and water is welling in his eyes. 'His son's eighteen. They have a good relationship. He'd never bully him or get his friends to. And what do kids know about futures markets? What do they *care*? Hesketh, I'm so sorry. I—'

Lars Axel has started to cry. Huge sobs disrupt his body. He leans forward and hides his face in his hands. Swiftly, I start to fold paper in my head. I know I should do something else, but I'm at a loss. Then, before I can even begin to configure the etiquette of the situation, he has sprung up and walked out of his office, openly weeping. Through the glass panelling, I watch a female colleague attempt to console him. A man joins her. Then together they lead him away slowly and with great gentleness.

I stay where I am for a long time. Then I open my briefcase and take out some origami paper, and select a sheet of Classic Ivory.

Japanese tradition requires one, on a first visit, to present a gift to the host. I'm not Japanese and nor is Lars Axel, but I think: Lars Axel will see that I wanted to make a gesture of some sort, to mark his pain and my awareness of it: a memento of the few awkward moments that we spent in one another's presence. I know that Sunny Chen appreciated his praying mantis. I make a lotus flower, and balance it carefully on his desk. It's not much by way of consolation, I suppose. I realise I'm not talented in this department, in the way Lars Axel's Swedish colleagues are. But nor am I 'a robot made of meat'.

Then I leave.

Back in the hotel I sift through the financial files a second time and sort them into piles according to their relevance. I read more on the *acte manqué*, which leads me into medical descriptions of the psychogenic 'fugue' state, in which part of the mind can 'dissociate' from the rest and make its own independent decisions. Trauma or heavily suppressed negative emotions such as guilt, jealousy, resentment and rage can play a role in triggering the mind going behind its own back in this way. Most interesting to me are those cases which involve self-sabotage, such as the man who sends an anonymous letter to the police, accusing himself of his wife's murder, and then denies he ever wrote it, or the nurse who injects the wrong drug 'by accident' to five different patients on the same day and cannot explain why, or the bride who sets fire to her wedding dress as she prepares for the ceremony. I sketch out some Venns. If I am on to something, my blood feels it before my brain and I get very hungry. I raid the mini-bar. Dried fruit. Salted cashews. The inevitable Toblerone. As I eat, I shut my eyes and wait for the connection to materialise.

But instead, along comes Freddy. He does this more and more.

I open my eyes and check the time. He will just be home from school now.

My body-clock remembers his schedule.

For my birthday back in February he gave me the dinosaur that subsequently became my one souvenir of him. It has toilet-roll cardboard legs and goggly egg-carton eyes. Its skin is a crude layer of papier mâché painted green with red spots. When I asked him what it was called, he said, 'a Happybirthdayosaurus'. Children have no inhibitions about inventing words. The Happybirthdayosaurus stands on my desk at home next to the semi-assembled hermit crab. Freddy's exceptionally good with his hands, for a boy of his age. Kaitlin came up with the idea of getting him a big work-table for his bedroom, and a special chest of drawers which he filled with feathers, conkers, cardboard toilet rolls, scraps of fabric in different textures, sequins, busted jewellery, screws, nails – anything that could be fashioned into something else. He kept his tools in there too. I used to bring home odd bits of packaging and polystyrene chips, defunct cartridges, and broken computer parts for him to add to his collection. He likes to invent, and get messy. He is a fan of wood glue. He always has some on his hands. He peels it off at mealtimes. He calls it 'dead pirate skin'.

When I call Kaitlin's home number, nobody answers. This is usually what happens. She keeps her answerphone switched off. I hang on anyway, counting the rings.

I've made seven mental *ozuru* and I'm beginning an eighth. I'm just about to hang up when, on the fifty-ninth ring, someone picks up.

'Hello Freddie Kalifakidis speaking who is it?' His voice is breathless and loud: he must have been running.

'Hello Freddy K! It's me.' I am so surprised to hear him that I stall completely. But he doesn't.

'When are you coming back?'

I hesitate. 'What did your mother say?'

'She said you went abroad and we won't see you again for ages and ages.'

I start to rock gently. I gather that one of the rules with children, in the world I am not completely part of, is: 'spare them the truth'.

'Well I am in another country. But I don't live here. I have a cottage on the island of Arran in Scotland. So she got that wrong.'

'What do you do there?'

'I work. And I've got a goldfish. In an old bathtub.'

'Cool!' Freddy has always hankered after a fish.

'Maybe you can visit, and help me choose it a name.' He is very keen on christening things. 'Where's your mother?'

'In the garden. We were pulling up dandelions, but she got mad furious because I ate a woodlouse and she said I had to brush my teeth and it was disgusting, that's why I'm here to wash it off cos I've still got mud and stuff in my mouth, woodlouse blood.'

'You ate a woodlouse?'

'Actually lots of woodlouses. Maybe a hundred. You touch them and they roll into a ball. And then you eat them like peanuts. I found them in the ground, there was a whole nest under a stick. Some of them were smaller than a . . . a grain of pepper or an ant's bottom.'

'Freddy K. Irregular plural. So it's wood*lice*. Did they taste good?'

'*Nyet.* Crunchy. A bit sour. And they smell weird.'

'So what else have you been doing, apart from eating woodlice?'

'Making papier-mâché stuff. Mum said I could use your origami paper.'

'Of course you can. I was thinking of getting you a new Lego model. A big one that we can work on together.'

'Cool. A ship.'

'OK. I'll find one. How's school?'

There's a noise in the background and he breaks off for a moment. When he comes back his voice is different. 'Mum's here . . . She says she can't talk she's got muddy hands.' I hear her hissing *who is it* at him. He tells her. 'She says she'll call you back . . . I have to wash my face and brush my teeth because of the woodlouses.' His voice has changed. I'm losing him.

'Freddy K—' I rock harder. 'Remember the irregular plural. Louse becomes lice.'

I hear his mother say his name sharply, and he says, 'Got to go. Bye Hesketh,' and he's hung up.

I check the Svensson file again and draw up a mental list of questions to ask him and his doctors. Kaitlin doesn't call back. Freddy will be interrogating her about me, I am sure. He'll want to know why we can't see each other and she'll come up with a new lie which she will justify by saying it's a 'white' one.

Dulux has many whites in its range. Lily, Ivory, Orchid, Ice, Barely Grey, Pacific Mist.

We argued about Freddy before I left.

'I'm the only adult male he's ever been around on a regular basis,' I said. 'He thinks of me as his father.'

'That's exactly the problem,' she said.

'So you'll just go and find him a new one?'

She didn't say anything. I did a mental flow chart which brought me to the conclusion that this might already have happened.

★　　★　　★

It's six o'clock and I have gone down to the hotel bar where a woman is sitting alone drinking white wine. She is flicking through a demographics journal. This attracts my attention, firstly because population distribution is a fascinating field of study and secondly because the journal is in German, a language I speak passably. I like to practise it, so I introduce myself to the woman in German – *guten Abend* – and we get talking. She tells me she is an academic attending a conference on statistical projections in the wake of the UN's recent warning. It's called *The Perfect Storm: Climate, Hunger and Population*. She shows me a graph whose growth curve I am familiar with: it is applicable to any biological species with no significant predators and finite resources. I ask her when she sees the exponential growth phase being replaced by stationary and death phases. She replies that it is unlikely to be later than 2100 and could be sooner than 2050.

'Human civilisation faces a 90 per cent risk of collapse if the population rate isn't held in check. We're a species out of control. Do you realise, the world's population has more than doubled in my lifetime?'

I do a swift calculation. She'd have been born around 1960. 'You must be above fifty, then.' Her eyes change shape. 'That's OK. I like older women.'

Although she has no distinguishing features by which she can be readily recognised, she is reasonably attractive. I haven't had sex in two hundred and sixteen days and I feel the need with a sudden urgency. So I ask a few personal-information questions by way of a warm-up: where do you live, etcetera. I learn that she is based in Geneva but travels a great deal, which means she can't have a dog. But she would like one. I ask what breed and she says a King Charles spaniel. I tell her I have an as-yet un-christened fish. When I ask her if she'd like to join me in my room, she understands what I mean immediately, but claims she is *ein bisschen überrascht*, 'a little taken aback', and suggests we have another drink first *um sich kennenzulernen*, 'to get acquainted'.

I thought we'd done that. I don't want another drink, but I buy her a second glass of wine and wait for her to finish it.

'Don't you want one?' she asks. She is drinking her wine rather slowly.

Apparently I hadn't made myself clear. 'No. I just want you. I like older women. And sex too of course. I like sex. We won't reproduce.'

This prompts the blush reflex and she laughs. 'Not at my age, no.'

She looks down at her hands. Then she looks up and says, 'Hesketh. You're an incredibly good-looking man. But I expect you know that.'

I do, as women have often told me so before. 'My ex used to call me the tall, dark stranger,' I tell her. 'But she didn't mean it as a compliment.'

She smiles. I run my finger up the inside of her wrist, one of my favourite places on women. Then she finishes her drink in one gulp and we go upstairs and I get to sample some of my other favourite places: the nape of the neck, the breasts and nipples, and, of course, the *mons venus* area.

The sex starts well, but just as I've established a definitive momentum my phone makes its text-message noise, which is the cry of the peregrine falcon. I regret programming this in. Some rhythms are not meant to be broken, and certain sounds are particularly disruptive, so this causes a setback. The Swiss demographer gets me going again quite expertly, but once my penis is back in her vagina it's all over after twenty-two thrusts. She hasn't had an orgasm, and although she at first declines my offer to give her one, she then changes her mind and guides my hand and my movements. Every woman seems to have her own bespoke requirements here, and I consider it polite to pay heed to this. They generally appreciate my respect for the rules of reciprocity.

Afterwards, she suggests we have dinner together, but I decline.

'Sorry. In other circumstances I would, but tonight I have to work.'

'I could come by later when you've finished. Stay the night.' Perhaps she wants another orgasm.

'No, that's not possible.' Here I switch to English because I lack the vocabulary I need. 'I have RLS. That's an acronym for Restless Leg Syndrome. It means I kick women. In bed. By accident, of course.' I switch back to German. 'Don't worry,' I reassure her, as she finishes dressing. 'We don't need to see each other again.'

Her mood must have shifted because her smile vanishes. I've observed this before with women, post-sex. They want to linger, but they can't spell out why.

'Do you make a habit of this?'

'No, but I'd like to,' I tell her. 'It's just that I'm not good at being with other people for long. I know I don't have—' Once again I can't find the German term I need, which annoys me. So I say it in English. 'People skills.'

She switches to English. 'I noticed.' She is fiddling with a silver bangle on her wrist, decorated with a pattern of feathers. Indian, at a guess. I realise I have probably hit the wrong note again, but I don't know how to remedy it. I haven't memorised the phrases for it in any language. 'Tell me,' she says, 'isn't a problem with social interaction quite a handicap in your field? Didn't you say you were an anthropologist?' Her English is far superior to my German. I must take the time to study harder.

'When it comes to gauging human behaviour, it's an asset. It's like colour-blind people being deployed by the military to detect camouflage,' I reply. 'They look for the shapes rather than the colours.' This line is tried and tested.

Her features relax into a more forgiving configuration. All of a sudden, she seems to understand. Usually they do. I reach for my laptop and fire it up. She stands in the doorway watching me for a long time, just as Kaitlin used to.

At some point she gives up on me and leaves the room.

Kaitlin did that too. It was always a relief.

It's only later on, when I'm setting my phone alarm, that I see the text that interrupted sex with the demographer.

You have left Freddy very confused. He's not your son and you are out of his life now. If you want the best for him, then please leave him in peace and let's all move on.

Kaitlin Kalifakidis is a lawyer: we met on a case. I was instantly attracted to her. I liked her Greek surname, but it was her wild hair that struck me most. It seemed messy and a little unprofessional, given her sober job. Even tied up, there was — and is — a huge amount of it. So that's what I registered first: that confusion of Burnt Cedar hair piled high. I liked her mouth. The full lips, lipsticked a good, forceful red. Wide-set, animated eyes, a small neat body. There are certain colours I dislike intensely, so it suited me that she was largely a monochrome dresser. Blacks, whites and shades of cream or beige: she wore nothing that shouted. Everything was discreet and suited her. The only bright colour was on her lips: the rest of her make-up was a variation of her own hair colour and skin tones. 'Easier to make decisions,' she explained once. 'Anyway clothes should showcase you. Not the other way round.' I liked that in her: the choice to limit her wardrobe to what worked, and ignore fashion. Her practicality.

When the case was over she told me she found me very attractive and invited me out to dinner. Over this meal I learned she'd been brought up bilingual, so I tried out some Greek phrases on her. This made her smile, and led to her questioning me more, and what she heard seemed to excite her. She already knew all about Phipps & Wexman and she'd heard of Professor Whybray's work on mass hysteria. She was impressed that I'd worked so closely with him, and that he'd been my mentor. When she invited me back to her home after dinner I didn't need to draw a mental flow chart to know what this would mean. She had already told me about Freddy: he was five at the time. She described him as 'born fatherless', but changed the subject when I asked how that was technically possible. She did not have many taboos, but I quickly learned that Freddy Kalifakidis' paternity was one of them.

Kaitlin employed a live-in au-pair girl who had already fed the boy and put him to bed when we got in. This young woman then melted discreetly into her room. Kaitlin and I had sex that night and again the next morning. She had warned me we had to do it very quietly because of Freddy and the au pair, but silence is always fine by me. I find that women often make distracting noises during sex, right in one's ear, necessitating the deployment of various coping mechanisms. I liked grabbing her Greek hair in my hands. If the lack of eye contact bothered her, she didn't mention it.

I discovered that Kaitlin was very straightforward and business-like about what she wanted, in and out of bed. After a few dates, I grasped that I was being interviewed for a job I had not considered applying for. She told me she wanted a man in her life who could be a role model for her son, who respected her lifestyle and her work, who was compatible with her sexually and whom she could grow to love.

'Is that how it works?' I asked. It was not what I had gleaned from popular culture and empirical observation, or from anything Professor Whybray told me when his wife Helena was dying. When I expressed my doubts, she suggested a trial run of three months. I didn't ask how many other men she had considered or why she wanted me. But she did. The trial period worked: Kaitlin liked the way Freddy and I fitted together mentally. I did too. I felt at ease around him from the start. And he felt the same. He liked watching me make origami models. He liked the folk tales I told him, and he enjoyed pulling at the hairs on my arm, and being swung high in the air, and testing his strength against me. We had arm-wrestling matches and developed a game involving the hurling of cushions which Kaitlin called 'daily violence'. He had been starved of male company.

I put up some shelving for my things, folded Kaitlin a Hot Crimson Kawasaki rose with a Jungle Khaki stalk and leaves and moved in.

There is a popular theory that when a woman falls in love with a man, she falls in love with two men: the man he is, and the man she wants him to be.

It soon became apparent that I could not become that man.

By now I have studied Sverige Banken's financial documents closely enough to have established that Jonas Svensson's costly act of sabotage required him to make only five keystrokes on his computer. In or out of a dissociative state, it was the work of no more than eight seconds. More likely three. Tomorrow I will seek confirmation of this, and interview him accordingly. Pleased to have made progress, I allow myself the relaxation of watching the final part of a documentary on BBC World about Napoleon's pyrrhic victory over Moscow in 1812. It's followed by the late-night news. A disturbing murder has rocked France. A boy of ten shot his two uncles at point-blank range, in a forest. One died, the other survived with severe injuries. He used his father's rifle. They were out hunting wild boar. It was not an accident: eight witnesses – including the boy's father and some cousins – saw him do it. There was no obvious motive. Unsurprisingly, it's being linked to the case of the Harrogate child now known to the public as Pyjama Girl.

But to me she's Child One. And the French boy is now Child Two.

All night I kick.

CHAPTER 4

WHEN ASHOK SKYPES me in the morning the image is unclear. It gives him a cubist look which suits him. Whenever I think of the cubist movement, I think in particular of Georges Braque, because of all its adherents, he strikes me as the most mathematically aware.

'How's Sweden?' Ashok wants to know. My screen tells me it's 9.12 local time. It's Thursday 20th September. This was my mother's birthday. Had she lived she would now be seventy-one.

'See for yourself.' I angle my laptop to show him the view of the waterfront from my window, where ships, ferries and boats gleam dully under a low sun. 'The forecast says it'll be cloudy with light rain showers and a high of twelve.'

'Neat,' he says. 'Must go there sometime. What are you up to then, Maestro?'

'I had sex with a demographer.' That wakes him up.

'Well they don't call you the Pussy Magnet for nothing. She Swedish? I hear they're hot.'

'Swiss–German. Attending a UN conference on the population crisis. What are you supposed to do when someone cries?'

'You made her *cry*? You big, crazy heartbreaker!'

'No. I'm talking about Jonas Svensson's boss. Lars Axel. He cried when I interviewed him.'

'What did he say?'

'Not much. He cried. So what do you do, when it's a man?'

'Jeez, Hesketh. Same as a woman. You pat them on the arm or squeeze their shoulder or their hand or you might give them a hug. You tell them you understand this is a difficult situation and suggest you talk another time. Did you do any of that?'

'No. But I think his colleagues did. He left the room crying, so I made him a lotus flower. Then later his PA called to apologise.'

'OK. Well I just talked to the wife. Annika. Very dignified lady. She says you can visit Jonas in hospital this morning. She'll be there. But she says she won't guarantee you'll get any sense out of him. He's been in a confused state since he came out of the coma. Mental breakdown, whatever. But get what you can. By the way. Lotus flower: nice touch.'

After he has said goodbye, this remark puzzles me. The lotus is a perennial plant that grows from a thick rhizome in altitudes up to 1,600 metres. It is almost entirely edible, and is seen in some Eastern cultures as a symbol of purity, or the movement of the human spirit towards a state of enlightenment. Was this symbolism what Ashok was referring to, when he said, 'nice touch'? If so, he would be wrong. I constructed a lotus flower for Lars Axel because apart from *ozuru*, I work through my repertoire of twelve basic models on a rota system, and it was the turn of Model 8.

Outside, altocumulus and cirrocumulus clouds drape the sky. At ten o'clock, I take the fourteen-and-a-half-minute walk from my hotel to the hospital. It's an eight-storey modern structure with polished floors. There's a huge courtyard with a bronze sculpture of a lion, surrounded by glass-sided lifts. It doesn't have the sickly, claustrophobic smell of the British hospitals I visited during the years of my parents' physical decline, or later, when Mrs Helena Whybray was dying and I accompanied the professor to help him 'keep a grip'. This is an environment in which one can imagine people getting well at speed, where broken bodies are repaired and serviced by high-quality machines. At Reception I'm told that Jonas Svensson has been placed on the psychiatric ward where he is still being assessed. If he is deemed to be a danger to himself and others he will be moved to another unit. If not, he'll be allowed home.

Svensson has a room to himself, which I am directed to by a black male nurse with tribal markings on his cheeks. There's a woman sitting outside it, angled oddly on a chair, like a perched *ozuru*. Annika Svensson is probably in her mid-fifties, and quite wrinkled. She is wearing a jacket in a green I particularly like: Bamboo Classic. When she sees me she rises, all long limbs and hinge-like joints. My height is often a useful barrier to eye contact. Not on this occasion: she is exceptionally tall, so I focus on her earring and greet her in Swedish. People are always glad when you address them in their own language, I have found, even though your knowledge may not extend further than what you have memorised from a dictionary or phrase book. Annika Svensson has very clearly been crying, and her left cheek is bright red. She must see me noticing, because she puts her hand to it. Her fingers are very long.

'How is your husband doing?' I ask. 'I hope you don't mind speaking English.'

'I went in there a minute ago and he hit me in the face. He's never done anything like that before.'

Abruptly, through the door, we hear a man shouting something and a woman's voice trying to calm him.

'What's he saying?' I ask. I caught only one word: *fan*, or 'devil'. Scandinavian swearing is very tame compared to its Anglo-Saxon equivalent, which is why they import words like 'fuck' and 'shit' into their vocabulary. They use them liberally and with far less inhibition than native English speakers.

'It's all nonsense,' she answers. 'It's like he's gone back to childhood. He says kids forced him into it.' She shrugs. 'This is not the Jonas I know. He was never violent. Never. He's become another person.'

'Can I go in?'

'Ask Dr Aziz. She's in there with him. But keep away from him, he's very strong.'

I knock. No one answers, so I go in.

A young black-haired woman whom I take to be Dr Aziz is standing by the far window, speaking rapidly into a phone. She looks distressed and I can see why: Jonas Svensson, who is seated on the bed, is wearing nothing but a pair of sunglasses. When I saw his photo at the bank, he was not stark naked. He was clad in a quiet grey suit. And you could see his eyes: blue, like his wife's. The glasses are a ski-style wrap-around design with mirror lenses. I am not cut out for this kind of encounter. His bare skin is almost translucent, in the same way as a maggot's, and mapped with blue veins. The pale hair on his limbs and genital area catches the sunlight. His penis rests on his thigh, flaccid. He has a small pot belly. A hospital nightgown lies on the floor. He has apparently just removed it. Dr Aziz shakes her head and again points at the door, indicating I should leave. But just then Jonas Svensson turns his attention to me, shouting something in Swedish and motioning angrily at the chair. He wants me to sit. I hesitate. I don't mind not having eye contact with him. But his mirror sunglasses are distracting. I have no wish to see my own alarmed face. I look at the floor and say, 'I came to see you from London. I'm investigating what happened at the bank.'

'So sit down.' His Swedish accent is thicker than Annika's.

'I'll let you stay for a moment,' says the doctor, breaking off from her phone call. 'But as you see he is very agitated.' I nod, and she returns to her conversation. I sit on the plastic chair next to the bed, but I don't know where to look.

'There is a gang of them,' says Jonas Svensson. He seems manic. 'Anyway they are disgusting creatures, they just took my clothes off, those . . .' He can't find the word. Then he does. 'Trolls.'

'Trolls?'

'Yes. Little kiddie trolls. I must've swallowed one. That's how they get in, right? I'm just guessing. Like a tapeworm or something. They stink. Look at my hands. Do they look a normal size to you? Or do they look like they belong on a stinking kiddie troll?'

He shoves his huge hands towards me, clenched into fists. I recoil. On a parallel track, I'm folding paper in my head. I speed it up, but I can't do it fast enough to get the effect I need.

I say, 'They look a normal size. In fact they are on the large side.'

'On the large side, is that what you think? Well think again man,' he says with what seems to be contempt. 'It made me fuck things up. I didn't want to! Don't you see?' He's shouting now. 'It's in me! It's using me like a puppet!'

'Sir, you should go,' says Dr Aziz.

'What's using you like a puppet?' I ask, hesitating.

'The fucking . . . creature. It's still in here.' He thumps his chest. 'It's going to kill me.'

'We won't let that happen,' says Dr Aziz, in English. Her voice is reassuring. She is preparing a syringe. 'You're safe in here, Jonas.'

He laughs. 'You think they came all this way for nothing? You think they're just having fun? Ha!' He whips off his sunglasses. I wish he hadn't. My breath catches in my throat. His eyes are so bloodshot that there's no white to be seen. Just two pale blue irises swimming in a sea of red. They are leaking a kind of glue. 'And how do you think it feels to go blind, ha?' he asks.

'You're not going blind. You just have a bad infection,' says the doctor. 'And a pressure build-up. The antibiotics will help, you'll see.' She addresses me. 'Why don't you come back another time when he's calmer?'

Svensson puts a fist to his brow next to his bulging right eye, then suddenly opens up his hand. It's a baffling gesture. I think of a spread starfish. 'That's what happens next. Pop. Do you think we like what you did to us? Do you think we wanted to be the last?'

Dr Aziz addresses Svensson fast, in Swedish. I understand none of it, except '*du*', meaning 'you', and '*nu*', meaning 'now'. He shoves his sunglasses back on then lifts his hands high above his head, splays his fingers again, and with a swift movement catches hold of my upper arm and digs his fingers in deep. The pain is shocking. I cry out sharply and the doctor buzzes an alarm. 'You fucking grown-up,' he says.

'Security's coming,' says Dr Aziz, trying to pull Jonas off. But he shakes her away and tightens his grip. I start rocking. As I rock, I can see my own face moving back and forth in his distortive mirror lenses. My mouth is open, as if I am trying to shout but can't. He's remarkably strong. I can feel the tip of each finger digging into my flesh through the fabric of my sleeve. He digs in deeper and hisses, 'Do you think we like starving, and fighting over food? You fucking *lap-sap*.'

I freeze. *Lap-sap* isn't Swedish. It's Cantonese. It means rubbish. Just then the door opens wide and a tall blond security guard enters with the black nurse. At this Jonas utters a yelp, releases his grip on my arm, jumps up and dodges past the guard. The nurse grabs his hand, but he breaks free and hurtles through the open door and out. Dr Aziz slams at a button on the wall and the wail of an alarm sets up: the guard has already gone. Outside the door, I hear Annika screaming at Jonas to stop.

Dr Aziz rushes out and I follow. There's no sign of either Jonas or the nurse or the guard, but the swing doors are closing as Annika Svensson reaches them. She pushes them open again and bursts through, still calling after Jonas: *Hold op Jonas! Hold op!*

When Dr Aziz and I reach Reception a cluster of people is pointing through the revolving door and staff are yelling into walkie-talkies. Annika speeds out and I follow. Outside, others are chasing him: some wear white coats. The nurse with tribal markings is crouched on the ground, groaning and clutching his stomach. Jonas must have punched him. Then I see him, far off, racing across the parking area in a zigzag sprint, his pale buttocks jiggling as he manoeuvres past the cars, occasionally ducking and popping up again. Everyone's shouting. Jonas is still well ahead of everyone else, and clearly heading for the vehicle exit and the road beyond. I am a fast runner, but I know it's hopeless trying to close the gap. I keep running anyway. Up ahead, Annika screams again.

A different kind of scream.

I have never seen a traffic accident actually happen before.

The truck is a big one, with eight wheels. Dirty. Underneath the dirt, it's red and yellow. It must weigh eight tons. There is a high screech of brakes as the driver sees Jonas and swerves to avoid him. He fails. The noise when it hits him: *BAM* or possibly *KERTHUNK*. The impact hurls Jonas sideways and upward, on a diagonal trajectory. He could be one of Freddy's Action Men, flung gaily aside. I don't see him land. But I see the truck smash into the wall on the opposite side of the road. There's a huge reverberative thud and then the engine dies.

In the silence that follows, my mind goes blank. I stand there rocking. I register a security guard shouting into a walkie-talkie; Annika Svensson sinking down on to the bare tarmac; paramedics rushing past with a stretcher; a man taking a photo on his mobile phone. Within seconds, blue lights are flashing everywhere and the site of the accident is seething with people.

There's nothing I can do, so I walk at high speed back into the hospital and find a bathroom where I vomit copiously. What comes out is dark because I ate Swedish crackers for breakfast, and these are made of rye. I also had smoked salmon, plus some fresh blueberries and redcurrants. There are traces of those too, making for a repellent colour mix.

Back at the hotel, I call the hospital to find out the news, then take a long shower. I think about how I'd tell Freddy the story of Jonas and the truck.

A Swedish man said that kiddie trolls made him ruin his work. He tried to kill himself with poison. When that failed he was locked away in a safe place. But it wasn't safe enough. He ran under a truck. They're operating on him now. He has suffered massive blood loss. The driver of the lorry has a broken clavicle and fractured ribs. And here's what I know about Scandinavian trolls, Freddy K. They steal people and carry them off into the mountains. The English expression 'off with the fairies' stems from that belief. Trolls can change shape. Some can appear very dapper. Troll-women seduce men, but they can be spotted because they are only facades: they never show their backs. They come in all sizes. Some have tails. They never divulge their names.

I Skype Ashok and fill him in briefly on my abortive interview with Jonas Svensson and what followed. When I tell him about Jonas' prognosis – not good – he puts his head in his hands. When he looks at me again, his hair is sticking out at odd angles.

'Jesus. You're sure earning your bucks on this one, Maestro.'

'In the Chen file, there's an envelope containing a specimen. I think it's something mineral. Can you have it analysed?'

'Sure. Might take a few days.'

'And the suicide note?'

'Is just some weird little drawings. I've sent you a PDF. Stephanie Mulligan's got a theory. About Chen and Svensson. Want to hear it? Belinda, get Steph in here, will you?'

'Sure,' says Belinda, picking up the phone.

'No. Don't,' I say.

'Why?' says Ashok.

'It might cloud my judgement.'

'You're not thinking straight.' He leans closer to the screen, but I can't make out his expression. 'And you could do with a shave. You've missed some on your neck. You need to keep it together, bud. A lot's riding on this. Hey, Steph.' He turns as she enters. 'Come join us.'

If he had any idea what Stephanie has been to me, and perhaps still is, he would not be doing this.

I'm aware of the pale hair, the stark, unadorned face, the white neck, the eyes demanding contact. The small, mean breasts I have often fantasised about, against my will, and which, in combination with other things, have brought me to orgasm forty-seven times to date. I focus on her hairline. She raises a hand, smiles and says 'Hi'. She can be very professional. By this I mean she is very good at pretending. She is popular at work. People call her 'modest' and 'insightful'. I nod back. She pulls up a chair next to Ashok, who adjusts the screen so they are both visible.

'So, Steph. I was just telling Hesketh you have a theory.'

I shift my eye line to the rim of the laptop.

'You've probably thought of this yourself already Hesketh,' she

86

begins. 'But here's my take on it, for what it's worth. What strikes me is that there's such a big split between the men's actions and their personalities that something's got to be going on behind the scenes. Some kind of outside pressure.' The connection is a bad one: her voice is patchy. 'Chen and Svensson are what I'd call the drone type. They're conscientious about their work and they're loyal to their firm. They don't fit the saboteur profile. We know that from your report on Chen, and from what Annika Svensson told Ashok about her husband.'

'Who just threw himself under a truck, by the way,' Ashok tells her. 'Hesketh saw it happen. Guy's fighting for his life.'

She pulls back slightly and her face changes. Her voice too. 'Hesketh. I'm so sorry. Perhaps we should talk another time. You must be in shock.'

'No. It's a bad connection, but let's just get it over with.' They look at each other.

'OK,' she says. 'So someone's got to these men, and forced them into doing something that went against their nature. They felt manipulated. Like they were at the mercy of someone or something. Suicide was their only way of protesting and taking back control. Does that make any sense?'

I start sketching a new Venn on the hotel notepaper in front of me. I press too hard and the pencil lead breaks.

'Yes. As far as it goes.' She hasn't mentioned the possibility that Chen and Svensson's subconscious minds were in active rebellion against their conscious selves. I could raise the notion of dissociative fugue myself, but I'm not going to. This is my investigation.

Ashok says, 'In the meantime, we've warned all our past clients that if they get any motiveless sabotage, in view of what's happened we're offering surveillance and counselling. Stephanie's idea. Nice touch, eh?'

'Sounds lucrative,' I say. Stephanie looks away.

The careless way she stirred up my life.

Ashok grins. 'All part of the elite service we offer. Look, Hesketh. We've got two clients so far. But I'll be frank. Word's going around, there are others. A lot. There's some seriously weird global shit going on. I'll send you some outlines, if I can get them. But for now just do your thing. Usual strategy: describe, process, prevent slash eliminate.'

Just as Stephanie starts to say something else the image freezes. So I say, 'You're breaking up,' press End Call, download Ashok's PDF and go offline.

I open the file. Sunny's suicide drawings are striking. I can see why Mrs Chen refused to associate this odd legacy with her husband. I can't picture him producing them either. Their boldness and brashness seems out of character. The three images are large and crudely executed in broad ink strokes. Freddy could have done them.

There's a human eye with what might be rays of light shooting out of it, reminiscent of the all-seeing eye depicted on top of the pyramid on an American dollar bill.

There's an ellipse that resembles a necklace strung with elongated beads. Their tips are spiked, like narrow bones.

And at the bottom right of the page, where an artist would put his signature, is a hand-print. The fingers are together, with only the thumb separate from the rest. The effect is that of a stop sign.

Have the police checked the fingerprints against Sunny Chen's? His wife may have demanded it. She had insisted, after all, that the drawings could not have been left by Sunny. The jagged ellipse and the eye are large in relation to the hand. I pull the Jenwai folder back on my screen and call up the image of the smear that Sunny Chen was so keen for the police to fingerprint at the factory, yet so reluctant to discuss: the smear he later claimed he'd made himself. He'd called it 'evidence'. I stare at it for a long time. Then I text Ashok asking for the dimensions of the original 'suicide drawings'. If I know the scale, I'll know if the hand-print is a normal size for a man. If it is not, then how could Sunny have made it? He said 'they' had pressured him, and made his body disobey his mind. And Jonas claimed 'little kiddie trolls' used him as a puppet to sabotage the system. He thought he might have 'swallowed' one. He used the analogy of a tapeworm.

They are travellers, said Sunny Chen. *They go wherever they like.*

They came all this way, said Jonas.

Who did? And from where?

Later that evening, I go on the net. There's been another attack, this one in southern Spain. The culprits are twin boys, aged nine. Child Three and Child Four, as I immediately think of them, pushed their father off a stone staircase in full view of the rest of the family, who were gathered in the courtyard of their farmhouse for a meal, celebrating a younger child's birthday. Afterwards the boys would not speak. Again, there was no apparent motive, but on the morning of the attack, they told their parents that they had woken abruptly in the night, from the same nightmare.

The father died.

I reach for a pencil and sharpen it with six turns, inhaling the scent of the long, pristine shaving that emerges. Pine and graphite. It's very pleasing. Then I reach for a pad and start drawing.

Men attacking institutions that they love.

Children turning on their families.

Two overlapping circles, with irrational violence at the intersection.

What else connects them?

Something has lured my old mentor out of retirement. Mass hysteria is Professor Whybray's field. Something *hush-hush* at the Home Office, Ashok said. *He hinted at a contract.* Is the old man thinking along the same lines as me?

At 8.15 I go to the hotel restaurant for dinner, where I learn the Swedish word for crayfish: *kräfta*. When I come back I see there's a message from Annika Svensson. They are still operating. She's going to fetch her son, then go to the hospital and wait. She'll call me if there's any news.

My upper right arm hurts where Jonas dug his fingers in. I run a hot bath, hoping to ease it. You can adjust the temperature on the taps: I set it to forty-one degrees. Steam fills the room. I slide into the scalding water. It's cramped; in order to lie with my arms beneath the surface, I have to stick my legs out the other end. I inspect the bruising, exaggerated by the water's heat and the bright lighting of the bathroom: it's Victory Purple in the centre, and there are several shades of yellow, from Soft Butterscotch to Ochre Bisque at the edges, nudging into the green range. The pattern of the oedema is unusual. Jonas' grip spanned much of my upper arm. But the marks – four surprisingly small blotches made by his fingers across the bicep, and a thumb-print on the triceps – are condensed into an extremely limited area.

If you didn't know that a grown man had gripped me there, you'd think the bruising came from the clutch of a child.

CHAPTER 5

BEFORE I GO to bed, I call Ashok and update him on Svensson. As I talk, he keeps raking his fingers through his hair, which he always does when he is rattled.

'Did you get the dimensions of Sunny Chen's suicide note?' I ask.

'Yep, it's A4.' He shifts the chewing gum in his mouth. Numerous studies have proved gum to be a useful concentration aid.

'Which means that the hand-print's too small to be Sunny Chen's. So his wife was right. Someone else made it.'

'Well I'll be happy to hear where that leads. Looks like a blind alley to me. In the meantime, here's the thing. Tomorrow you're heading for the airport.'

'I'd prefer the train.'

'That won't work for where you're going.' He removes a wad of gum from his mouth and squishes it into a Post-it note. 'Dubai. New case. I told you there were others. Construction industry.

Guy named Ahmed Farooq. Killed himself yesterday. The client's his employer. Eastern Horizons.'

Two thoughts cross my mind. The first is that I don't have my Arabic dictionary. But I only voice the second. 'At least he's already dead.'

Ashok cocks an eyebrow. 'No more ugly surprises, right? I hear you. Let's hope Svensson pulls through.'

'Tell me about the new one.' I'm stirred.

'Straight sabotage. Farooq removed a whole string of zeros from some vital sales agreement after it'd gone past the lawyers. Managed to screw up his company's business across five continents. Seems totally random. Nothing in it for him. No motive. If he hadn't killed himself he'd have gone to jail. Got a theory yet?'

'Humans have a highly evolved neurophysiology of self-deception. Under pressure, the subconscious can take charge and force you to succumb to your true desires. The deep ones that your conscious mind rejects. Dissociation enables you to commit acts that your conscious mind won't acknowledge. Later, you'll turn a blind eye to what you've done. To deploy a metaphor.'

'So how does that work? You're awake, but sleepwalking?'

'Yes. I think Sunny Chen was in a dissociative state when he sent the documents exposing Jenwai. Jonas Svensson claimed he sabotaged the bank against his will. This sounds similar.'

'So that's what you're working on?'

'Part of it.'

'So what's the rest?'

'I anticipate that you'll object to it on principle.'

'Try me.'

Sure enough, I've only just begun my line of speculation when he pronounces that I am 'barking up a seriously wrong fucking tree'. He thumps his desk for emphasis, and I see Belinda Yates jump in the background. 'Just go there and you make some sense out of this mess that doesn't involve . . . what d'you call it?'

'Indigenous belief systems.'

'Yeah them. I don't care if you've got a PhD in it. Our clients are international corporations run by grown-ups. We've got rivals out there. So no fucking little people.' Ashok is a child of the Age of Reason. As such, he cherishes the notion that we have cast off the superstitions and fears which dominated the lives of our medieval forefathers. 'Got it? Don't let me down on this one bud. You're paid to think out of the box, but not that far. A lot's riding on this one.'

'When humans dare to think in new ways they are set free,' I tell him.

'Come again?'

'That was Kant's motto in the Enlightenment. But we're not completely enlightened, Ashok. There will always be dark corners. Humans like to believe they're rational. But the capacity for super-stition is part of our DNA. It can't be purged. All the things we fear − all the *little people*, if you like − are as present as they ever were. But they're no longer external. They've been chased indoors. Where we can't let them go.'

He sighs. 'OK. But bottom line, they're not popping up in Phipps & Wexman reports. So no Harry Potter bullshit and no goddam . . . ectoplasm. Got it?'

★   ★   ★

In bed, I scroll through the news. A headline catches my eye. In Seoul, a boy of nine tied up his grandfather, turned on the gas and left him to die in the kitchen. In Argentina, a girl of seven dropped a flowerpot from a fourth-floor balcony on to her aunt's head, killing her instantly. A leading child psychologist is calling for an international conference on 'this unprecedented phenomenon'. He says that before their attacks, many of the children reported vivid dreams or nightmares. Afterwards, they either remained silent, or claimed to have no knowledge of what they had done.

The Venn diagram in my head bursts into rapidly expanding life. I need to talk to Professor Whybray. He's more of a lateral thinker than I am and less of an *incurable materialist*, so he'll have gone further, and faster.

He and Freddy never met. But they'd get along.

Together we'd make a satisfying equilateral triangle.

It's Annika Svensson who takes me to the airport the next afternoon. She has been crying again. I tell her she should not be driving, and offer to take the wheel myself, but she insists. She is going there anyway, to meet her sister Lisbet. Lisbet is flying in from Minnesota to help Annika prepare for the funeral and afterwards to sort out the family's administrative and financial affairs in the wake of Jonas' death. Yes, Jonas died. So today, Friday 21st September, is Annika's first day as a widow. He survived the operation, but an hour later he suffered a catastrophic heart rupture. Technically speaking it wasn't Jonas' blood that flooded out of his burst aorta. It was somebody else's, or to be more precise a mixture of several other people's, because he'd received a transfusion.

She says, 'I just want to know why. What it was for.' I don't answer because I can't think what to say. I do believe, however, that everything must mean something. That even the most random events have significance, on some level. 'Something happened to Jonas to make him act that way. I told you, it wasn't *him*. He behaved like he was someone else. Someone . . . *possessed*. And he's not the only one. I know that, Hesketh. Isn't that why you came here?'

She must have heard rumours about other cases. 'There are always a thousand connections when you look for them,' I say. We've reached Departures. 'The trick is to work out which to follow up and which to reject.' She still recalls the elegant *ozuru* I first saw outside Jonas' hospital room. But suffering has altered her angles and folds.

'Please, Hesketh. Find out why all this happened.'

'Can you try to note down everything Jonas said about why he did it? Even if it makes no sense?'

She draws in a long breath. 'He said a lot of things. I'll talk to my son and I'll send you a mail.'

We say goodbye, first in English and then in Swedish. She hesitates, then plants a dry kiss on my left cheek. She turns and I watch her walk towards Arrivals.

I text Ashok.

Request Jonas Svensson autopsy report

I buy the *New Scientist* and while queuing for the security check, read an article about the threatened extinction of honeybees.

Colony collapse disorder is affecting swarms worldwide. The repercussions of the species disappearing would be catastrophic for farming – the meat and cotton industries in particular – and wildlife. The isolation of unaffected hives is posited as one solution. While I am deep in Marie Celeste syndrome, which refers to hives found inexplicably abandoned, a woman in a red coat – what Dulux, in 1984, called Carnation – comes up to me.

'Well this is quite a coincidence,' she says, waving a passport case. 'I'm leaving today too.'

I look around. 'Well so's everyone in this queue,' I say. 'It's for Departures.'

The woman's smile looks crooked. I can't identify the emotion it corresponds to.

She looks familiar, but I'm not good with faces. I return to the article: the group dynamics of social animals always interest me.

'Ingrid,' she says. I am not good with names either.

'Hesketh,' I say.

'I know.'

It's only when she puts her hand up to flick back her hair – women often do that when they're anxious, I've noticed – and I see the feathered pattern of her Indian silver bangle, that I remember who she is, and smile.

'Got it!' I'm happy to have placed her. 'The Swiss demographer. Wednesday. The Perfect Storm conference. Climate, Hunger and Population. You'd like a King Charles spaniel. We had sex.'

She takes a step back and her face changes shape.

'Well, enjoy the rest of your life, Hesketh Lock,' she says.

Then she walks away very fast towards the other queue for departures. If she'd addressed me in German, or worn the Carnation coat in the hotel, I'd have known her straight away.

'*Auf wiedersehen!*' I call after her. But she carries on walking and doesn't look back.

There's a five-hour stopover at Charles de Gaulle in Paris, where I'm changing planes, so I go to an airport hotel gym and run ten kilometres on a treadmill, then buy some new clothes: sandals, cotton trousers, three white shirts. In Departures I eat a meal (I choose the 'menu gastronomique'), do forty-seven sudokus and download the new document Ashok has sent.

In Dubai the native population believe in djinns or 'jinn'. A djinn is an evil spirit which taunts people and renders their lives intolerable. It can possess them without their knowledge, and cause them to behave out of character. Like Sunny Chen's Chinese ancestors, djinns need placating and appeasing.

When I told Ashok that I considered it logical to suspect that the Dubai case would involve somebody losing their reason and blaming some kind of native evil spirit, i.e. a djinn, or a demon child, he shut his eyes and breathed out and said *oh man*.

'I am sure Farooq will have mentioned djinn.'

'And what kind of fucked-up weirdo place does that take us, Maestro? Do we tell the client his construction empire's spooked?'

'No. We tell them that something caused one of their employees to regress and invoke negative childhood archetypes, and that this behaviour's part of a mass hysterical phenomenon we have yet to fully identify. Sunny Chen. Jonas Svensson. Same pattern. In order to explain what they did in the dissociative fugue state, they conjure manifestations of indigenous belief systems. Ancestors in Chen's case. In Svenssson's, trolls. In Farooq's, I predict djinns.'

That's when he banged on the desk and made Belinda Yates jump.

But sure enough, according to the police report on Farooq's death, which Ashok has very typically not bothered to read thoroughly, I now discover that Ahmed Farooq did indeed mention djinns. It is right there, in his wife's statement.

Halla Farooq claims he worried that a djinn 'who looked like a small beggar' had 'possessed' him. Annika Svensson also used that word. Unlike her husband, Halla Farooq did not claim to see the djinn herself, but the natives of the United Arab Emirates – known as Emiratis – are very superstitious, and she believed in it as fervently as he did. It was the djinn, she insisted, that made him behave oddly and drove him to his death.

If I believed in the resting of cases, I would rest my case. I know what Ashok will say when I tell him.

He'll shout, 'Jesus Christ, Hesketh. Fucking Arab goblins. This is all I need, man!'

And he will bang on his desk and scare Belinda Yates some more.

It's an overnight flight to Dubai. On the plane there are several children, some working their way through the airline's complimentary puzzle books. I am congenitally incapable of coming across a puzzle without trying to solve it, but Freddy can take them or leave them. His imagination is big and free. If he were here, he'd draw dinosaurs and talk to himself in his favourite dinosaur voice, the archaeopteryx. *'Hulooo, aya am a flooing fossil and aya weigha fifteen foosand zillion tons.'*

The little bruises on my arm ache when I press them.

Freud once said 'sometimes a cigar is just a cigar'. He was making a point about what is or is not significant.

He was a wise man.

I take a sleeping pill and fall in and out of that insubstantial, restless aeroplane sleep that fails to nourish.

When I told Kaitlin I was leaving, I knew I would not miss her. We did each other no good. If our relationship were an organisation, Phipps & Wexman would classify it as dysfunctional, toxic or 'hollow'. Her good looks no longer attracted me. In fact, illogically, they did the opposite. For her part, she had become impatient of aspects of my behaviour that she once claimed to find endearing.

But Freddy had done nothing wrong.

Once, driving home from the countryside, we hit a rabbit. Freddy had been staying with Kaitlin's mother – this was before her cancer – and I'd gone to fetch him. The creature darted out of a hedgerow into the road and was under the wheel before I could react. The crunch was soft and decisive. I hoped Freddy hadn't noticed – he'd been watching a DVD and seemed on the verge of sleep – but he saw it and yelled out. I wanted to keep driving, but he insisted that we must stop.

'We have to help it, we have to help it!'

In the time it took me to reverse back, he'd made wild plans: he'd nurse its injuries, keep it as a pet, give it a name, keep it in a cage, find it a mate, let it have litters of baby rabbits, and then they'd have babies and soon there'd be thousands of them and we could sell them to pet shops. He had the creature's whole life mapped out. But of course when we got there and inspected the lump of mashed fur it was stone dead. The hind quarters were completely crushed, but there was surprisingly little blood. Freddy cried and stroked its ears and stared into its death-glazed eye, and I rather helplessly tried to comfort him with some head-patting and shoulder-punching and calling him Freddy K, Freddy K, Freddy K, over and over. But he wouldn't stop crying. Finally, a little desperate, I suggested staging a funeral. Immediately, he brightened up: we had a project. I found a plastic bag in the car and we put the dead body in it, still warm, and resumed our journey. He was now full of energy: the idea of a ceremony had galvanised him.

'I'll bury it and put a cross on the grave and say some words.'

'What kind of words?' I was curious about what notions he might have, at six, of burial rites.

'I don't know.'

'You don't know when?'

He laughed. 'Yet. So go on then. Tell me.' Freddy didn't realise it, but his child's perspective provided me with a cognitive path to the world we both lived in. So I quoted him the 'ashes to ashes and dust to dust' lines of the Christian burial rite, and explained how in other countries and religions they say other things. But how a lot of the words are very similar no matter where you live, just as the types of prayer are, and the things people pray for. Then he wanted to know how long it would be before the body became a skeleton which he could dig up and glue together, to keep in his bedroom. I explained how dead bodies rot in the earth. How insects and maggots would come and eat the rabbit. We went into life cycles and protein and the food chain and he fired more questions at me. Those straightforward exchanges of information about the world always made me feel more at home in it. Who and where, how and why, when and what. Nothing slippery. No double meanings.

'So it rots and it feeds the earth and the earth feeds the plants and then the plants grow and then we eat the plants,' he summarises.

'Yes, Freddy K. Correct.'

'So why don't we just eat the rabbit?'

'Good idea. Rabbit stew. We can find a recipe.' That took us on to knives and blood and skinning techniques. We'd look up how to do it. We'd remove the guts, and inspect them. We might see its heart, and we could compare it to the one in my da Vinci book, which he loved. We'd identify and dissect its liver and its kidneys and its brain too.

Back in London, Freddy burst into the kitchen brandishing the plastic bag and gabbled the story of our adventure and our intentions to Kaitlin. She was in a good mood. She was glad when we did what she called 'boy things' together. The creature's skin came off like a coat. We cured it by staking it to a piece of chipboard and covering it with salt and then leaving it on the car roof in the sunshine to dry. Then we butchered the meat and Kaitlin made a stew with prunes and Armagnac, which Freddy declared 'epic', but left largely on his plate.

I wake in time to see the sunrise over the city as the plane comes in to land. It's Sunday 23rd September. I don't know the weather forecast, but I can guess it will reach well above forty degrees later in the day. Sprawling next to a glittering sea, pincushioned with construction cranes, the city gives the impression of an unfinished and unfinishable project.

Outside, it is indeed hot. My taxi driver is Afghan, so I try out a few words in Pashtoun. On the drive to the hotel, I get the impression of a city of gleaming, sun-baked glass and metal, of broad highways, improbably green lawns, of vast clean malls and building sites at every turn. I know that virtually nothing that I see around me is made here: that virtually everything except the sand is imported, and that in one of the shopping malls there is an indoor ski slope. The tall palms that line the roads are kept alive by water from desalination plants. Dubai uses more water than any other city in the world. It consumes more carbon per capita. It is home to the world's tallest structures. The slender needle of the 800-metre-high Burj Khalifa rears into the sky, the sun glinting pinkly off its glass and steel. It is magnificent. It looks like CGI.

I remember a story from Arab tradition.

A young man falls in love with a princess. He marries her, but when he touches her on their wedding night she turns into a pillar of flame. It turns out that she is not a princess at all, but a djinn in disguise. Djinns are created from smokeless fire. The fiery djinn-bride is cruel. She burns the young man's flesh to punish him, but he never finds out what his crime was, and why he was so viciously barbecued on what should have been an evening of sexual passion.

The story does not tell us, so we can only guess.

From the hotel, I email Annika Svensson my further condolences. Sunday is a work day here, so at 8am local time I contact the legal

team at Eastern Horizons' lawyer to ask for the translated tran-
script of Farooq's confession. I am told that this will take longer
than the rest of the documentation because it contains complex
technical terminology. I then visit the company's headquarters and
talk to several of Farooq's colleagues – largely Europeans, Indians,
Americans and Australians – who all express their horror at his
act of sabotage and subsequent suicide. The phrase 'out of character' is used eighteen times. After witnessing Annika Svensson's
grief I am not enthusiastic about meeting Halla Farooq, but I press
for an interview nonetheless. This is refused so adamantly that I
suspect I have made a gaffe with respect to her grief, or that Eastern
Horizons is embarrassed by her 'small beggar-djinn' allegations. Or
both. However, this afternoon I have an appointment with Farooq's
immediate deputy, Jan de Vries, who has agreed to my request to
see one of the current construction projects Ahmed Farooq was in
charge of when he died.

I have time to kill before this meeting, so I return to the hotel and
sit by the infinity pool – nineteen storeys up, with a view across the
waterfront – and read about the crisis in particle physics. Since the
Japanese verification of CERN's famous neutrino experiments the
furore, with string theory at its centre, has been raging on an epic
scale. 'Einstein's laws of cause and effect have so far meant that time
can only travel in one direction. But now that is questioned, the
paradoxes flood in,' says a theoretical physicist. 'Maths has known
for decades what physics is only just discovering: that there are
dimensions we can't see, and possibly never will.'
    I like this idea, but it unsettles me because how can one get the

measure of something that's apparently destined to remain immeasurable? I would like to discuss it with Professor Whybray.

The article ends by quoting a joke:

The barman says, sorry we don't serve neutrinos.

A man goes into a bar.

It takes me a little while to 'get' it. But when I do, I enjoy its cleverness in obeying the rules of the classic 'man goes into a bar' joke format, while simultaneously upending it. When the waiter comes to ask me if I would like a drink I consider trying it out on him, but decide against it because I am not a natural joke-teller and I fear it may fall flat as he may not have read enough about particle physics to appreciate it.

I order a Coke. Most of the hotel staff come from the Philippines. On the construction sites they tend to originate from Pakistan, Bangladesh, Sri Lanka, India or Afghanistan. Ninety-seven per cent of Dubai's ever-shifting population is non-native. So only a small percentage of them will be familiar with djinns: they will have their own spirits. How significant this might be I do not know.

While the neutrino experiments have shown that there are dimensions that we cannot yet grasp, because they operate outside the membrane we inhabit, I have never fathomed the notion of faith, or recognised the dividing line that the traditionally religious draw to distinguish their own belief systems from those of superstitious people who believe in ancestors, goblins, djinns, trolls and other legendary manifestations. Anthropology shies away from juxtaposing religious faith and non-religious belief. But to me, there is no difference: irrational belief is irrational belief, no matter what the creed or how much money its followers can raise to build and maintain their houses of faith. Perhaps it is precisely because of my immunity to belief systems that they fascinate me. Having studied those in thrall to non-existent forces which they generally claim represent either good or evil, I know that there's always a pragmatic explanation for their terrors. But often it's one they'd rather not face. So if their baby has altered beyond recognition it won't be thanks to a blow to the head, but because he's a changeling. If they lose something, a goblin stole it. If a woman gets pregnant when she is supposed to be a virgin, it's holy intervention. Superstitious conviction is born of an unconscious decision, in the face of the unthinkable, to fabulate.

This is something I could never do.

'Which is why you chose to study it,' Professor Whybray said, when I told him of my decision.

He was usually right.

At 10.30 I am heading upwards in a shaky construction elevator to the thirty-first floor of a half-built multi-storey skyscraper with Jan de Vries, who smells of stale beer, partly masked by aftershave, and who is now talking to me about his boss Ahmed Farooq: Ahmed Farooq who is dead, who swallowed rat poison on the alleged provocation of a small beggar-like djinn, and therefore died in extreme agony like Gustave Flaubert's fictional anti-heroine Madame Bovary.

The nominal ban on alcohol in Dubai has the effect of turning most of its Western inhabitants into moderate drinkers, but I have read that there are still plenty of alcoholics. Because of the smell of beer on his breath, I suspect the blond-haired, red-skinned Mr Jan de Vries to be one of them. His South African accent is very thick. He calls me 'man' a great deal, which he pronounces 'mun'. He is an Afrikaner from Cape Town, he tells me in the elevator we share to the building site. When it finally comes to a shaking halt on the thirty-first level of the skyscraper-in-progress, de Vries and I step out on to the floor where the construction continues. The site is open to the sunlight, with very little shade. I count twenty-six very dark-skinned workers in thin vests and hard hats at work in three separate areas. Many are small and wiry: Sri Lankan, I guess. Others look more like they are from Pakistan. Eleven are pouring cement and sand into a row of concrete mixers, while the rest are erecting and dismantling scaffolding. Concrete has its own particular smell, and here it manifests itself in a variety of forms: raw powder, sand-mixed, wet, damp, drying and hardened. This part of the floor is in shade, thanks to a stretched white tarpaulin. But bizarrely, Jan de Vries seems to prefer standing in the sun.

It must be heading for fifty degrees.

De Vries waves at a man who is standing apart from the others, consulting a chart. 'Foreman,' he says. 'Pakistani.' The foreman waves back. 'So, Hesketh. Take a look.' De Vries points towards the edge.

'I can't. I get vertigo.'

'That's too bad. It's quite something.' He strides over to the edge, leans his meaty bulk against the security rail and gazes out at the panorama. I shift a little closer, near enough to catch what he says, but not so close to the drop that I can see what's below. The rail is made of aluminium so it must be burning hot, but he doesn't seem to notice. He hasn't stopped talking since we met.

'Ahmed was a goddam diamond, I tell you,' he calls to me, continuing the theme he began in the lift. 'This just was not Ahmed. Not one single element of this bloody mess was him, mun. I mean, he wasn't a saboteur, no way. Plus, bloody rat poison, what kind of shit is that, mun? If he had to do it what's wrong with Valium or paracetamol?' De Vries is one of those men who become aggressive when they are upset. He sweeps out his big muscled arm to show me 'the world's most fantastic city. It's just gonna keep on expanding and expanding. Why not, eh? D'you realise we have the most advanced desalination technology in the whole goddam world?'

No, I tell him. But it comes as no surprise.

De Vries speaks very fast, so I have to concentrate. His eyes are hidden behind very dark sunglasses that cling tightly to the bridge of his nose, making the flesh bulge to either side. I find myself almost lip-reading him, focusing on the rapid movements of his fleshy mouth. Above it, the moustache pours from his nostrils like blond lava. I am faint-headed from jetlag.

'Sure, we had a bit of a dip in the economy, and we were reeling for a while there, I mean truly reeling. But look at it now, it's all happening. This is a happening place, a vibrant place. Ahmed was part of that big vision, mun. I just love this city, mun. Lived here twenty years. I mean how can you not be crazy about this place?'

He says this is just one of fifty-seven construction projects managed by Eastern Horizons. Farooq was personally in charge of it. As De Vries grips the scaffold-rail and expounds on Dubai – 'This city. It's what the future looks like, mun' – I begin to feel thirsty. The sun is unbearably hot. 'I don't know what bloody Farooq got into his head. I just don't know. So much to live for, mun. The world was his oyster. And his wife, how d'you think she's feeling, mun? Gorgeous lady, Halla. Very traditional. Can you imagine what it was like breaking the news to her? It tore me apart, mun.'

I want to tell him: Halla Farooq thought her husband was possessed by a small beggar-djinn. She believed that the djinn didn't wish her husband well, just as Sunny Chen believed the ancestors stamped their curse on him with a tiny dirt smear and Jonas Svensson believed that small creatures – 'kiddie trolls' – had used him as a puppet. And I have a baffling set of bruises on my arm.

There is a pattern, you see, Mr Jan de Vries.

The problem is, it's so outlandish that it makes no sense to any logical, rational, scientifically inclined mind. I am thinking specifically of my own.

As Jan de Vries carries on moving his fleshy mouth and saying things in a vehement manner I am asking myself, as per Ashok's angry instructions: what are your other lines of inquiry, the ones that don't have something to do with 'fucking little people' who are menacing enough to make men resort to desperate measures after doing something against their will? Death by wood-pulping machine, death by oncoming vehicle after a failed attempt with aspirin, death by rat poison: I see no connection there. What about timber, finance and construction? Money links them all, but money is as vague and pervasive as oxygen. Taiwan, Sweden and Dubai: again they have nothing obvious in common except in my own mind, where they feature as recent additions to a list of places I will not rush to visit again.

★   ★   ★

Now we are up here, Jan de Vries is keen to show me the other Eastern Horizons sites. You can see four from here, he says. 'I want you to see them in the context of the whole Dubai project.'

The land around the building site resembles a dusty, clogged tray of cat litter. I have read that many of the immigrant workers live in giant metal containers stacked like cages. I personally like confined spaces, but not everybody does. The air is far hotter than anything I have experienced beyond a sauna. Despite my sunglasses, my eyes hurt. I'm trying to block out de Vries, but his presence is insistent and I can't concentrate on my little *ozuru*. His voice seems to be spiralling higher and higher in pitch until he's almost screaming. Desalination and the future.

Fucking miracle, mun.

The world has so much to thank this company for. Proud to be here, proud to be part of Dubai's future. Think of our grandchildren and their children, they'll look at us like we look at the pharaohs, have you been to Egypt, mun, have you seen all that amazing shit over there? Magic.

Something is wrong. His voice is getting higher and higher. The pitch becomes unnaturally elevated. I'm too hot. I start to rock. I can't think straight when people shout or screech at me in a high unnatural voice. I get overloaded. I am overloaded now. I rock harder and harder. There is something out of kilter. The noise de Vries is making does not sound normal. And now, suddenly, he is doing something as grotesque as it is incomprehensible.

He is licking his bare forearm.

He is still making the screeching noise, but it's muffled by his lips meeting his own flesh. The gesture isn't human: it reminds me of a dog gnawing at a bone and growling, or a parody of a kiss. But it is not a bone, or another mouth, it's the hairy flesh of his own arm. It's as if de Vries has a small motor inside, operated inexpertly by another person, or malfunctioning. I can't be alone in getting the impression that something is awry with de Vries because just then one of the workers comes up with a hand raised, signalling at him to stop. The little figure is different from the other workers. No hard hat. And long hair that reaches beyond the shoulders. From this angle, which must be immensely distortive, it seems no bigger than a child.

I lift my sunglasses for a moment, but the glare of the sun scalds my eyes and I shove them back. I blink rapidly and look again.

It is a child. Dressed in rags.

Male, I thought at first—

But no.

Female.

A small girl. In filthy, torn clothing. Her dark round eyes stare at de Vries, unblinking.

When de Vries catches sight of the ragged child he stops licking his arm, he catches his breath and then spits out a word, or a repeated series of words, that sound Japanese – *toko-loshi-toko-loshi-toko-loshi* – and his face distorts like a chimpanzee under attack, with a terrible pleading grimace that reveals his teeth and gums.

'You can't come in!' he screams. It's not clear if he's talking to her. Or if he is, what he means. 'You are not coming in, you fucking creature!'

The child's eyes narrow. Then, without moving her mouth, she starts to make a sound: a high insistent noise that has too much of an edge to be musical. A monotone humming.

Why would they allow a child up here? Is she the daughter of one of the workers?

Just then, still humming, she puts her fist next to her eye and opens it out in a sudden starburst, palm out.

This has a dramatic effect on de Vries: with a sharp, pained squeal he lurches his big body around so that his back is to me. A cry goes up from the group of workers on the other side of the building, then more urgent shouts.

Jan de Vries' meaty hands grip the rail decisively.

He is still screaming as he lifts his entire body up – it looks effortless – and vaults over the protective railing.

He does it like men in old films leap over gates in the English countryside, in a single smooth and gymnastic movement.

And then he is gone.

Later, when I am being interrogated by Detective Mazoor, I will call his suicide leap 'surprisingly elegant'.

His vanishing is clean and complete. I am too far from the edge to see him fall. Not that I would wish to.

I stand where I am, rocking.

There is more shouting among the men. Then one of them – I recognise the foreman – yells an order. They cluster together, arguing and gesticulating. Above their cries I can hear the hum of traffic thirty-one storeys below.

There are sections of my brain that are stupid. By which I mean slow and sometimes quite incapable of spotting the obvious. Belatedly, it strikes me that if de Vries jumped over the railing then – *ergo* – he must now be dead. *Jan de Vries is dead, Jan de Vries is dead, Jan de Vries is dead.*

I sink to a crouching position and hold my head. I'd like to crawl into a confined space, but there's nowhere to go in this place of ferocious light and heat and soft cruel breezes. So I stay where I am and rock.

I don't know how much time passes. I construct three *ozuru* in my head and send them fluttering up into the searing hot air. I rock. My mind is blank. I rock harder. After a while I become aware of the foreman shouting at me and pointing downward.

Jan de Vries is dead.

'I didn't push him,' I say. 'I didn't push him. I didn't push him.' I say it again and again and again. I can't seem to stop. I'm very overloaded.

'I know,' he says, approaching. 'Calm down, sir. Take deep breaths.' It's a good suggestion. 'I saw it happen. I saw him go over. You were nowhere near, sir. I called the site boss. He's called the police.' His phone rings. 'Excuse me.'

While he talks I think about Tom and Jerry. Freddy and I are fans of this cartoon. When an animal hits the ground, in Tom and Jerry, its body is flattened by the impact. But in real life, this doesn't happen. When an object drops vertically from the sky, the speed of its descent will be slowed to some extent by air resistance. I wonder if a height of thirty-one storeys is enough for a falling object to achieve terminal velocity. I imagine de Vries' skull will be split open like a coconut, with the brains exposed and perhaps a quantity of blood pooling beneath. Blood would dry fast in this heat: a skin would form, like a membrane. Its colours would travel through the chart: Gala Day, Postbox, Shepherd's Delight, Mombasa, Heritage Maroon. Will de Vries' body break open likewise, or will it remain intact? Death at the moment of impact would be instantaneous. They use the carcasses of pigs to determine exactly what happens in violent accidents. Or sometimes real human bodies. So be aware that if you donate your corpse to science it may be dropped from a great height, to test what happens to it. It won't matter as you'll be dead. But some people object to the idea out of squeamishness.

Or on aesthetic grounds.

The foreman has finished his call.

'What happened to the little girl?' I ask. 'I don't see her.'

He takes a step back. 'What?'

'There was a child. Half your height or less. She scared Jan de Vries. He told her she couldn't come in.'

He looks at me, but I can't work out what his face means. 'Sir. It's just you and me and the workmen over there.' He nods at them.

I start counting. They're in a large cluster, and engaged in energetic argument. This involves much pointing downward at the street below, and at the rail de Vries sprang over. Others are kneeling on their haunches, their heads down, apparently praying. One stands alone, sobbing and wailing. When I arrived there were twenty-seven, including the foreman. Plus me and de Vries. That makes twenty-nine. The girl arrived and de Vries jumped so we should still total twenty-nine. But we are twenty-eight.

'You see?' says the foreman.

'But I know what I saw.' I count again. Still twenty-eight. 'She was right in front of me. She made a noise. A kind of humming. And she gestured at de Vries. You must have seen her too.' He licks his lips, but he doesn't speak. He's sweating heavily. 'Good Muslims don't lie. Now did you or did you not see her?' I seem to be shouting.

I don't usually shout. I also want to shake him.

I grab him: he blinks rapidly, then puts a hand on top of mine. It's gentle.

'Take a deep breath, sir. Easy. Calm down.' He lowers his voice. 'OK. I will level with you. There appeared to be a girl. But the heat often makes people see things.' He nods his head in the direction of the construction workers. All are small compared to me, but none is child-sized. The crying man is being comforted by another. The child has gone and so has the perspective from which I saw her. Or did not see her.

I am confused. This is confusing.

I say, 'She was here. She must have jumped.'

'No. I just talked on the phone to the boss down there. Just one body. Mr de Vries'.'

He jerks a thumb towards the security rail. Far below, there will be people clustering around that big, beefy shape by now. The site boss he mentioned. The police. From here they'd all look like ants around a big crumb.

'So where is she?'

His jaw fights before he speaks. 'Sir. Like I said. We must have all made a mistake.' He blurts it. 'There was no child. Let us go down now, sir. The police will want you and me down there first. For statements. The men will wait here. They'll get statements from them too. Come this way.'

The breeze wafts through the bars of the construction elevator. Its slow shaking progress down the side of the building soothes me. It is a limbo I could happily stay in.

'If we didn't see a child, then what did we see?' I ask the foreman.

He looks at his shoes. They're leather, and coated with a fine film of cement dust. 'The men say it was an evil spirit. I don't know.'

'There's no such thing as an evil spirit.'

'I know, sir. But the men, they believe in them.'

'You saw her too.'

'I *thought* I did. But the light and the heat, they play tricks. Create false impressions. Very common here in Dubai. A lot of people imagine things that are not there.' He shrugs. 'Fifty degrees plus does that to you.'

'But I never imagine things that aren't there. Not even when I have a fever. What else did they think they saw?'

'Some of them saw the child jump or fly.'

'Jump or fly where? Over the edge?' He is still looking at his dusty shoes. 'Where? Where, where, where, answer me!'

He wipes sweat off his face. 'Into him.'

Jonas Svensson said, *I must've swallowed one.*

'That's not possible.'

'I know. And it can't have happened. I am just reporting what they said. But there is no evidence.' He is speaking very fast. 'I will be very honest with you now, sir. I don't like to tell lies. As you say, it's against my faith. And it's not in my nature either. But I will not mention this little girl in my statement to police. The others will do the same. Nobody wants to be called crazy and lose his job. It looks bad for us to say we have seen something we cannot prove. Understand this, sir? That's where we stand. You will have to do what you like and follow your own conscience.'

'Did you see her or not?'

'I saw her. But I am sorry, sir. If you tell the police this, I will deny it. Please. Understand me here. My men think this skyscraper is haunted. This is going to be a big problem for me.'

'Did you see Mr de Vries lick his arm?'

He nods. He looks very distressed. 'Yes I did, sir.'

'Why do you think he did that?'

'I cannot understand. He was behaving in a very strange way sir. I do not know why a man would lick his own arm. An urge must have come upon him.'

'Just before he jumped he said, *You can't come in,* and then he said some foreign words. They sounded Japanese. Did you hear that?'

'No. I didn't hear anything. I was far away.'

He said *toko* and he said *loshi.* I am sure of it. 'And what about Ahmed Farooq. Did he behave oddly, last time you saw him?'

He looks at his feet again. 'Yes. He did. Very oddly, sir.'

'How?'

'He asked one of the workers for some water. The man gave him his own bottle and he crumbled something into it. He had it in a plastic bag in his pocket. Then he drank it down. I asked him what it was, and he said medicine.'

'Did it look like medicine?'

He makes a face. Disgust, distaste, something like that. 'No. I recognised it. The desalination plants produce it like that. In blocks. It was salt.'

At the police headquarters I call Ashok but he is in a meeting, so I leave a message with Belinda Yates explaining what has happened. She expresses shock and sympathy.

'My God, poor you, Hesketh! Look, shall I get one of our psych people to call you?'

'No.'

'Stephanie Mulligan! She's specialised in workplace suicides.'

'There's nothing she can help me with,' I say. 'Do you have Svensson's autopsy report yet?'

'It's just come in.'

'Good. Send it. And I'll need you to get hold of Jan de Vries' too.' And I hang up.

Salt is born of the purest parents, wrote Pythagoras. *The sun and the sea*. It's the only kind of rock we consume, the thing we cannot do without. Salt deprivation, as well as a salt excess, can cause medical conditions. 'Sodic soil' or 'dry-land salinity' is on the increase, due to salt in the water table being drawn to the surface by the sun's heat. Shakespeare based King Lear on an Italian folk tale about a king with three daughters. One said she loved her father bright as sunshine, the second said she loved him wide as the sea, but when the third said she loved him as meat loves salt, he banished her. But she returned in disguise and gave the king a banquet in which the food contained not a single grain of salt. When he complained about the taste, she revealed herself. 'Just as meat is tasteless without salt,' she told him, 'so is life without my father's love.' And they were tenderly reunited. Atmospheric change over the last fifty years has caused chemical imbalances in the world's oceans, causing both increased acidity and 'a large-scale, rapid rise in salinity, particularly in tropical regions'. Some marine species are reported to be adapting. Most are not. In India, a gift of salt brings good luck because it is solid when dry, but invisible when dissolved. Jesus called his disciples 'the salt of the earth'.

The purest parents.

It has a melodious cadence to it.

I spend the afternoon with Detective Mazoor, who questions me gently, mercilessly, sympathetically, aggressively and in many other styles. Arab men are often very masculine-looking, with a great deal of hair on their wrists. I focus on his Rolex watch as he speaks, and observe the tiny second hand tick through the revolutions. His professional life must be lacking in excitement, because he wants me to confess to murder, which I presume would afford him kudos. If I had pushed de Vries then Mazoor could solve the case, and get the glory for it. And I would go to jail or even be executed. This would be a big 'feather in his cap'.

One of the studies Professor Whybray generated – it linked into what he affectionately called 'the Paranoia Index' – mapped the stress levels of innocent detainees according to time held in custody and faith in the justice system. Predictably, there were impressive variations according to culture. Thanks to this study, and news reports I have read, I know enough about the Dubai justice system to have cause for alarm. Yet I do not feel nervous under Mazoor's interrogation. The mesmeric second hand of his watch has a role to play here. So do the facts. I did not push de Vries, and if Mazoor has not already heard corroboration of this from the other witnesses, he soon will. Because of the detective's intense focus on my hypothetical guilt, it is very easy for me to omit any mention of the ragged girl who signalled to de Vries and scared him into vaulting into the blue sky. When the foreman told me that he and the workmen would not mention her in their statements, I did not doubt him. Those men would have families back home. Losing their jobs would have catastrophic repercussions.

But I saw the child. She was probably no higher than my waist, and she was dressed in rags. The sight of her made the workmen agitated and she scared de Vries so badly that he killed himself. That's how it seemed. And I heard her too. She generated a high, tuneless humming that grated on my ears.

Her presence didn't frighten me.

But the impossibility of it did. I have no strategy to deal with something that so adamantly defies categorisation, quantification and logic; something that so stubbornly refuses to fit into any of the diagrams I've been constructing in my head.

As Mazoor interrogates me, I rock in my seat as gently as I can, so that he doesn't notice. I keep calm and I do not get overloaded. There is a plastic water bottle in front of me. I reach for it and unscrew the top.

'You have children,' he says suddenly, changing tack. This throws me.

'A stepson.'

'Hmm. A violent little boy.'

'What?'

'Like you maybe.'

'No. I'm not violent. Nor's Freddy. Freddy's a great kid.'

'Oh, but I think he is violent.'

'What do you mean?' He reaches across and shoves my shirt sleeve a little higher to reveal the bruise on my arm. I regret not wearing long sleeves. 'That wasn't Freddy.'

'How old is this Freddy?'

'Seven.'

'So who grabbed your arm?'

'A man in Sweden. A mentally disturbed man.'

Mazoor puts his hands on the desk and observes them, then looks up at me.

'You are lying, Mr Lock.'

'I don't lie.'

'So how do you explain those bruises?'

'I'm not violent. I never touched de Vries. If you're implying we had a fight, then you're wrong. Ask the others.'

He laughs. 'I am a detective, Mr Lock. Not a fool. That bruise is at least two days old. So whoever made it does not concern me. Though as you guessed, your violent nature does. I will ask you again, why did you push de Vries off the edge?'

'I didn't push de Vries off the edge, or threaten him in any way. I was never alone with him. There were twenty-six workmen plus the foreman on the rooftop at the time. I am sure they can all corroborate my testimony. He vaulted. It was surprisingly elegant.'

'Elegant?'

'Yes. *Elegant* is the word I would like to use in my statement.'

'Poetic,' says Mazoor. 'You are fond of your language.'

'Yes, I am. My own, and others. Especially when coaxed into a rhythm.'

He smiles and leans back. He has a small gap between his front teeth. In African cultures such a gap is considered lucky and a sign of sexual potency. 'So quote me some English poetry.'

I clear my throat.

"'Who would have thought my shrivell'd heart

Could have recovered greennesse? It was gone

Quite underground, as flowers depart

To the mother-root, when they have blown;

Where they together

All the hard weather,

Dead to the world, keep house unknown."

It's from "The Flower" by George Herbert. I can also quote you some Shelley.'

'Go on.'

"'My name is Ozymandias, King of Kings.

Look on my works, ye mighty, and despair."'

'Well, Mr Lock. You certainly keep interesting things up your sleeve.' He nods at my arm. He means the bruise. He has made a joke. I force a smile, but can't manage a laugh. He shifts in his seat, sighs and shoves some paper at me. 'OK, that's enough entertainment. Draw me what happened.'

This I can also do. I show where I was standing in relation to de Vries. It's clear he wants to hear the story yet again in order to spot an inconsistency. So for the fifth time, as I draw, I tell Mazoor about de Vries' strange behaviour at the site: the screaming and the arm-licking and the fact that he had clearly been drinking alcohol.

'In conclusion, in my opinion Jan de Vries was inebriated. He was also upset about Ahmed Farooq's suicide, and having to break the news to his wife. I think he was having a mental collapse that nobody spotted or foresaw.'

He comments on the excellence of my sketches. He is right to. My 2-D representations are highly accurate. If we were in a different setting I might tell him about my admiration for da Vinci's anatomical drawings, shared by my non-violent stepson Freddy. But we are in this setting, and his mission is to find a hole in my story. He is probably used to dealing with drugs cartels and alcohol smugglers and political assassinations, not stories of alcoholic Afrikaners who get 'tipped over the edge'.

'But there must have been a trigger,' he keeps saying. 'Something that happened.'

He is no fool.

I shrug. 'The symptoms of mental imbalance are always unpredictable. Mr de Vries started behaving oddly. He worked himself into a crescendo. The elegant vault was part of that crescendo.' I am thinking of *toko* and *loshi*.

'It is a strange situation, do you agree, Mr Lock?' asks Detective Mazoor.

'I agree that it's strange. But as I said. Disturbed people behave in unorthodox ways. It's well documented.'

Next he questions me about the nature of my consultative work for Phipps & Wexman and I explain a little about behavioural patterns in the workplace, and methods of targeting anomalies. I list some of the multi-national corporations I have dealt with over the years and he nods in recognition. 'Specialised troubleshooting,' I summarise. This being part of his job too, I detect the beginnings of an understanding. He leans forward attentively as I tell him about the direction my investigation has been taking, and the speculations it has led to.

'I believe de Vries' death fits into a pattern involving indigenous superstitions,' I tell him. 'I don't know if he believed in djinns, but the look on his face before he jumped over the edge was one of terror. Farooq certainly believed in them. And his wife apparently thinks he was possessed by one. It's in her statement. Jonas Svensson talked about trolls. And Sunny Chen was afraid that the spirits of his ancestors were angry. All these men feared something which they were convinced was absolutely genuine. I suspect this is all part of a global outbreak of hysteria that goes well beyond the cases I've investigated.'

At this point Mazoor shakes his head and the corners of his mouth turn down. The demographer who called herself Ingrid had this expression on her face at the airport. Kaitlin wore it often.

I have disappointed him.

In my head I make a lotus flower, a frog, a pelican, a basic water-bomb, an ox, a fish, a swan and five *ozuru*. I drink some water from the plastic bottle. It tastes very bland, like it's missing something. I long for the island. For the smell of burning logs and the sound of gulls and crashing waves and the squeak of my swivel chair.

'That second piece of poetry you quoted,' says Mazoor, after a long silence.

'Ozymandias.'

'Is that a comment on Dubai?'

'Dubai is very special. It is like a body on life support,' I tell him. 'Or a honeybee. Serviced by a million drones and producing royal jelly.'

He laughs. 'A good comparison,' he says. 'This place is the future.'

'That's what de Vries said just before his elegant vault,' I tell him. And his face changes again.

After Mazoor has finished with me I am allowed to call Ashok Sharma who says, 'OK. Being witness to a suicide, that's beyond the call of duty, man. You're getting backup.'

'I don't need it. I'm fine.'

'Too late. No argument. The client's requested it. Oh, and listen: the chemical analysis on the sample from Taiwan: get this. Human blood. Bits of insects. Legs and wings. Plus mineral deposits.'

'Whose human blood?'

'I don't think the machine's that sophisticated, bud.'

'What kind of mineral deposits?'

'Trace elements. Salt. It's dirt. So who cares?'

'I do.'

'Why?'

'I don't know yet. What does Svensson's autopsy show?'

'It's in Swedish. But I spoke to the guy who did it. He said there was nothing chemical that would've provoked mental disturbance. He had an eye infection that wasn't responding to treatment. Some pressure problem. And abnormal kidneys. Congenital anomaly, he said.'

'What kind of congenital anomaly?'

Ashok chuckles. 'Seems he had an extra one. Quite rare, though it's on the increase in some parts of the world. Remember that story not so long ago? Some guy in Ohio discovers he's got four kidneys, decides to sell two of them. Easy bucks for Johnny Multi-Organ, and everyone's happy.'

He's waiting for me to react, but I'm thinking. The kidneys process salt. I remember seeing pictures of Orumieh in Iran: the country's biggest lake turned to salt. A boat marooned on a shelf of whiteness that twinkled like hot, hard snow. Pyjama Girl dreamed about *a beautiful white desert that sparkled*.

'Ashok, Ashok, Ashok. Listen. I asked Belinda for de Vries' autopsy report. Well I need Farooq's too.'

'I'll see what I can do.'

'Can you get me a kidney expert and an ophthalmologist to consult?'

'Whoa, slow down. Is this developing into some medical theory?'

'Again, I don't know yet. I need more evidence. Can you do it?'

'Hey. Glad to. Anything beats little people. So finish with the police, then go back to the hotel and wait for our guy. By the way, Old Man Whybray?'

'Professor. Professor Whybray. That's his name. Professor Victor Whybray FRS. What about him?'

'You'll never guess what he's doing for the Home Office.'

'Yes. I can. He's researching the epidemic of child violence.'

'So you also know we've been sub-contracted, and he wants a meeting as soon as you're back in town?'

This day has not been a good one so far. But it has just got better by several thousand per cent. I remember a young student thumping a table in a Cambridge pub for joy. He has just got his PhD. Next to him sits the white-haired man who handed him 'the keys to the castle'. Not long after that, the professor's wife Helena became very ill and I sat with him in waiting rooms. He asked me to. He never said why. He had many other students, all of whom had better conversational and social skills. But I was glad to help. Over the weeks, we jointly completed 271 *Times* crosswords.

After my phone call, it's Eastern Horizons' turn to question me. This is a more bureaucratic affair, and it also involves a statement, though of a more legalistic kind. Ashok has hired a Phipps & Wexman 'associate' lawyer to take me through this process. Rachid Omar is quiet and soft-spoken. His features are indistinct, as though molten. You see this on antique plastic dolls. Plastic is in fact a very dense liquid: this shows with the passing of decades. It's a problem for Barbie doll collectors. I tick the boxes he tells me to tick and I don't mention the little girl to him, the little girl whom de Vries and I and the others all saw, whose presence filled the Afrikaner with a lurid fear, a fear that had the face of a threatened chimpanzee. The work with Rachid Omar takes four hours and eight minutes. By the time a woman called Angela Monroe from the British Embassy comes to escort me back to my hotel, it's late evening.

'I'm afraid it won't be possible to return to London just yet,' she says. 'But maybe by tomorrow. There's a lot more paperwork to be cleared. But you can relax now, Mr Lock.'

Of course I can't relax, I tell her. Relaxing is inconceivable under these circumstances. For one, I am concerned about the hermit crab. I've left the model in the cottage untouched for too long.

'Origami paper is susceptible to damp. It can suffer.'

She pats my arm. 'The good news is that your colleague from Phipps & Wexman managed to get the midday flight out of London. She should be here soon.'

'She?' I ask. 'Did you say she?'

'Yes,' she says, consulting her iPhone. 'It says here Stephanie Mulligan.'

Wait for our guy, Ashok said. Did he not even know who he was sending?

A piece of paper crumples inside me.

CHAPTER 6

THERE IS AN explanation for everything. But it is not always apparent at the time.

In Meno's paradox Plato asked, *And how will you inquire into a thing when you are wholly ignorant of what it is? Even if you happen to bump right into it, how will you know it is the thing you didn't know?*

In 1783, people believed the world was coming to an end when Europe was smothered beneath an oppressive and unchanging lid of black cloud. The resulting social upheavals lasted the best part of a year, from late winter into the following autumn. Crops were ruined and many were driven to madness and self-harm. Religious mania exploded. Slowly, the climate returned to normal and the sun's brightness returned. But it was over a hundred years before the 'summer without end' was fully explained. Meteorologists confirmed that a conjunction of volcanic eruptions near Iceland and Japan had dimmed the stratosphere, stifling Europe with an eiderdown of ash.

At the time though, there was no convincing explanation.
Just superstition and the terror it gave birth to.

Stephanie Mulligan has left me a message suggesting a drink in
the Aldeberon Lounge at eight o'clock. I order room service and
go online. Ashok has sent me a PDF of Svensson's autopsy report,
along with the names of a renal specialist and an ophthalmologist
who have agreed to be consulted. I glance through the autopsy
report, then forward it to each of them, with a request for an assessment. There's also a mail from Annika Svensson.

> *Dear Hesketh,*
>
> *You had some questions about salt. When I showed your email to my son
> Erik he told me that one day he borrowed Jonas' car. There was a plastic
> water bottle in there. Erik said he took a gulp but had to spit it out. It was
> salty. Like seawater, he said. Why would Jonas keep seawater in a drinking
> bottle? Can you also explain why the garden shed is full of seaweed and
> jars and sacks of grain and bottles of Coca-Cola? In the last week of his
> life my husband was not my husband any more. I think he was under the
> influence of an idea which frightened him and which he could not share. He
> said children were trying to get inside him. As you can imagine the worst
> burden is not knowing why this change in him happened. So I pray that
> your admirable focus will shed light on this darkness.*
>
> *Many greetings,*
> *Annika.*

There's no hotel Bible, which is perhaps not surprising in Muslim
Dubai. So I go online to look up a reference from the book of

Genesis in the King James version. Lot and his wife and daughters have been hastened away from the iniquity of the city of Sodom. *And it came to pass, when they had brought them forth abroad, that he said, Escape for thy life: look not behind thee, neither stay thou in all the plain; escape to the mountain, lest thou be consumed. The sun was risen upon the earth when Lot entered into Zoar. Then the Lord rained upon Sodom and upon Gomorrah brimstone and fire from the Lord of Heaven. And he overthrew those cities, and all the plain, and all the inhabitants of the cities, and that which grew upon the ground.*

But his wife looked back from behind him, and she became a pillar of salt.

I search for the Japanese words *toko* and *loshi*. *Toko* can mean endless or barber shop or floor or bed. *Loshi* doesn't seem to mean anything.

In any case, where's the logic in an Afrikaner speaking Japanese? The words he'd reach in a crisis would be in his own tongue, the guttural Afrikaans spoken by descendants of God-fearing Dutch colonialists. I do another search.

But I'm wrong there too.

I try again, spelling it not as two words but as one. *Tokoloshi.*

This brings success. A *tokoloshi* is a figure from Bantu tradition. This is something de Vries himself could have told me, had he lived. I should have known all along. It wasn't Afrikaans that came to Jan de Vries' lips just before he died. It was Xhosa, a language spoken by many tribes of Africa. He'd have grown up hearing it. And very possibly speaking it too. It involves throat clicks which sound like delicate machinery changing gear. In Zulu the word is *uthikoloshe.*

It means demon dwarf. *Tokoloshi* are small and humanoid. They live near pools and springs. They like to kidnap. They hide under beds and grab you. If you are asleep, they will bite off your toes. If you are female they will rape you.

So this is what de Vries believed he saw.

He was scared into suicide not by a little girl in rags, but by something he identified as a demon dwarf.

The Aldeberon Lounge has a Thousand and One Nights theme with tiny halogen stars recessed into the ceiling. Stephanie Mulligan is already seated at a corner table in a booth. I count seven other customers, all of them men. Five are sitting alone, the other two are together. All of them are looking at her, some openly, others furtively. Men tend to do this around her. Stephanie is slim and in her early thirties, with blonde hair. Her face is narrow and symmetrical and she is wearing an Azure blue dress and an unusual white necklace — bold and jagged — which looks familiar: I have to drag my eyes away from it. Or perhaps it's her neck that preoccupies me, that has always preoccupied me. Her skin is very pale, as though she never goes out in the sun. It seems to glow.

Is she beautiful? Most of my male colleagues think so, emphatically. They also claim to like her 'as a person'.

The men stare as I walk over, and answer her hello with a hello of my own. Forcing myself to concentrate on the fact that we have a specific job to do, I settle opposite her on a leather banquette and I begin the mental reconstruction of the praying mantis I made for Sunny Chen. It is fiddly and it might just see me through this.

Between us is a shiny lacquered table overlooking the blue neon of the waterfront thirty-seven floors below. Stephanie has the reputation of being a good and tactful listener. People who feel the need to talk a great deal about themselves might find themselves drawn to that aspect of her. I'm not one of those people. I intend to be in charge of this meeting.

'Eastern fairy tales are often about young men who sit around doing very little until huge fortunes unexpectedly fall into their laps,' I tell Stephanie. 'Aladdin's an example. Fate decrees that whatever shall be shall be. Destiny versus free will is a recurring motif. You'll also find that—'

She interrupts. 'Hesketh. Before we begin, we need to talk about a personal issue.'

Where is her professionalism? 'No.'

'I'm sorry, Hesketh. I don't want to open old wounds, but there really is something I need to tell you.' She clears her throat. 'Something you should know.'

Stephanie puts her pale, slim hand on top of mine, but I pull it away. I say, 'Whatever it is, now is not the time.' If it comes out bluntly, I don't care. I signal to the waiter. I'm not as in charge as I had intended. 'You and I are going to have to co-operate. We're here for one thing. To find the pattern, and work out what's happening and why. So we should behave like colleagues. Let's just do that, OK?'

I stare at her necklace. I often fixate on the wrong thing, and I only realise it afterwards, when it's too late. The waiter is heading towards us. He is a Filipino with skin the colour of Dulux's 2010 Cointreau. I begin rocking. We order. Double Scotch for me.

Chardonnay for her. Classic gender-based choices. I abandon the praying mantis and get to work on a basic water-bomb.

'We do actually need to talk, Hesketh.' I open my mouth to speak, but she raises her hand, indicating she's going to continue anyway. 'Look, if you want to begin by discussing the sabotages we can do that.'

'It's why you're here. It's the only reason we're in the same room.'

'But we *will* come back to it, because actually we have to.' Perhaps she pities me. It's a frequent mistake. People misunderstand who I am, and assume I want to be like them. I don't. Our drinks arrive. The waiter arranges them on the table with some small dishes of nuts, olives and crisps. Stephanie thanks him and I take a large gulp of Scotch. Too much, too fast. It burns my throat.

She straightens up. 'So. The sabotages. Ashok wasn't very keen on your speculation, I have to tell you. As you'd expect. He talks about blue-sky thinking but . . .' Unexpectedly, she smiles. I can't tell if it's genuine or what kind of smile it is. She has very regular teeth. Her lipstick is Dusk Rose.

I say, 'Ashok doesn't hire me to tell him what he wants to hear. He hires me to spot behavioural trends.'

She raises her glass to me and takes a sip of Chardonnay. She leaves a lipstick mark on her glass. 'Hesketh. Please. We're on the same side.' I don't know how to begin replying to this. She straightens up and sighs. 'OK. The first thing you need to know is that there have been new cases of this, everywhere. I'm talking about motiveless sabotage followed by suicide. A Brazilian pharmaceutical company. A man and two women. Wrecked three years' work on some wonder-drug. Destroyed the database and trashed the lab.' I don't say anything. 'It wasn't a joint suicide: they were all found separately, at different times of day. The man shot himself, the women took pills.'

More classic gender-based choices. 'And the others?'

'An engineer in Namibia, installing some big pipeline. Destroyed the whole project in an explosion. Then he killed himself. With a blowtorch of all things. How does that fit into anything? And Ashok's hearing of more every day.'

I shut my eyes, focus and think it through at speed. I can't not. I open my eyes and concentrate on the whisky in my glass as I speak.

'With Chen it's deforestation and with Svensson it's futures trading and the Farooq case is about construction. Now pharmaceuticals and energy. You could argue they're all part of the same . . .' To my frustration, I can't find the right word. She has weakened me.

'Corrupt franchise?' she smiles. I don't smile back. The old wound is as bewildering and raw as on the first day. If I don't focus on the puzzle, I will get overloaded. 'If we're looking at institutions or spheres of commercial activity that people bear a grudge against, all of these might fit. But there are other so-called bad guys. Why not them? What makes this epidemic, or whatever it is, attack one organisation and not another?'

'Maybe it hasn't had time,' I say. 'Maybe there's a list.'

'And whoever is orchestrating this is ticking them off one by one, as part of a crusade with no discernible message?'

I don't want to work with her. 'Anarchists, possibly.'

She shrugs. 'That makes it just plain childish.'

I say, 'If these are just the cases that Phipps & Wexman has heard about, there'll be thousands of others we haven't.'

She nods. 'Exactly. Look at it. It's a can of worms. Which is why Ashok's keen to move on. Clients aren't going to pay for investigations if these sabotages turn out to be part of some mass psychosis. Or weird moral witch-hunt. Or anarchist uprising. And there are other things going on. Equally bizarre.'

'And equally childish?' I ask. She looks up.

'What do you mean?'

'Those children,' I say. 'Pyjama Girl. And the others. The violent children and the suicidal saboteurs aren't two separate epidemics. They're one. Although since it's a global phenomenon, it's a *pan*demic. Technically.' She should have realised this by now. Professor Whybray will have done. She stretches out her fingers and inspects them. They are thin and plain. No jewellery.

She says, 'Go on.'

'Both groups commit uncharacteristic acts. They do so in a dissociative fugue state so they're unaware of what they're doing at the time. But when they see the consequences, they realise they're culpable. The children distance themselves from their attacks by not speaking. While the saboteurs claim they weren't in control of what they did. Sunny Chen said the body doesn't always obey the mind. And Jonas said he felt like a puppet.'

Stephanie takes another sip of wine, leaving a second lipstick imprint on top of the first. The cosmetics industry should rectify that sort of thing. 'Whose puppet?'

Why am I collaborating with her? Of all the people Ashok could have sent—

Or did she volunteer?

'He talked about trolls. And creatures. But mostly about children.'

She takes a breath. 'But how do they fit together?'

I grab a napkin and draw two overlapping circles. It's a rollerball pen: the ink bleeds into the paper.

'OK. Example. This one is children who attack,' I point to the circle on the right. 'Call it K for kids.' I write in the K. 'And this is families with adults who sabotage. Call it A. Both the K and the A circles are part of a general picture of violence.' I draw a third circle labelled V to encompass the other two. I think of the tiny finger-marks on my arm. Stephanie is the last person I would show them to. As for the little girl in Dubai, she has no place in any diagram I could draw. 'Dissociative fugue could fit in there too.' I start draw-ing a circle called F overlapping all the others. 'But we don't know where the boundaries lie.' I finish off the F region with a dotted line going through both K and A. 'See? You can have dissociative behaviour without any of the violence, so some of F must lie in the region outside V. In Venn terms, fugue may even be the universal, enclosing everything else.' I draw a stronger dotted line encom-passing everything. Another thought strikes me. 'But children who destroy their own families are committing sabotage too. Maybe economic and emotional destruction are one and the same circle.' I sketch it out.

'So this is how you work.'

'When the problem calls for it.'

We sit for a minute, not saying anything. Then she points to the circle marked K. 'The Home Office has set up specialised Care Units for them. Drafted an army of specialists and volunteers. The biggest one's in Battersea. A former colleague of mine's running it. Naomi Benjamin. Some ex-academic hotshot came and head-hunted her.'

Of course. I find myself smiling. 'I would guess that's Professor Whybray. He's a medical anthropologist. He's a world expert on mass hysteria. He was my supervisor.'

Two men in a hospital ward, one helping the other 'keep his grip'. *Your materialist focus saved me*, he said afterwards. *I needed to be with someone who wasn't going to spin me fairy tales.*

'Well, his team's based in Naomi's unit in Battersea. Pyjama Girl's there, apparently.' She reaches in her handbag for a small red laptop, sets it on the table next to our drinks, fires it up and stabs at the keys. 'This is just today's news.' She turns the screen to face me. It's the Reuters website. *Children in Violent Killings – latest.* It takes me five seconds to skim through it. In a single day there have been eight reported murders by children in the United States, five in Korea, two in Russia, one in Latvia and another in Morocco. The children are all under ten.

The victims are mostly, but not always, family members. Last week in Egypt, it has been revealed that a boy of four stabbed his mother with a kitchen knife.

Stephanie says, 'Naomi tells me that the kids won't talk about what they did. The parents say they're not the same children. A classic distancing technique. You have to agree: on the social observation front, it doesn't get much more dynamic than this.'

I was thinking that too. But it doesn't make us friends.

I say, 'There's another factor in all this. Which might have a bearing.' When I tell her about Chen's soy habit, and Svensson's bottle of seawater, and Farooq crumbling a block of salt from a desalination plant into a plastic water bottle, and de Vries licking his arm, she puts down her drink and she sits very still.

'Have you told anyone else about this?' she asks when I have finished.

'No. It's only recently I made the connection.' *And it's my investigation. Not yours.*

'Pyjama Girl has a salt craving. Naomi told me last time we spoke. Her parents found a stash of dishwasher salt in her bedroom. If other kids do too, there could be other parallels. Let's find out.' She starts typing again. Her fingers fly over the keyboard like a pianist's. She presses send and looks up. 'OK done.' She looks at her watch. 'I told Naomi we've made some connections, and asked her to call us. With your Professor Whybray, if he's there. In the meantime, here's what we've got,' she says, pointing at the napkin. 'An epidemic of some kind.'

'Pandemic,' I correct her.

'Involving children and adults. They attack something they care about. Be it a corporation or a loved one. And then either refuse to speak or blame a figure from their local folklore.'

'A small figure,' I say. 'Child-sized. They call them trolls or ancestors or djinns or *tokoloshi* or whatever corresponds to the superstitions of the culture they grew up in. But they're children. And then in the case of the adults they kill themselves. Having swallowed a lot of salt,' I continue. 'A salt craving can be a symptom of various medical disorders. Adrenal cortex diseases, diabetes, Addison's. Nothing these people had, that we know of. And it came on very suddenly, in all the cases I've come across. When de Vries started licking his arm, it resembled an animal instinct. Like a sick cat eating grass. And Farooq,' I remember. 'The foreman said he called it medicine.' Did he and de Vries have abnormal kidneys too? 'So what the kids and the saboteurs have in common is that first of all, they commit dramatic acts of physical or economic violence. Secondly, they have no obvious motive. Quite the contrary in fact.' She nods. 'Thirdly, they won't talk about it afterwards, except to blame children. I'm thinking of Svensson in particular. He told his wife that children were bullying him. But in general they can't or won't speak about it. Which implies that someone is scaring them into silence or that they've wiped it from their minds.'

'That's certainly the case with the kids,' she says.

'And fourthly, they crave salt. All of the saboteurs and at least one of the kids. Possibly several. Possibly all. Chen wasn't autopsied. De Vries' and Farooq's results I'm waiting on. It may mean nothing, but Svensson had an extra kidney.'

I am spiralling towards a new connection, but I'm jolted away from it by the noise of the Skype ringtone from Stephanie's laptop. She pats the seat next to her, signifying I should join her. I'm reluctant to get closer to her, but I shift across and she presses answer. Eight seconds later a woman materialises on the screen. Behind her, through a window, I can see some tiny red-clad figures milling about. Children.

She says, 'Hi, Steph.'

'Hi, Naomi.'

Naomi Benjamin has large breasts. And a close-cropped helmet of dark hair and dark eyes. She is wearing a vivid green sweater and a scarf of a similar green with gold stripes, and although it is not one of my favourite greens – there is too little saffron in it – the overall effect is exotic. She must be aware of my eye line because all of a sudden she adjusts her scarf to hide the view of her cleavage.

Stephanie says, 'This is my colleague Hesketh Lock. One of our most brilliant investigators. Behavioural pattern expert.'

Naomi Benjamin nods and smiles, and two small grooves appear, bracketing her mouth. 'Yes. Victor's been talking about you. He'll be along as soon as he's finished in a meeting.' She jerks her head, indicating the children. 'You know, after Angola I had the feeling that nothing could faze me. But I've never seen kids like this before. It's like they're damaged in an entirely new way.' In addition to the red uniforms, some of them are wearing sunglasses or plastic goggles: this gives them a jaunty look, as though they're in fancy dress. I can't make out individual faces. But I can see enough of them to gauge a pattern. 'We're trying to figure out how to get them back to normal. But we don't really understand what it is we're trying to cure. It's a very fluid and distressing dynamic.'

'How many?' asks Stephanie.

'Just over fifty at the moment, at this unit. Ours is the most advanced. But the arrivals are accelerating and I know it's been chaos elsewhere. The Home Office has put in an order for eighty thousand more uniforms. But it's already looking like that won't be enough. No one's geared up for anything like this. The managers are having to make it up as they go along. There are new press restrictions, so you won't be hearing about any new British cases. With any luck that'll slow it down. Whatever I tell you isn't for public consumption.'

Stephanie says quickly, 'Of course.'

The door opens behind her.

'Professor Whybray!' I call out. 'I'm over here!' It's frustrating to be 3,396 miles apart because I would very much like to shake his hand. He's more stooped than the last time I saw him. Either the colours are odd on this screen or he has a tan. But his white beard and moustache are the same. When he sees me he breaks into a smile.

'When the hell can I get you to call me Victor?' That familiar cracked and reedy voice makes something swarm in my chest. 'I know you're not a hugger.' He spreads his arms wide in a gesture of embrace. 'So consider this poor substitute a lucky escape.'

'Good to see you, Professor.' I make the hugging gesture back – Stephanie has to duck – and he laughs. I am happy. It's a clean and fine feeling.

'Hello, Professor. I'm Stephanie Mulligan.' She raises her hand. 'Also from Phipps & Wexman.'

'Good to meet you,' he says, smiling. 'Ashok Sharma told me about you. You'll both be working with me from now on, if you're agreeable.'

Both? Why both?

'On the single pandemic theory?' asks Stephanie. 'Hesketh mentioned it.'

'Yes, I thought he'd get there,' he says, smiling. Naomi pulls up a chair for the professor and he settles next to her with a sideways smile. He is what the French call *bien dans sa peau*: at ease with himself. Or literally, 'good in his skin'. Often he used to drape his arm over my shoulder and call me 'son'. He made me feel *bien dans ma peau* too.

'So let's get started. Children and adults wreaking havoc in a dissociative state. Different methods, same result: sabotage. Family and wider social structures in one case, economic in the other. Hesketh, what do you observe in the adults?'

Still watching the red-clad children milling about in the background, I give Professor Whybray and Naomi Benjamin a brief summary of my three investigations. When I mention the salt, Professor Whybray's eyebrows go up.

'Well here's what I can tell you about the salt from our end. Worldwide, we know of a hundred and twenty-five confirmed cases of children who've attacked and who have a salt craving.'

Stephanie asks, 'What form does it take?'

'All kids go for sugar and salt,' says Naomi. 'It's fundamental. But we're talking high excesses of whatever they can get hold of. Crisps, salted popcorn, peanuts, the usual snack food. In coastal areas we hear they're eating seaweed.'

'Jonas Svensson collected seaweed,' I say. 'And drank seawater. He also had a food stockpile.'

'In some kids it was apparent for weeks before they attacked,' Naomi continues. 'And parents are reporting finding food-hoards and salt-stashes in their kids' bedrooms.'

'When it comes to the violence there's a memory blank in most cases. But interestingly, when they learn what they did, they seem indifferent. Possibly a shock reaction. Later they become hostile towards adults. Or just contemptuous. The families claim they don't recognise them. Some say it's not the real version of their child.'

'Changelings,' I say. 'Alien possession. Exchange for a replica. A very common explanation for uncharacteristic behaviours.'

'Superstition was part of Hesketh's field,' Professor Whybray tells Naomi. 'Before he moved to the dark side.' Just then a door opens behind them and a narrow-faced young man with a ponytail walks in.

Naomi swivels in her chair to address him. 'Hi, Flynn, what's up?'

'Sorry to interrupt you guys,' he says, addressing us. 'But I'm going to have to drag Naomi away. We have a situation.'

'Off you go, Naomi,' says Professor Whybray. 'I'll fill them in on the rest.'

When she and Flynn have left I ask Professor Whybray, 'Could it be the excess salt consumption that's making them behave like this?'

'That's the first thing we addressed in terms of treatment. At the Unit we've eliminated it from their diet completely. No impact so far. We can't police their homes, and some's being smuggled in. We're seeing some very odd behaviours. Which are changing by the day. Hard to keep up.' He angles the screen so that we get a better view of the children in the playground behind him. 'So. Tell me what you observe.'

'Unusual patterns of movement. It looks co-ordinated by instinct. Like birds, or the shoaling of fish.'

Stephanie points to the top of the screen. 'I can see some fighting over there.'

A blonde girl and a black boy are tussling in the background. The boy is wearing swimming goggles.

'So who'll win?' asks Professor Whybray.

'The girl,' I say. 'If she's blue-eyed.' As if in confirmation, the girl wrestles the boy to the ground, tears off his goggles and runs away.

Stephanie glances at me questioningly. 'Jonas Svensson wore dark glasses,' I explain. 'He was blue-eyed. He had an eye infection. The fact that many of these kids are wearing sunglasses or eye goggles tells me they're either protecting their eyes from sunlight, or hiding signs of infection. Since children don't tend to be vain, I suspect the former is more likely. And pale irises need more protection than dark ones. Any deaths yet?' I ask. I am thinking of the autopsies.

'Still waiting.'

I tell him about Jonas Svensson's renal anomaly.

'In normal circumstances I'd call it a long shot,' says Professor Whybray. 'But given what's going on . . .' When he frowns you can see the furrows. 'The whole thing's unprecedented. Anyway, I'm glad to see you've kept your edge, Hesketh. I'm looking forward to working with you again. And you too of course, Stephanie. Ashok praises you highly.'

We start discussing arrangements. Today is Sunday. Our flights are open. I agree to meet Professor Whybray and his team at nine o'clock on Thursday. Stephanie will join us if she is back from Dubai by then. Before that, I'll find a moment to tell the Professor I can't work with Stephanie 'for personal reasons'. And he'll agree to this because it's me he wants. I am confident about this. We say goodbye and Stephanie presses End Call.

She takes a sip of her drink. 'I'm glad we got the contract. Though it's not a classic Phipps & Wexman case.'

'Yes it is. Ashok's a disaster capitalist. He follows the money.' I finish my drink in one gulp, and signal to the waiter for the bill. I stand up.

'Where are you going?'

'To do some research and make notes for Professor Whybray.'

'Wait, Hesketh. If this thing continues to spread, there's a lot at stake here and we'll need to collaborate. So we have to clear the air on the personal front.'

I sit down opposite her and reach for a napkin. 'Five minutes. Starting now.' I point at my watch. I begin folding an *ozuru*. The material is thin, but not ideal.

'Hesketh?' Her hand is on my arm.

I shake it off. 'Don't touch me!' It comes out louder than I intend. The waiter has been approaching: now he backs off.

'OK. OK. Please Hesketh.' Stephanie is aiming for eye contact but she won't get it. Kaitlin likes direct people. She admires them and says they have 'guts'. I like direct people too, but only if they are children. 'We need to have a conversation about Kaitlin.'

Kaitlin Kalifakidis. The woman who Stephanie drove crazy with love and lust. The woman who told me lie after lie after lie, and turned me into two ugly birds, a cockerel and a cuckoo. At the Phipps & Wexman reception I saw them talking and laughing together, but failed to identify their sudden, intense camaraderie as courtship behaviour. I hadn't even known that Stephanie was a lesbian. Or that Kaitlin was, to use her repellent expression, 'bi-curious'.

I say, 'No. There's nothing we need to discuss. It's in the past.'

The best man won! said Sunny Chen, the day he burned his Hellnote effigy. But no one won. It was all wreckage.

She shifts. 'But that's the thing, Hesketh. That's what I've been wanting to tell you. It's not.'

'What do you mean?'

'Kaitlin and I are back together. I've moved in.'

I say, 'Oh.'

She fingers the spiked shards on her necklace. It's still mesmerising me. The material isn't plastic. And it's certainly not mineral. But it has the sheen of a polymer . Varnish, maybe. It might be more lightweight than it looks.

'When?'

'Two weeks ago. Perhaps I should have told you earlier.'

I complete my *ozuru* and stand it on the table between us. It observes her with its head cocked slightly to one side.

'No,' I say. 'Now is fine. Now is quite early enough.'

The waiter slides the bill on to the table, then melts away. She speaks quietly. 'You know there was something between us before. Well. We began seeing each other again. She rang me when you split up.'

I'm overloaded. I stand and pick up my briefcase. The whisky has gone to my head. I need to get out of here. Breathe some outdoor air.

'Hesketh, stay!' she calls after me. But I can't.

Men generally find the idea of two women together sexually exciting. This is well documented. The fact that I was no exception only deepened the horror.

There. It is said.

CHAPTER 7

THE POOL IS a relief. They put ice cubes in the water to cool it down. That's what the attendant told me yesterday. I swim crawl, sloshing the water over the edges, which are flush with the sides. It disappears noisily down sunken runnels. I forget myself. I forget everything except the intense pummelling of my muscles.

I've done fifty-three lengths, almost the equivalent of 0.75 kilometres, when a thought strikes me. It should have come to me before. But I was too busy reliving my cuckoldry to see Stephanie's revelation as an opportunity.

Now that I do, I must act immediately.

I get out and dress hastily. Five minutes later I'm banging on her door. There's a tray on the floor outside. She must have ordered room service. I have read that women often do that in hotels on business trips because they feel self-conscious eating alone in restaurants. It's half past nine. I bang harder.

'Open up!'

She opens the door a crack, leaving the chain on. 'Oh. It's you.'

She lets me in. Next to the bed is a photo of Kaitlin with Freddy. It looks recent. I haven't seen it before. It fills me with rage. She stole my family.

She looks nervous, as though I might have come to rape her. Women on business trips worry about that too, according to the same article. It contained a list of Dos and Don'ts While Travelling. Opening the door to me would have counted as a Don't.

'How can I help you?' Her voice is very cold.

I go over to the big picture window and turn to face her. My hair is dripping: I can feel the water running down my neck, chilled unpleasantly by the air conditioning.

'I want to see Freddy. You can make that happen. Kaitlin's wrong to stop me seeing him. I was a father to him.'

'Why don't you sit?' She indicates an armchair, but I stay where I am. 'Look, Hesketh. I know what you mean to Freddy. He talks about you a lot. He misses you.'

'So you admit that much.'

'Of course. Why wouldn't I?'

'So admit that it's wrong.'

She takes a breath. 'Actually I think it is. Wrong.'

'What?' She waves again at the armchair, but I stay standing. 'You think it's wrong? You admit it?'

'Yes. You heard me. And you might have heard me say it earlier if you hadn't stormed off.'

'So why can't I see Freddy?'

She shuts her eyes for a moment. 'Kaitlin has her reasons.'

'Name me a single one that's justifiable.'

She pauses. 'Kaitlin's a good mother. But she brought Freddy up on her own. And basically, she feels comfortable with that.'

'That's not justifiable. And it's not even a reason. It's an excuse.'

'Please, Hesketh. You're shouting. Sit down.'

She sits in an armchair and points at the other one. Reluctantly, I sink into it. 'Anyway this isn't about what Kaitlin feels comfortable with. It's about Freddy and his entitlement to a father. It's a question of justice.'

She looks at her hands. When she speaks, her voice is low and I have to strain to hear it. 'Don't think I've felt good about all this, Hesketh.'

I bang the glass table between us and she jumps. 'So don't be a coward! Stand up for the boy's rights! Do whatever you want with Kaitlin. I don't care. But don't let her stop me being Freddy's dad.' She turns away, so I bang the table again. 'Is that a yes?' She nods again. 'Then say it.'

'Yes.' Her eyes are reddening. I don't care.

'I'm going to hold you to that.'

'You can.' She gets to her feet quickly, goes to the bathroom and emerges blowing her nose into a tissue. She's carrying a white hand towel which she chucks in my direction. 'Dry your hair.' She sniffs and blows her nose again. 'Now let's have a drink.' She goes over to the mini-bar and throws open the door.

'Thanks.' As I start towelling my hair, my head begins to buzz with what might be joy.

She comes and sits opposite me, pours out our drinks. Whisky. She hands me a generous glass. 'Well I'll be honest with you, Hesketh. Things haven't been easy with Freddy.' She takes a big gulp and flushes. I see that this must represent a betrayal. I am glad. 'He's confused, inevitably.' I remember Kaitlin's text: *you have left Freddy very confused.* 'I'm not kidding myself. I can't afford to in my job. I want to do what's right. The thing is, the thing I wanted to discuss with you is, well . . . The day before yesterday he—'

She breaks off and takes another big swig. Something's bothering her. And she seems slightly drunk. Did she have another drink after I left the bar? An image hurtles back to me: Freddy aiming his catapult at Kaitlin's heart. And its signature noise: *zoooshhh.*

'Has he been violent?' My own question startles me.

Her face reddens. Her neck too. The necklace glows white against it. 'How did you know?'

I shrug. 'A guess. I've barely spoken to him since I moved out. What did he do?'

'He attacked a teacher. He threw a flint at her in the playground. She was badly hurt. It was . . . pretty shocking. Five stitches.'

As she speaks, I find myself staring at her necklace again. Those shapes: bones. Vertebrae. Knuckles. Something like that. I made a printout. A4. Sunny Chen's suicide note is in the side pocket of my laptop case. I reach for it and open it. I pull it out and when I see the thing confirmed I feel instantly sick and shove it back. I help myself to another swig of whisky and bang my glass down too hard, so that some of it spills out. Stephanie wipes it with her napkin. I make a mental *ozuru,* and then another. I feel the horrible swoop of vertigo. I'm overloaded. And still too hot. There's no breeze here. Not even a breath of wind.

'Hesketh, who on earth gave you that bruise?' She is looking at my arm.

'Jonas Svensson. In the hospital. He grabbed me.'

'But those aren't adult finger-marks. What's going on? Are you OK?'

No. I am not OK.

I clear my throat. 'Where does your necklace come from?'

'Hesketh, you're changing the subject.'

Can't she see this is urgent? 'I said, where does it come from?'

She sighs, then reaches up and fingers it. 'Do you like it?'

'That's irrelevant. I need to know exactly where you got hold of it.' She's smiling. Doesn't she realise I am incapable of making small talk? She leans forward, as if to divulge a secret. But I know the answer before she says it. Of course I do. Even so, I feel my chest tighten when I hear it confirmed.

'Hesketh, what's the matter?' I pull out the piece of paper again from my laptop case. It's crumpled at the sides. I flatten it out on the table and spread it out in front of her so she can see it properly. But she doesn't look. She needs to. She should. 'He's so clever with his hands,' she's saying. Then she stops and sees what I'm showing her. 'What's that?' She looks puzzled. 'How – did Freddy draw it?' She picks it up. 'But it's ink. Freddy doesn't use ink, does he? And this hand-print here, how could he—'

'Freddy didn't do it. Do you remember Sunny Chen?'

'The Taiwan whistle-blower.'

'He left this for his wife before he killed himself.' The sheet starts trembling in her hand. With care, she sets it down on the table between us and shifts back in her seat, as though the paper is contaminated. 'His wife insisted he couldn't have done it. The hand-print's too small to be a man's. Can you see that this pattern here matches your necklace? Exactly?' I point to the spiked circle.

She clears her throat and begins to fiddle with the clasp at her neck.

'Help me here, will you?' I can hear the panic. She wants to get rid of it. She can't do it fast enough. 'Please. Just get it off me.'

She bows her head, and I reach over. It feels very intimate to look at the nape of this woman's neck. This might be a place that Kaitlin has kissed, while cupping Stephanie's breasts from behind. The place an executioner's blade would target for a clean kill. The clasp is the classic kind, a metal one which locks on to a plain ring. Freddy cannibalises Kaitlin's old jewellery for beads and fastenings. I undo it and free the necklace. It weighs surprisingly little. Papier mâché. Of course. Not the pulp variety, but small shreds of paper glued on in layers. Freddy has tiny fingers, like the claws of a bird. The workmanship is accomplished, even for him. Most of the paper is plain white beneath the varnish, but looking closer I can see a few yellow streaks of a different texture. It's origami paper. The shapes – you can't really call them beads, though that's their function – are reminiscent of skeletal fingers, connected by a length of nylon fishing line. I lay it on the table next to Sunny's suicide drawings.

There's no doubting it. The configuration is the same.

'There's no way Freddy could have got hold of this and copied it?' asks Stephanie. 'I mean, that would explain—'

'Not unless you gave it to him.'

'But I've never seen it before.'

'Did you look at the Chen file?' I ask.

'I read your report, that's all. But it didn't mention this.'

'No. I hadn't seen it. Not then. And when I did, I didn't know what it meant. I still don't. When did he give you this?'

'Last month. For my birthday. On the twenty-second.'

'That's before Sunny Chen died. It's before he even exposed Jenwai.'

'And what about this eye?' she points.

'I don't know.'

'And this hand-print?'

'I don't know.'

'Can't you hazard a guess?'

'It might mean stop.'

'Stop what?'

I slam my hand on the table. 'I don't know!'

I'm getting overloaded. Stephanie must be too because she just says softly, 'Jesus, what's happening here, Hesketh? What the hell's going on?'

And once again I don't know. I rock and rock. *I don't know I don't know I don't know.*

CHAPTER 8

KAITLIN'S HOUSE, BUILT in 1910, is part of a classic London terrace of faded red brick off Fulham Palace Road. The front door is the same French Grey I painted it when I moved in. But the metal containers with trailing ivy and miniature box trees are new, and the blinds have been replaced by curtains. I arrive at 11.16, fourteen minutes earlier than agreed. I've been staying at an airport hotel in London since my return from Dubai two nights ago, so I've brought my suitcase with me. It's Wednesday 26th September. Temperature, fifteen degrees centigrade. Moderate to light winds. They're shuffling branches, stirring up dust, making litter dance.

Freddy must have been looking out for me because I don't even need to ring the bell: as I approach, he throws the door open wide, yells 'Hesketh!', launches himself at me like a monkey, and clings. 'Freddy K, Freddy K, Freddy K,' I laugh into his hair. He feels heavier, more substantial than last time. I get a surge in my chest, not dissimilar to pain. Wellbeing. I am *bien dans ma peau*. I carry him through the narrow entrance hall into the kitchen and sit him on the table to take a better look. I inhale the old-fashioned floor-polish smell of Kaitlin's house. A brand called Pledge. My mother used it. The boy's mop of dark curly hair is the same, but his face has altered subtly: its angles more defined, its planes cleaner, and there's a sprinkle of freckles on his nose, the colour of muscovado sugar.

'Hi Hesketh.' I swing round. Stephanie's paler than ever. 'Kaitlin's visiting her mum at the hospice. She's gone all day.' I have no idea what she has told Kaitlin about my visit. It's an irrelevance. 'Why don't you guys go through to the living-room while I heat us up a pizza?' Before I left Dubai we had a short, practical conversation about how to proceed with Freddy. The strategy we agreed on: food; Lego; questions.

'Hey, Hesketh. Come and see what I can do,' says Freddy. And he's dragging me through to the living-room to show me his 'nearly' headstand on the sofa. He makes ten attempts, each of which requires a star-rating from me, on a scale of one to six. Then he's perched on the back of a chair almost doing the splits and holding forth in his sparky, energetic way, flexing the power of being a boy aged seven. I'd forgotten his grasshopper mind, the eccentricity of his questions. If I had to decide between being tied to an ant's nest and being stuck in a giant spider's web what would I choose? Can people microwave themselves?

The Kawasaki rose I made for Kaitlin when I moved in has disappeared from the alcove by the mantelpiece. But it's easier than I anticipated to function within the new parameters.

'If you stuck your hand in a volcano, you'd get a ninth-degree burn,' he's saying a little later, through a mouthful of pepperoni pizza. 'From the lava. It can kill you. And it's glow-in-the-dark. Sometimes red and sometimes orange and then it's blue at the edges. Blue fire. You can get that.' He reaches for another slice and does the archaeopteryx voice. '*Huloo, Froodoh, wooda you lika anootha slooce of poopporoni pooza. Yos Ploz.*' Then he throws back his head and laughs at his own entertainment: a throaty, dirty laugh. He spills his juice; Stephanie mops it up without complaint. His flow of speech is directed largely at me.

'Did you bring me a present then?'

'As a matter of fact I did. Guess where it is.'

'Up your bottom. Jokes. Suitcase, *duh. Foonk-you-fonk-you-fank-you!*'

Soon we're at work on a Lego cruise ship. Principal colours: red, white, blue, beige and grey. It has a swimming pool, a tennis court and a mini-golf course. On the top deck there are ranks of solar panels, a wind turbine and a helipad. Under my tutelage, Freddy has learned the importance of studying the instruction pamphlet before beginning a job like this, and of arranging the small plastic bags containing the different elements in the right order. But he likes to improvise. It's secretly a pirate ship, he insists. So we need barrels of explosive. Weapons. Rigging. A flag. Potted palms. He has a box of Lego pieces from which to add to the basic template. Occasionally, we look out of the window and check the sky for changes. Today there are the flattened cumuliform elements that characterise stratocumulus. I've long been trying to teach him the scientific terms for clouds, but Freddy prefers his own. Bacon rashers. Popcorn. Fuzzaluzz. Double blob. Mega-poo. Ha ha ha.

'It's an ark,' he tells Stephanie as she comes in and settles on the sofa opposite us. It has new cushions. There's also a lamp I don't recognise and a rug whose weave I identify as West Moroccan. There's more feminine clutter than when I lived here. 'Look.' Freddy points to the animals he has lined up ready to board the vessel when it's complete. Plastic farm animals, mostly, scuffed from over-zealous play. But also llamas, lizards, wolves, vultures and a giraffe. A few dinosaurs. 'Hey Steph, is there anything else to eat?'

'What do you want?'

'*Crosps! Crosps! Crosps!*'

'Hmm. The thing is, they're for treats,' she says. 'I don't think Mum would like that.'

The deep voice again: '*Moom's not hoyah. So gov me som crosps.*'

'If you want something, what do you say?' She wants to please him more than she wants to please Kaitlin. That makes sense. She already has Kaitlin.

'I say, *ond som jooz. Ploz.*'

A moment later she's setting a packet of crisps and a glass of orange juice in front of him. '*Foonk-you-fonk-you-fank-you.*' Outside, a police siren wails, and he mimics it: *weew-weew-weew-weew!* then tears the packet open and starts feeding himself. They're cheese-and-onion flavour.

Stephanie nods at me. *Now.* I start rocking very gently, gearing myself up.

'I've got a story for you, Freddy K,' I say.

'Cool,' he says, shifting closer. He likes my stories. Maybe he thinks I make them up. But I never do. I would be incapable of it. Stephanie is sitting very still.

'A man called Sunny Chen spotted that some people were breaking the rules at work. So he told on them. But then he died. Just before he died he did some drawings.'

'Cool. Is he good at drawing?'

'You can decide for yourself. I'll show you them.' I'm about to open the folder when he says suddenly, 'So did he say "AAAAGH" when he fell in the machine?' Soggy crumbs fly out as he speaks. The smell stings my nostrils. I put the folder down.

I ask, 'What did you say?'

Freddy grins. 'Did he die like this?' He reaches for a little red Lego figure in a white hard hat and holds it up in front of his face between finger and thumb. 'I'll be the machine.' Then quickly he tips his head back, opens his mouth, still full of half-chewed crisps, and drops the little figure in. It happens almost too fast for me to register. Stephanie's face is rigid, but she draws in a sharp breath as Freddy pretends to chew on the Lego man, making loud eating sounds. I just watch him and rock. 'Mmmm,' he says. 'Delicious. Nice crunchy bones. *Nyca-crooncha-boonz.*'

Then he spits out Sunny Chen with some saliva and pieces of crisp and licks the salt from his lips.

I need to make some *ozuru*. From the corner of my eye I can see the little Lego figure in a pool of spittle, with blobs of mashed crisp attached. When Stephanie speaks I can hear she's struggling to keep her voice level.

'Freddy, how do you know how Sunny died?'

He shrugs. 'I just do.'

She glances at me. *Now you.* Still rocking, I say, 'And then after

163

that, another man died. In another country – Sweden.' No reaction. 'Do you know where Sweden is?'

'*Schwoodoon?* Nope.'

Freddy's globe is on the sideboard: Stephanie gets up and passes it to me. I settle it on the coffee table next to the ship.

'Geography lesson,' I say. I show him Taiwan, and then Sweden. Stephanie's paleness almost glows. She is very talented at keeping perfectly still. Lizards and other reptiles can do that. Freddy, apparently unaware of the impact he's made, munches more crisps and takes a glug of juice which trickles down his chin. Stephanie tries to wipe his face with a tissue, but he wriggles out of her reach.

'So then the Sweden man died,' says Freddy.

'Swedish,' I correct him. 'People from Sweden are called Swedish. Or Swedes. Like the root vegetable.'

'*Shwoodoosh,*' says Freddy. '*Schwoods.* I bet they talk like that. *Hulloo, yoi um a Shwoodoosh man from Schwoodoon.*'

I pass him a second Lego figure. Yellow. Still holding the bag of crisps, he settles the man on the carpet, then roots around in the Lego and pulls out a green truck.

'Here's the road. And here comes the truck, and here comes the Schwoodoosh man. *Come on da trucka-ducka, and run Mister Swoodoosh over!*' The truck in one hand, and Jonas in the other, he makes classic noises, like the 'kapow' of my childhood comics: '*Nrrrrr, nrrr, nrrr, vroom, ka-donk, aaagh.*' He slides them towards each other on the floor until they collide. '*Oooh, ooh, the kids hate me, says Mister Schwoodoosh, I must run under a trucka! Boof! AAAGH! Noo oi am DEAD!*'

'How do you know he died like that, Freddy K?' My voice is a croak. 'You weren't there.'

'One of us was.' He rummages in the Lego pieces, then looks up. 'Maybe the one who did that.' He points at my left arm, then pokes it with his small finger. 'You made us be born and then you made us live like that. So you should go to prison.'

'What do you mean, Freddy?' asks Stephanie.

'What?' Suddenly his face goes lax and his body slumps slightly. He yawns, as if exhausted, then blinks rapidly several times. 'I don't know.'

'Freddy?' she repeats. He gives his head a small sharp shake, as though an insect is bothering him, and fingers another crisp. 'Freddy? Can you answer me? Can you explain what you're saying?'

'Is there a football match today?' he asks me. We used to watch sport together sometimes, at weekends. ''Cos I'd like to see one. I'm really tired now.'

'No. But you can lie on the sofa and have a rest for a bit. How about that?'

'No. Wait.' He takes a deep breath and a shudder runs through him. It's clearly visible: a wide current working its way down his body. Then he sits up very erect, smiles, grabs the crisp packet and downs a huge handful in a single go. 'So what about the other man?' he says. All his energy is back. 'Come on. Let's do him!'

Stephanie says, 'What other man?'

'The other man! In the other place!' Freddy says excitedly, scrabbling around in the Lego.

Stephanie licks her lips. They seem very dry. Her lipstick has disappeared. 'But how do you know there was another one?'

Freddy shrugs his tiny bird-boned shoulders. 'I just know. There's always three, in stories.' This is true. Perhaps it's even something I have told him. Three brothers, three wishes, three chances. Three ways to die. 'Except there's lots more. You just don't know about all the others.' He grins. 'Say it Hesketh. Go on.' He pokes me in the ribs with his tiny finger. He means, say *yet*. But I don't want to. He picks up the little Jonas figure and then makes the truck run over him again. And again. And again. *Nrrr, nrrr, nrrr. Ka-donk! Aaagh!* 'They got scared. We scared them. It was cool. We made them stop.' He rummages in the box until he finds the figure he wants. It's brown. He holds it up.

Stephanie says, 'What do you mean, we scared them? Who's we?'

'And then *this* one died.' He licks the crisp salt around his mouth. It's burned a pink halo on his skin. The colour alarms me. There's a tightening in my throat. Often, this is a sign that I am feeling something. It might be deep and terrible. I make a swift mental *ozuru*. Then at high speed, a frog, a water-bomb, a kite and a lotus flower. But I botch them and they crumple.

I say, 'What do you mean, Freddy K?'

He sticks his finger on the globe. 'There.' Freddy has left a greasy little fingerprint on the Arabian Gulf. Ahmed Farooq. 'He ate something poisonous. But his eyes didn't pop. Then the other one jumped off a tower that wasn't finished yet.' He fishes a pink man out of the plastic box, sets a green hat on his head and fits a spanner in his hand. He stands the man on the edge of the ship and tips him off. De Vries.

I ask, 'How do you know?'

He shrugs. 'You saw the girl with him. I've got that skyscraper in my bedroom. It's called the Leaning Tower of Pizza.' He turns to Stephanie expectantly, but she doesn't speak. 'That's a joke. It's really called Pisa. It's in Italy. Hesketh thinks she wasn't real.'

'Who wasn't real?' says Stephanie.

'But she is. She was there on the skyscraper. He saw her. She's one of us.'

I know what is real and what is not real. I have forged a career out of knowing the difference. Stephanie looks at me. There's a question on her face, but I can't answer it.

Freddy's busy arranging another Lego man near the edge of the table. He wriggles himself so that his mouth is level with it, settles his chin on the surface, puffs out his cheeks and blows hard. Crisp crumbs come flying out, and twinkles of salt. The white Lego man tumbles off the edge.

I ask, 'Did Mum tell you about these men?'

'*Nyet*,' he says. He's tearing his crisp packet apart and flattening it out.

'Stephanie then?' I sense her shift. 'Or maybe Stephanie knew about them and she told your mum and you overheard.'

'No,' says Stephanie. 'That didn't happen.' I glance across at her. She is paler than ever.

'*Nyet*,' agrees Freddy. 'That didn't happen.' Then he does the archaeopteryx voice again, even deeper this time. '*Thot dodn't hoppon.*'

I ask, 'So who told you about the men, Freddy K?'

He wipes his nose on his sleeve. 'The other kids.'

'Kids where?' I ask.

He shrugs. 'Everywhere. We talk about killing grown-ups.'

'And why would you do that, Freddy?' asks Stephanie.

'What?' he slumps again. 'I'm tired. You're being a weirdo, Steph. And you're being a weirdo too, Hesketh. I don't know what you're talking about. I want to lie on the sofa and watch football.'

I pick up one of the ship's tiny solar panels and hold it between finger and thumb. Stephanie stays perfectly still on the sofa. She doesn't blink. Just then there's a sound in the hallway. The front door opening, then closing shut. If Stephanie registers it, she doesn't let it show. Her eyes stay concentrated on Freddy.

Stephanie says urgently, 'And how do you feel when you and your friends talk about how to kill grown-ups?' Freddy looks up and crumples his empty crisp packet and grins slowly. Who is he now? His eyes are panes of blue light.

'It's epic,' he says. 'We feel good.' And he smiles wider. You can see all his teeth and the gaps between.

The door opens. It's Kaitlin. She sees me right away. Her voice is cold. 'Well hello everyone.'

Raindrops glitter in her hair.

'Hello Kaitlin,' I say. She looks older than when I last saw her, three months ago. But she is still beautiful and her hair is still messy and piled high, like a bird's nest. I see some grey in it now, at the temples. She's brandishing a bouquet of white roses.

'Hi Mum,' says Freddy. He's looking in the Lego box for a plastic cog.

'Hello pumpkin,' says Kaitlin.

Stephanie leaps to her feet. 'Hey. Lovely that you're back so early.'

She reaches to touch her, but Kaitlin blocks it by flinging the bouquet and her handbag on to the sofa, then turning her back to remove her raincoat. She is dressed differently from usual, in bright colours: Jade Mist and Sea-Burst. I quote Sanderson, 1993. They hurt my retinas. Stephanie must have had an influence.

'Mum and Steph are lesbians,' Freddy tells me matter-of-factly, still rummaging. 'Mum didn't used to be a lesbian but now she is. They sex each other.'

There's a silence. 'Yes I heard about that,' I say. My throat feels very dry. I would like to run away and drink water. In a café. A large bottle of it. With ice.

Kaitlin says, 'Well it's a surprise to see you, Hesketh.'

'Not for me,' says Freddy. 'Steph told me he was coming.'

'Did she now?' She addresses Stephanie in a voice I know well. 'Has he eaten anything but crisps this afternoon?'

'*Pooporooni pooza*,' says Freddy in the archaeopteryx voice. I think of the mess not cleared up. 'And the crisps was just one packet. I wanted salt and vinegar, but I got cheese and onion. So can I have another?'

'No,' says Kaitlin. 'You know the rules Freddy.' Outside, a police siren wails in the distance. Freddy mimics it: '*Weew-weew-weew-weew! Nee-naw, nee-naw!*'

'How was your mother?' asks Stephanie, folding Kaitlin's coat. She is good at appearing calm.

Kaitlin looks at me again and shakes her head, then addresses Stephanie. 'Actually, I never got there. The train was cancelled. It's chaos out there. Have you heard anything?' For a moment I think things may work out after all. If there's an external distraction it might deflect the tension.

'We haven't seen the news,' says Stephanie. 'But there's something we really need to talk about. Freddy, perhaps you could go upstairs so the grown-ups can have a chat.' Her mouth shapes a smile, but her eyes don't join in. 'Me and Mum and Hesketh.'

Kaitlin's face flushes. 'Of course. I'm very keen to hear what you have to say. Freddy, say goodbye to Hesketh.'

'Why can't he stay and finish the ark with me?'

'Because it's not something we agreed.'

I'm still holding the piece of Lego between finger and thumb. Very slowly, I put it down.

Freddy persists: 'So when can he come again? When? You have to say when.'

She won't make a scene in front of him. But I can see the fury. She doesn't speak.

'Maybe we should work out an arrangement,' says Stephanie evenly. 'If Freddy and Hesketh both want to see each other, why don't we agree that they spend time together whenever Hesketh is in town?'

Kaitlin flushes. I know that later she will refer to this as an 'ambush'.

'Cool!' says Freddy.

Kaitlin puts a forefinger to the bridge of her nose: her default 'stress' gesture.

'We'll talk about it.' She claps her hands. 'Come on, Freddy, up-up-up! I'm counting to ten and then I'm coming up. One. Two. Three.' When he has run off she says angrily to Stephanie, 'I'm not opposed to discussing it. I'm not a monster you know.'

'No one ever said you were,' Stephanie replies in a low voice. 'But that's not actually what this is about. Something's come up. That's why Hesketh is here. It's urgent.'

Kaitlin makes an impatient noise. 'OK. But whatever it is, I'm talking to Freddy first.' She raises her voice. 'Nine, ten! Freddy, I'm coming!'

'I could do with a big drink,' says Stephanie, when Kaitlin has disappeared upstairs. I tell her I could do with one too. We go through to the kitchen. Stephanie hunts about for a vase, but can't find one, so she shoves the bouquet into the sink and runs some water. Kaitlin must have bought the flowers for her mother. I jettison the remains of our pizza and wipe the table. 'Now that you've shown your face here, and Freddy's had his say, she'll come round,' Stephanie continues, pulling a bottle of Australian Shiraz from the wine rack. 'But in any case, given what he's just told us, all that's going to take a back seat.' She twists in the corkscrew – its handle is a vine root, from a vineyard in Portugal – and pops out the cork. She pours out three glasses, but we don't wait for Kaitlin. 'Cheers.'

The wine is excellent. It energises me. 'There's no way Freddy can have known about Chen and Svensson and Farooq and de Vries,' I say.

'Or the girl on the tower,' she says, taking a large gulp and looking at me hard. I don't say anything. But she won't let it go. 'Come on, Hesketh. Was there really a child up there when de Vries jumped?'

'I don't know.'

She's still looking at me. 'That's not like you.'

I drink some more wine and wait for the warmth to spread. 'I know what I think I saw. I think I saw a child. The others thought the same thing. I didn't mention it in my statement because she vanished. She was just ... gone. It was very hot up there. And stressful.'

'Why didn't you tell me about this in Dubai?'

'I hadn't processed it. I still haven't.'

There's the sound of movement upstairs.

'She'll be here in a minute. We'll come back to it,' Stephanie says quickly. 'Look, we can't keep her in the dark. She needs to know everything. If what Freddy says is true, then kids everywhere are discussing how to kill people. So this is potentially huge. It'll expand and peak. In which case—'

She's cut short by a scream.

There are moments in life – so few you can count them – when time's perspective seems to shift quite literally. In those moments, a second can last a minute, or freeze to near-eternity. Soldiers know this. But homes can be war zones too.

The scream is so grotesquely extended that it seems to require more air than two human lungs can contain. Shooting up from the table, Stephanie knocks over two glasses and they crash to the floor, spattering wine everywhere.

Finally, the screaming stops to an abrupt halt and there's a brief silence. Then Kaitlin shouts, 'NO! Freddy, don't! NO!'

Then she shrieks. There's a scrambling sound then a huge thud, followed by banging. Then more thudding. We rush through to the hallway. Kaitlin's lying halfway down the narrow staircase. There's no sign of Freddy.

Stephanie groans and says, 'Oh my God.'

Everything about Kaitlin is wrong. If she were origami, she would be a write-off.

She is trapped transversely on the stairs, with her legs splayed at an odd angle. Being vain, she would not like to be seen like this, with her staring white face and her hair in a tangled cloud streaked with grey. Her brightly coloured Oceanic Range clothes, and the fact that her skirt has flown up around her neck, disturb me. Her eyes are wide open, as if she's transfixed. She doesn't blink.

Stephanie rushes over and cradles her head. She presses her finger to Kaitlin's neck and begins to whimper. I am about to ask if Kaitlin is dead when something makes me look up.

A movement at the top of the stairs.

'Hey, Hesketh.'

There, as rigid as a little Lego man, stands the boy I love.

He still has a sore pink halo round his mouth where he licked the salt from his lips. He doesn't seem to notice his mother lying sprawled and motionless on the stairs. Or Stephanie holding her head.

'I'm still hungry.'

I can't speak.

'I said I'm hungry!' he shouts. Then he shifts to the deep archaeopteryx voice. '*Hoskoth, oi sod oi om still hongra!*'

It's a command.

Due to the unexpectedly high number of emergencies, we can respond only to life-threatening situations. Check that the situation you are calling about is life-threatening. If it is not, you must hang up. If you stay on the line, your call will be put in a queue.

I lived in this house long enough to know that normally at this time on a Sunday there is a loose pattern of activity in the street. You'll see the last shoppers coming home, the first cinema-goers heading out, a few kids on bikes and skateboards in the sinking light. But when I go to the window I see only one person: a large woman standing in the middle of the street swinging her head heavily from side to side. She seems distressed. A car swerves to avoid her. *To confirm that your situation is urgent, press the hash button.* I press it and begin to rock. *Be aware that any hoax or non-urgent calls will result in prosecution. Please hold.* Some narcotic music comes on: I recognise Josef Strauss' *Sphärenklänge,* The Music of the Spheres. If its intention is to soothe, in my case it fails. I put the phone on loudspeaker, shove it in my jacket pocket, shut my eyes and visit the same inner panic room I went to on the construction site in Dubai. I don't know how long I stay there.

'Hesketh.' It's Stephanie. 'Hesketh. Look at me.' I take a breath, open my eyes. 'Listen. I'm going to phone Felicity. My sister. She's a nurse. Get Freddy downstairs. Keep him in the kitchen till the ambulance arrives.'

Yes. Freddy is not a stranger or a *tokoloshi.* He is Freddy K and he is hungry and the part of me that can function can go and supervise him until help comes. Stephanie punches at her phone and goes into the living-room.

'Come down now, Freddy!' I shout. He must have gone back

to his room. I shout again and he reappears. He looks very small. His face is flushed and pink. I wonder if he has a fever. Might a fever explain what has happened? What he did? 'Come down. You'll have to step past Mum. We'll get an ambulance for her. I'll make you spaghetti. Out in the kitchen.'

He hesitates and says in a small voice, 'OK.'

He looks disoriented as he picks his way past his mother. He doesn't stop to look at her or glance back. He is panting slightly by the time he reaches the bottom of the stairs. He glances from side to side, as if unfamiliar with his surroundings.

'This way.' I put my hands on his shoulders and march him into the kitchen, where a message interrupts the Strauss in my jacket pocket: *you are now number twenty-nine in the queue.* I start calculating, then give up. I don't know enough about the local healthcare infrastructure to guess what number twenty-nine might mean, in waiting terms. 'Stay here,' I tell Freddy.

'OK,' he whispers.

Back in the hall, Stephanie has finished her call. The muscles in her face are drawn tight. I watch her lips move as she speaks.

'My sister says we have to move her or more blood will go to her head. We just have to hope there's no spinal injury. Come on. Let's do it.'

Wordlessly, we shift Kaitlin as the tinny music – in normal circumstances an oeuvre of distinctive beauty – crackles away in my pocket. The stairway is narrow and manoeuvring Kaitlin's unresponsive body is hard work. At one point, she kicks out, then goes limp again. A sign of life, surely: of a body still responding to the pump of blood. We lay her in the recovery position.

Stephanie says, 'My sister says it's not just Freddy. It's other kids too. They're attacking people.' I begin more impossible calculations. Epidemics can adhere to certain models, but mass hysteria can't be mapped. 'I'll see to Kaitlin and you deal with Freddy. Just keep him right away from both of us.'

When I go back into the kitchen Freddy is sitting on the floor with the contents of a cardboard box spilled on to the tiles. His usual paraphernalia: empty toilet rolls, pigeon feathers, felt pens, paper clips, blobs of Blu-Tack. But he seems uncertain what to do with them, or even how to handle them. It strikes me that he's even more spatially confused than he seemed earlier. His eyes zigzag across the ceiling as if searching for something. He squints at the light fixture, then opens his eyes wide and blinks repeatedly. He grabs a tube of wood glue, clutches it to his chest and spins around on his bottom, like a human compass finding north. When he stops again, his face is completely blank.

'Freddy K?'

Then out of the blue, he's crying. Big angry sobs that shake his small frame. His face is smeared with snot and tears. I step over to him, crouch down, put my hands on his shoulders. He falls against my chest and put his arms around my neck. We stay like that. I pat his back and he sobs.

'Freddy K, Freddy K, Freddy K,' I say. 'Let's sit at the table and talk about all this. I'm here. I'll take care of you. I love you. We'll work out what to do.'

But for reasons I can't fathom, this jolts him into another mood. He pulls away from me and leaps to his feet. 'I'm hungry!' I grab his shoulder: with a rough and surprisingly strong movement he squirms free. 'I said I'm hungry!' His voice wobbles, but it's forceful. As if there's anger in it. Or some kind of violence.

I hunt in the food cupboard, find the spaghetti and think about sauce. The minutiae will save me. Lipids, proteins, fibre, sodium. *Ingredients: wheat flour, water. Put water in pan. Turn on gas. Bring to boil.* At some point the Strauss is interrupted by a voice and I speak to someone from the emergency services. I answer the questions she asks, assure her it's serious, give the address, say can you hurry. *Please hang up now sir. We are doing our best.* The hot water goes milky and forms a gelatinous scum. Carbonara. He likes carbonara. I find a packet of bacon. I tear it open with a blunt knife and get my hands covered in grease, which brings me to the edge of panic because there are certain textures I find it hard to endure. I throw it in a pan then separate the yolks and whites of two eggs over the sink. I make what my mother would call 'a hash' of it. When I finish the sauce I mix it with the spaghetti and put a plateful on the table and point to it. I provide a bowl and a fork and knife and spoon and a glass of milk. I might vomit.

He reaches for the salt and pours it on in a steady stream. *Ssshhhhhhew.* I don't stop him. I feel an inner vertigo.

Child One dreamed of a sparkling white desert. Is that what he wants? Is he waiting for something in the world to tip, something that will send civilisation hurtling back into a dark age of djinns and trolls and *tokoloshi* and vengeful ghosts, of what Ashok called 'fucking little people'? Or forward into a new kind of darkness? What does the boy want? He spills his milk. I don't mop it up. I'm glad he doesn't say anything. What could there be to say? He is a seven-year-old boy who falls asleep listening to CDs of *Captain*

Underpants. He drops spaghetti all down his T-shirt and smears it all over his mouth. I don't tell him to wipe it. By the time the doorbell rings – *ding-dong, kapow, aagh, kapow, aagh, kapow, aaagh* – I am fighting down a ball in my throat that is a stopper for noise. Perhaps sobbing, perhaps cartoon noises. Stephanie opens up and I hear two men asking her questions, and the murmur of her answers, and the sound of equipment being manoeuvred. Freddy shows no signs of interest. I hear Stephanie talking in distress and then a man – Southeast Asian, possibly Malay – puts his head around the kitchen door. He seems shocked to see I have been cooking, but I point at Freddy.

The man says, 'Just to tell you we're off. We're taking your friend Stephanie with us, is that what you agreed?' He thinks I am Kaitlin's husband. I see no point in correcting him. 'Normally this would be a police matter. But they're snowed under. I understand your son's committed a serious crime. That means he'll go on the list and be assigned to a Care Unit. In the meantime there's a curfew on all kids below twelve. The net's down, so I'd keep the radio on, if I were you, sir. Listen out for announcements.'

I look at the clock. It has been an hour and ten minutes since we found Kaitlin on the stairs. I am not an expert in medical crises. But I estimate that this is far too long for any good outcome to be likely. Forty seconds later the front door slams shut and two minutes and fifteen seconds after that the ambulance siren has started up, *nee-naw, nee-naw*. And then I am left alone with Freddy.

A new timescale begins.

I sense it will have different rules.

CHAPTER 9

FREDDY IS STILL showing signs of disorientation when I send him to bed an hour later. For once he makes no objection. Downstairs, I turn on the TV, but it isn't working and the net's still down, so I try the radio.

The Home Office has ordered a curfew on all children under twelve in the wake of increased domestic violence across the nation, and made a plea to all families to stay calm but vigilant. Public helplines are now open to those with concerns, and the army has been mobilised. Care Units to house disturbed pre-teens have been established in empty office compounds and school premises, and the government's emergency committee, COBRA, is meeting now to expand the conversion programme.

The news continues with reports of a train crash near Leeds that has claimed more than fifty lives.

If it's sabotage, I think, it will be played down. As will subsequent incidents. But whatever censorship the official media is subjected to, and however strenuously commerce and industry stifle evidence of their crises, the scale and nature of the phenomenon – which

179

I would guess is peaking – must be public knowledge by now. I have little doubt that social-networking sites are already awash with potent theories invoking alien invasion and the supernatural.

Of course Professor Whybray came back from retirement. How could he resist a job like this? And how can I? It may be a long time before I can return to Arran, to my coastal walks and my dictionaries and my origami hermit crab. But while the prospect of working alongside my mentor, on the biggest challenge of both our careers, fills me with excitement, there's anxiety too. It centres on Freddy.

At five, Stephanie calls from the hospital. Kaitlin is still unconscious. There is a risk of more swelling and further bleeding into the brain which may trigger seizures. She has been given drugs to reduce the chances of these secondary injuries.

'The hospital's inundated. And the casualties are still coming in. So she isn't getting the care she should. I'm spending the night here. I reported Freddy. Naomi's fast-tracking him into the Care Unit in Battersea.'

I feel a wash of relief. Professor Whybray and I will work on this. We can't reverse what has happened. But we will come to understand it. And then solve it.

'Hesketh. If Freddy acted in a fugue state, it's quite possible he won't realise what he did. But if he does ask, we have to think about what Kaitlin would want.' Stephanie says nothing for a while. When she speaks again, it sounds as if she has gathered herself. 'Tell him it was an accident and it wasn't his fault.'

Quickly, she wishes me luck with Freddy, and hangs up.

★　　★　　★

I am planning to wait until the morning to talk to the boy, but when I go upstairs to check on him he's still awake, pink-cheeked and feverish-looking, listening to a story on headphones. A small night light illuminates his jumble of stuff: the big Lego crane lifting a basket of dinosaurs; his crude, lively paintings of animals and battle scenes; the bulbous shapes in dirty plasticine and cracked clay and a few of the origami models I folded for him: a lobster, a flamingo, a turtle, some big water-bombs and Satoshi Kamiya's fiendishly complex dragon. I turn off the CD, remove the headphones, get him to sit up.

He grins. Three gaps. Upper right incisor, upper lateral incisor and lower cuspid.

Human teeth develop in the womb, at embryo stage, long before they push through the baby's gums. All twenty milk teeth are lined up inside, long before birth.

What else has been biding its time?

'Mum's still unconscious,' I tell him. 'The fall caused some bleeding inside her skull. We don't know when she'll wake up again. Or if.'

The smile disappears and his eyes open wide. His mouth struggles with words that won't come. When they do, he's clearly confused.

'But – but Hesketh. But. I mean, Mum. What did you say about . . .'

He stops, then blinks and takes a deep shuddering breath. His body gives a brief spasm before settling. Then he sits up very straight.

'Hello Hesketh.'

Hello? 'Freddy K? Did you hear what I said about Mum being in hospital?'

'Yeah. Cool.' *Cool?* It can't have sunk in properly. I wait some more. But nothing comes.

'Freddy K?' His head gives a small involuntary jerk.

'Yep?'

'It was an accident. Not your fault.' Telling a lie turns out to be easier than I imagined. Mental preparation helps.

'Why would it be?' He seems genuinely puzzled.

'Well Freddy K. You were there at the top of the stairs. You were the only one there with her when it happened.' Without saying it more clearly, I can't say it more clearly. 'Do you remember that?' He shakes his head. 'So you really don't know why she fell?' He shakes his head again. On an engagement scale of one to ten, if one were not engaged at all, and ten were extremely engaged, he would score a zero. Professor Whybray would expect notes. But I don't even have a pen. 'Do you remember seeing her fall? Or – *making* her fall, by pushing her? Accidentally?'

He wipes his nose on his pyjama sleeve. 'Nope.'

'A skull trauma is a serious injury.' He grunts and shifts his pillow, bashing it into a new shape. In case he hasn't understood, I translate: 'I mean it's bad.'

'Was it before I had spaghetti? Or after?'

'Before. Look, Stephanie and I don't want you to worry about her.'

He yawns and reaches for his headphones. 'I'm not worrying. Can you put the CD back on again?'

I'm about to get up to leave when something in the corner by the door catches my eye.

'That looks precarious,' I say, pointing. Freddy is a collector, and tins are always useful to a child with plenty of small items to store. So there's nothing unusual in the fact that he has piled them high. What's strange is that he hasn't processed them in his usual meticulous way. Normally he'd soak the emptied tins in hot water, peeling off the paper labels and running the tin-opener around the edges twice, to make sure none is jagged. But these are clearly unopened. I see baked beans, rice pudding, pineapple chunks and various soups. I think: *an embryonic stockpile.*

'It's the Leaning Tower of Pizza,' he says. He mentioned it earlier. In connection with de Vries. He said he had it in his bedroom. 'It's not finished yet. I need more. It's going to reach the ceiling.'

'Then you need to build the base thicker. You need to work mathematically. There's a rule. I'll show you tomorrow.' I go and ruffle his hair, the way I used to.

'Goodnight, Freddy K.'

'*Goodnooght,*' says the archaeopteryx. '*Sloop toight, Hoskoth.*'

I lie awake. It's not a good sofa for sleeping on. I dislike physical upheaval. Staying anywhere other than my own surroundings requires inner resources I'm unable to muster tonight. I kick about on the sofa, then give up and shift to floor level, battling with cushions, shuffling my wide-awake legs. What if Kaitlin dies and Freddy is left motherless, as well as fatherless? He'll be an orphan. Who will put the eleven raisins on his yoghurt? Who will answer his questions about the world? Somewhere out there, Freddy has a biological father. Does the man even know he has a son? If Kaitlin doesn't recover, Stephanie is unlikely to want to take her place, after what he did to his mother. In the absence of a birth father, might a de facto stepfather become the boy's guardian?

It has taken me a long time to understand what I want.

Freddy needs a father. And I need to be that man.

The cry of the black guillemot wakes me. I have installed it as the ringtone on my mobile. It's 7.18 on Thursday 27th September. Stephanie and I were supposed to meet Naomi Benjamin and Professor Whybray at nine. That won't be happening.

'Can you get on Skype, Hesketh?' It's Ashok's PA, Belinda. 'Sorry to call so early.'

'I don't know if I have a connection. Give me five minutes and I'll get right back to you if I can.'

I go and check on Freddy, who is still asleep, then put on coffee and start up my laptop. The net is working again. Forecast: thundery showers and temperatures varying between eighteen and eight degrees. Onscreen, Belinda's face is pale and lacks definition. I adjust the contrast, but it doesn't help. Finally, I realise that the issue is not technical. The presence or absence of make-up can change a woman's face dramatically.

Belinda says, 'Hesketh. Look, can you come in and hold the fort? Ashok's going to be away for a few days. He's dealing with a family crisis.'

'No. Not today. I have a crisis of my own.' I tell her what Freddy did to Kaitlin.

As she expresses her sympathy, her voice falters. 'OK. I'll ring around some more. I was starting with the staff who don't have families. I'll try Stephanie.'

'Don't bother. She's at the hospital with Kaitlin.' I don't explain why. 'What's up with Ashok?'

My question triggers tears. While Belinda sobs and apologises, I take a sip of coffee and wait. Thirty-four seconds pass.

'He's looking after his sister.' I recall the family photo on Ashok's shelf, next to my paper *ozuru* pecking at hole-puncher confetti. The women and girls in traditional dress, the men and boys in suits.

'Last night, the two younger kids killed their dad with a kitchen knife.'

'Ashok's sister is called Manju,' I remember. 'It means sweet or snow or dewdrops.' I'd asked him to explain the origins of all their names.

'Hesketh, did you hear me? I said last night—'

'The sons are Birbal – that means Brave Heart – and Jeevan, which means Life. And Deepak. Lamp or Light. The daughter is Asha. Which translates as Hope or Aspiration. Her husband is Amit, which means limitless or endless.'

'Well it's Amit who's dead. Her youngest two killed him.'

So Amit is not endless. He has been murdered by Lamp or Light and Hope or Aspiration. She's looking at me questioningly.

'Dead. I see.' There's a silence. 'I'm sorry. I'm slow. It's taking me a while to—' I stop. More silence.

'Don't worry,' says Belinda gently. 'I can't believe it either.' She gulps. 'I rang the official helpline. All the kids' attacks have to be reported. There's a Families at Risk register. If you take Freddy to a Care Unit they'll take charge of him during the day. That's what

Ashok's doing with Deepak and Asha. They can't guarantee more than twelve hours because they don't have enough staff or beds yet.' I am trying to muster a coherent reaction when Belinda's eye line shifts. 'Anyway, Hesketh. Perhaps we should say goodbye.' I turn round: Freddy has entered the room, his hair ruffled, yawning. Belinda flashes her teeth in an unlikely smile and uses a new voice, louder than before, to say, 'So, Hesketh. Ashok may call you later. He's working from home today.' With another sidelong glance at Freddy she adds, 'Good luck with everything on the home front,' before switching herself off.

On 'the home front' the boy is tired and grumpy. I ask him if he wants to go back to bed for a couple more hours. No, he wants to eat, he says. He wants porridge. He also wants eggs. Scrambled. While I make the porridge – the habitual movements of pouring and stirring are soothing – I try to make sense of what Belinda told me about Ashok's brother-in-law. But I can't. All I can picture is colours. A Desert Sand carpet in Ashok's sister's home, stained Heliotrope with blood. Freddy eats his porridge ravenously and then, when I present him with the scrambled eggs, pronounces: 'That's not enough. I want more.'

'Eat them and then decide.'

The eggs are gone in seconds.

'I told you,' he says. I switch to observation mode. He still hasn't mentioned his mother. He jumps down from his chair, swings open the door of the food cupboard, and pulls out a can of tuna. 'Pass me the tin-opener,' he commands. A moment later he has expertly opened the tin and is reaching for the salt-grinder: a huge, heavy cast-iron thing that Kaitlin bought in a junk sale. She is a magpie that way. He can barely lift the thing, but he persists, grinding far too much on to his plate of tuna. He devours it fast and messily. 'Oi woont more. Oi woont more.' The deep throaty archaeopteryx voice again. He makes short work of a plateful of mashed potato which I find in the fridge and reheat in the microwave. This he salts heavily. He chews with concentrated haste. I don't stop him. I just watch and take mental notes. I wonder if this counts as fieldwork.

'Freddy K. Did you know that lots of salt can be bad for you?'

He laughs. 'That's like saying lots of *air* can be bad for you!'

'No. Air and salt are different.'

He looks at me, head cocked to one side. 'I'm not the weirdo! You are!'

'How?'

'Do you want to have the wrong kind of blood?'

This is interesting. 'What's the wrong kind of blood?'

He gives me another sideways look, but doesn't answer. When I repeat the question he asks, 'Why are you talking about blood? You're a freakman, Hesketh.'

I say, 'You mentioned it first. Not me. You said, did I want to have the wrong kind of blood.'

'Is this a game or something?'

'No.'

'Then you *are* a freakman. Can I watch TV before school?'

'Freddy K, you won't be going to school today.'

'Cool. Why not?'

'Because we're waiting to hear about how Mum's doing in hospital.'

He stops and blinks. There is a three-second pause. Then he says, 'OK. Can I watch TV?'

In normal life, Freddy would become hysterical at the thought of his mother being in hospital.

'No.' I don't want to risk him seeing the news. 'Choose a DVD.'

He scuttles out and to my surprise comes back with a nature series about desert life called *The Dry World*.

I call Battersea. It's permanently engaged. The net connection has disappeared again. I text Professor Whybray – *My stepson Freddy attacked his mother last night. I plan to observe him until we meet* – and join Freddy in the living-room, where he's already engrossed in scorpions, snakes, cacti and scuttling rodents. He settles on the sofa and I throw a rug over him, and he says 'Foonk-you-fonk-you-fank-you'. For a brief moment I begin to think normality has returned. But when I fetch him a glass of milk and put it on the coffee table in front of him he reacts with a cry of alarm.

'Hey! What are you doing? I don't want that white stuff!'

'Freddy K, Freddy K. Calm down. It's just milk. You usually drink it. What's wrong with it suddenly?'

He's looking at it with fear and disgust. 'It might be poisonous!' His alarm seems quite genuine.

'It isn't. Look.' I take a sip to show him, but he won't be swayed. This too is odd.

'It isn't poisonous to you because you're from the Old World. But we have a different kind of blood. We need Coke or Sprite or Dr Pepper,' he insists.

Again, I think of Jonas' hoard. Coca-Cola, Annika said. *We.*

'What do you mean, we?'

'Kids like me.'

'What kids like you?'

'I want something from a can.'

'Mum doesn't buy them, you know that,' I tell him. 'So it's milk or nothing.'

'If you eat something poisonous you go blind!' he calls after me as I leave. Curious, that he should make a connection between poisoning and blindness. Jonas also mentioned blindness, when he was raving in the hospital. He had good reason to: his eyes were alarmingly infected.

I leave him with the DVD blaring at the volume he likes it and enter what used to be my workroom. I know exactly what's in the boxes. Books, a set of shaving things, three pairs of shoes, some casual clothes. Origami supplies. All useful. I sit there for a while, just rocking, then make five *ozuru* in my head. I hesitate, then slowly create a lotus flower for Kaitlin. She always liked those.

Then I get to work.

I arrange my thoughts best when I can physically touch and shape each idea, and endow it with tangible dimensions. My whiteboard and my paper supplies, including the large sheets of coloured tracing paper I intend to use, are still in what used to be my cupboard. Though easier to set up and faster to manipulate, computer models offer none of the sensual gratification that paper does. Within minutes I have made decisions about the basic set categories, and picked a colour system that will not jar on me. Soon enough, new connections will reveal themselves, and I will move on to combine the templates. I feel calm yet energetic. My best state of mind. I have a project. I've brought the radio with me: I keep it on as I work. Every five minutes I stop and call Battersea – I need to talk to Professor Whybray – but the line's still busy. I want to know if the kids there have mentioned blindness, or having 'different' blood, or expressed a fear of poisoning. Whether their physical examinations show anything unusual. Do they mention the Old World?

At 11.18 I call Annika Svensson. I am in luck: she answers her phone after eighteen rings, breathless.

'How are you, Hesketh? Is it as bad there as it is here?'

'Numerically speaking, it will be worse here because we have a much bigger population.'

'I was just with my neighbour. She's been going crazy. Her son attacked his sports teacher last night. With an ice shovel.'

Briefly, I fill her in on what happened with Farooq and de Vries in Dubai, and what Freddy did to his mother last night. She shows her shock and horror in a typically Scandinavian way, by expressing denial: 'No!'

'The kids who attacked have salt cravings like Jonas. Can you tell me exactly what else he kept in the garden shed? You mentioned seaweed and jars and sacks of grain and Coca-Cola.'

'Yes,' she says, still breathless. 'Which he never even liked. And these big lumps of seaweed. God knows what he wanted that for. It's not all properly dried out, and it's full of things that crawl around.'

'What else?'

'There was chocolate. And sacks of nuts. I don't know where he got hold of them. And lots of seed packets.'

'What kind?'

'Vegetables. All vegetables, different kinds. Which is strange because he was much more into flowers. Hollyhocks and lupins and sunflowers. He liked the tall ones.'

'You mentioned grain before. Do you know what kind?'

'It says on the sacks. They're imported from India. Ara-something.'

'Amaranth.'

'That's it. Does it mean anything to you?' she asks.

'It's high in protein. Also in lysine, which you don't get in most cereals. It's a relative of pigweed. Its leaves can be eaten. It's not suitable for making raised breads, but you can make a flatbread. Was he into survivalism?'

No, she insists. He wasn't.

After we say goodbye I picture her in her Bamboo-green jacket, with her wrinkled face and her teenage son Erik, and her going-crazy neighbour and her dead husband Jonas whose penis I saw resting on his thigh, and whose death I witnessed, who found beauty in tall things. Back in the living-room, Freddy is curled up on the sofa, asleep, with his bottom in the air. The glass of milk is untouched.

I spread my circles on the floor and begin experimenting with sets. After a few moments, tenuous connections begin to manifest.

At 12.41 my phone rings.

'Hesketh.' That reedy, throaty voice.

'Professor Whybray.' I could show him these Venns and he would grasp them immediately. We played chess together. Battled with crossword clues. He liked to talk. He especially enjoyed running the theories of his rivals past me, to test my reaction. But he never minded silence.

'You still won't call me Victor?'

'No.'

He laughs. 'Good.'

'Why?'

'It means you haven't changed. Which is excellent. Because I require you to be exactly the same Hesketh you were before. Phipps & Wexman are officially on board. You can start in Battersea tomorrow. I don't just want you on the team. I actively need you. And if you have any clones out there, I need them too.' He pauses. 'Remember those times you were good enough to come to the hospital with me, when Helena was dying?'

'Of course.' There was a lot of waiting. We'd sit on the plastic benches and he'd make dark jokes about botched surgery and hospital superbugs. When he went in to see Helena or her consultant I bought us food and drinks from vending machines. 'You know why I never broke down?'

'Because British men of your generation and stature are traditionally proud and don't show their feelings in public.'

'That's true. But mostly because you stuck to the facts and never sugar-coated anything. That's what this task requires now. Someone independent who won't be swayed by the culture.'

'You once said I probably wasn't cut out for fieldwork.'

'Did I? Well. I was no doubt right. But this isn't fieldwork. See the Care Unit as a lab. And until you come in, treat Freddy's environment the same way. So. How's the boy doing?'

He's still curled up in his pyjamas like a tiny hibernating animal. I reach for the TV blanket and arrange it over him. He doesn't look like a child who tried to kill his mother. He doesn't look like a boy who would discuss murder with his friends.

'His behaviour's been atypical,' I say, moving into the hallway out of earshot. 'There was a short period when he seemed to realise what he'd done. And there was some distinct spatial confusion, just after he attacked her. Since then, he's been nonchalant. But his thinking's disjointed. He doesn't remember he did it.'

'That's the classic pattern.' He sighs and pauses. 'There's been terrible . . . *barbarity* in response to this. Almost a counter-epidemic triggered by panic. And spread by social networking of course. All that's exploded as you can imagine. It's similar to what we saw in some of the cross-species disease scares. Most parents are desperate for their kids to snap out of it and go back to normal. But so far we haven't seen a single case of that. Word's spreading that there's no cure. Even though there might well be, if we can just find it.'

'Secondary hysteria?' Is that what he meant by 'the culture'? It's good to be speaking to the professor again. To resume the old, effective patterns of communication.

'Exactly. The police are reporting they've come across parents driving their children out to the motorway or into the countryside and just . . . dumping them. There are already too many cases to prosecute. If we were equipped to have all the kids in Care Units full-time that wouldn't be happening. But most of them have to go home at night, if they live anywhere near. A lot of families can't cope with that. Especially if there are siblings.' He sighs. 'Anyway, talk me through the overlaps.' Quickly, I run through Sunny Chen's suicide drawings and the new permutations of the Venns.

'Blood. Violence. Eyes. Salt. Some of the elements seem almost Biblical,' he says.

'Which begs the question: if it's a shared narrative, are they collectively re-enacting an old myth, or creating a new one?'

'Go on.'

'Well I'm wondering. The phenomenon strikes me as going far beyond the physical. There's a collective subconscious at work here, and it has some kind of ideology or metaphysics that we need to identify. But the anarchist theory doesn't convince me. And it isn't terrorism as we know it. Even though I predict it won't be long before that word's used.'

'Well the human extinction lobby's having a field day, of course. Better Without Us is rejoicing. Any more predictions?' he asks.

I have already flow-charted it. I am sure he has too.

'There will be many more cases of sabotage than have been reported. If they continue, energy and communications systems will fail. And there'll be food shortages. Whatever disaster provisions are in place will themselves be at risk of random sabotage, so I see no grounds for whatever optimism the government may express. Regarding the children, the alien-possession theory will have started at grassroots level some time ago, after the first few attacks.' As I speak, I roll up my sleeve and inspect the flesh on my bicep. The tiny finger-marks are still there. 'The idea will first be reported in the news as an unfortunate and misguided rumour. But repetition, especially if it comes from someone in the public eye – most likely a so-called celebrity – will normalise and ratify it.'

'Go on.'

'In either case, you can be quite sure it's already in the public domain on some level. Superstition evolves with the times. So we'll hear more about figures from folklore. But my hunch is that among younger generations, aliens will come to dominate. They're more current. Have any of the children died yet?'

'Not in this country. But two in America. They're being autopsied now.'

I tell him about Svensson's anatomical anomalies. 'Any eye infections among the kids?'

'No, but as you've seen from their attachment to sunglasses, they seem to feel their eyes are vulnerable. But pursue this. Stephanie's out of the picture for now, I gather.'

'Yes. She and Kaitlin—'

'Don't worry. I know the, er, context. No need to discuss.'

Later, Stephanie calls to say she might be staying at the hospital again, but she might come home. She's not sure yet. There is no change in Kaitlin's condition. 'They want to take her home as soon as she's stabilised. So I'm talking to the medics as much as I can, finding out what to expect. Getting skilled up.' Her voice sounds very strained. I wonder if she is telling me the facts as they actually are, or as she would prefer them to be. There is often a discrepancy. 'I've agreed to help run a group here in the hospital for bereaved families. Crisis counselling. I've just held my first session.' She pauses. 'It was very difficult for me professionally. In normal circumstances, I'd be considered compromised.' She halts again and I hear her take a breath. 'I'm struggling, Hesketh. You should know that. After what Freddy did to her, whatever his reasons, or whatever his illness, I'm never going to be unbiased. I can't see him the way I did.'

After she hangs up, I sit and think about this.

I used to imagine Kaitlin vanishing from the face of the earth, and me and Freddy living in the cottage on the island. We would build and fly kites: proper ones that were not lopsided. Or boats, to float in rock pools on the beach. I'd teach him about birds and we'd get a chart to identify edible and non-edible fungi. We'd cook. He could go to the local school. If I had to travel on business for Phipps & Wexman, I could take him with me.

This scenario used to comfort me.

So why, when I conjure it now, do I get a lurch of vertigo?

Back in the living-room, Freddy has woken and is watching the DVD. I pause it – he doesn't object – and I slide Sunny Chen's suicide drawings on to the coffee table in front of him without comment. Then I press record on my little machine and wait.

His eyes quickly scan the page, left to right, top to bottom, and then back the other way, tracking the circle of the necklace, the 'all-seeing' eye and the neat little hand-print in the bottom right corner.

I say, 'Who drew this?'

'One of us.'

Freddy puts his own hand over the print. It's a perfect fit.

'Who's *us*?'

He shrugs. 'Us is us.'

'Children?' He nods.

'And what about this shape here?' I pull the necklace out of my jacket pocket and put it on the table next to the drawing. 'You made this for Stephanie. From papier mâché. It's just the same, see?'

'It's bones.'

'What do you mean, bones?'

I recognise the shudder that runs through his body because I've seen it before. It denotes a mental switch. 'Why are we talking about bones? You're being a weirdo, Hesketh.'

'But Freddy K, you just said—'

He slams the crayon down. 'Why are you asking me all this blibber-blobber? All this *lap-sap*? What's the matter with you?'

Blibber-blobber is a Freddy-word. *Lap-sap* is not. Jonas Svensson used it. He called me a 'fucking grown-up' and 'fucking *lap-sap*.' This can't be a coincidence.

'Freddy K, Freddy K, Freddy K. Because I want to know the answers.' I don't care how angry he gets. I need to get him out of this.

'Well I like it better when you just shut up and don't say anything, freakman!' He tips out all the pencils and they roll across the table.

'So the other kids. Where are they now?'

'How should I know?' Is he angry because he can't remember, or because he's confused? Or both? 'They're everywhere!'

I'd like to switch him off and then switch him back on again, forcing a basic reconfigurement. He's still Freddy, but he's not functioning normally.

Is he still Freddy?

Would I stake my sanity on it?

I go online. There are almost too many options to choose from on the BBC's home page. *Follow us on Twitter. Send us your stories and pictures. Crisis Helpline numbers. Watch live CCTV feeds from your area.* Worldwide, the attacks by children have lessened due to increased vigilance on the part of parents, but the UK government has urged all families with young children to observe the curfew and remain on the alert. It's estimated that as many as one family in four is affected. Religious leaders are appealing for calm, and urging their followers to pray for the children.

There is nothing from the ophthalmologist in my inbox, but the renal expert Ashok hired as a consultant has sent her response to Svensson's autopsy. In it, she reports that firstly, Svensson's eye infection at the time of death is highly unlikely to be related to his renal anomaly. Multiple kidneys, she writes, are by no means unprecedented. *The phenomenon is documented to be increasing globally, particularly in coastal regions. A recent (disputed) hypothesis points to an 'evolutionary shift' to cope with increased salt levels due to the Earth's accelerated water cycle, as already documented in many animal species. However, it is noteworthy that the subject's two supernumerary kidneys are significantly smaller, and in significantly better condition, than the 'parent' kidneys, which are unremarkable for a male of this age.*

Unless the other autopsies show similar anomalies, this information is unlikely to shed any light on matters, but I forward the mail to Professor Whybray, Ashok and Stephanie anyway.

Naomi Benjamin has sent me Battersea's standard admission form: it points out my legal requirement, as parent or guardian of the child, to accompany him slash her to and from the Care Unit according to the schedule agreed by the Manager on arrival. The parent slash guardian must agree to supply the child's doctor's name, address and practice code in order to obtain his slash her medical dossier. Recent height and weight measurements of the child should also be provided if possible. Each day-visiting child will be provided with two uniforms. *NB. Adult volunteers are welcome, especially those with medical skills or a background in psychology.*

Freddy's height chart is still in the kitchen, with little Post-its showing his age and weight on certain dates. Kaitlin used to record it every six months: on his birthday in January and his 'half-birthday' in July. Not for the first time, I wonder about his biological father. Whenever that happens, my heartbeat alters pace. How could a man opt out of his responsibilities in this way?

Or did Kaitlin never tell him?

The former is wrong. The latter is immoral.

Why can't I be Freddy's real father?

I fold three water-bombs.

While I'm completing the form, Stephanie calls again. She sounds exhausted, and describes her work with the family support group as 'extremely distressing'. I tell her about Freddy's behaviour, and the nature of our recent conversations. But she doesn't probe deeper.

'Are you avoiding him?' I ask.

'Yes. Since you ask.' She sounds very tense.

'Well that's unfair. He's just a boy.'

She sighs heavily. 'Tonight I'll come home and the three of us will talk.'

'Good. We need to.'

For the rest of the day Freddy seems listless, and is mostly silent. I can't lure him into conversation, so I let him watch four *Dry World*s in a row.

Stephanie comes home at six. Her eyes are red and when she takes off her jacket I can see her shoulder blades through her sweater.

'Freddy's in his bedroom,' I tell her. She flops on to the sofa. 'I'll call him down.'

'No. Don't.' Her voice is very flat. I can't read her.

'Why not?'

'Hesketh, Freddy needs to leave.'

'Why?'

'Because when Kaitlin comes home, I don't want him anywhere near her.'

'That's not for you to decide. He lives here. You can't say that.' I have not stopped hating her.

'Yes I can.'

'No. It's up to Kaitlin. She can decide as soon as she wakes up. I'm going to call Freddy down,' I say. 'You need to see him.'

'No!' she says sharply, sitting up. 'No. No. Not now. Hesketh. Listen to me. She's not waking up. Ever. Not properly, anyway. It's what they call a severe insult to the brain. Common in closed head injuries. It's inoperable.'

She breaks down.

I watch as her body shudders with sobs. She reaches for a cushion and holds it against her belly, as though she has been shot there and is staunching the blood.

With some reluctance, I go and sit next to her, and deploy Ashok's strategy. But I don't feel comfortable with it. After a while, she recovers a little and apologises and relinquishes her cushion. I stop patting her bony shoulder and fetch her a glass of water; she thanks me for it and she drinks it down. Then she reaches in her handbag, hands me a transparent file of printed papers and abruptly disappears upstairs. A moment later I hear the bath running.

There are seven printed sheets. Normally when I am presented with any kind of text I scan it in its entirety, and memorise what I deem to be its crucial elements. But on this occasion I don't read beyond the first set of bullet points. It is headed: *Severe Traumatic Brain Injury: What to Expect.* I think about Kaitlin's brain. A brain I once enjoyed knowing, along with the body that housed it, but then stopped knowing: a brain now traumatically injured and severely insulted. Kaitlin's brain is no longer the same. *Personality changes often occur in patients who recover cognitive function.*

Insult. The word – suggesting violent damage – is well chosen.

What happens to the rules of love when a person changes?

Are mother and son still the same people?

I will always love Freddy, I will always love Freddy, I will always love Freddy.

Out of Page One I make a butterfly. And Page Two becomes a frog.

I will love him no matter what.

CHAPTER 10

FRIDAY 28TH SEPTEMBER. I wake at 6.18. The net's working. Forecast: partly cloudy skies, a low front shifting westward, slight chance of rain. High of sixteen, dropping to twelve at night. The ophthalmologist has sent me her analysis of the autopsy report: I make a mental note of the information it contains.

I'd anticipated speaking to Stephanie before Freddy wakes, but she has already left. There is a brief note on the kitchen table next to the butterfly and the frog informing me that she will return Kaitlin's car tonight, after which it is mine. She signs it with an S, and a PS wishing me 'all the best'.

People can be very unspecific, when they are distracted.

I unfold the two origami figures, read the information about brain injury and mentally file it. It's geared to the non-medical reader, and neutral in tone. But when I rise from the table I'm aware of an extra weight on my shoulders. It's a very physical and concrete

sensation, like the pull of a fifteen-kilogram rucksack. This gives
me pause for thought. For a man of my size, fifteen kilograms is
bearable. I once loved Kaitlin. But Freddy's love for her is active and
current. So, I must presume, is Stephanie's. Each, in their own way,
is an unknown quantity: Freddy because his reality is inexplicably
'suspended', and Stephanie because I don't know her well enough
to be able to predict her reaction – though to judge from Elisabeth
Kübler-Ross's description of the grief cycle in her seminal work
On Death and Dying, she is likely to go through a process similar
to that of a bereavement, but with additional complexities stem-
ming from the fact that Kaitlin is not actually dead. This process
will doubtless involve the classic phases of denial, anger, bargaining,
depression and acceptance. But in what combinations will these
manifest, and in what order? I would expect her assessment mechanisms to be severely compromised and her volatility to increase.
She has already expressed hostility to Freddy.

'Which is irrational. Stephanie must realise that: she's a psychologist. Her resentment has no logical foundation,' I tell Ashok. I've
managed to reach him on Skype. His hair, normally sleek with gel,
is sticking up in odd tufts, giving him an agitated, vagrant look. He
shakes his head.

'That's what the textbook says, Maestro. But like I've been trying
to tell you, the rest of us are way off the page here. I'm ready
to personally strangle those two little shits who just destroyed my
sister's entire life. And I'm feeling less forgiving with every hour
that goes by. This is one fucked-up mess.'

'You're still a little manic, Ashok.'

'Sure. Sure I'm manic. What the fuck. What else can I be?'

'There are a number of options.'

'Yeah, well you do your thing, Spock, and I'll do mine. Either way, we're operating in a whole new dimension here.' In quantum mechanics, the most advanced theories are counter-intuitive, I think. 'How's Kaitlin?' I tell him the prognosis. 'Jeez man.'

'Stephanie's still with her in the hospital.'

'I didn't think you guys socialised.'

'We don't. But Stephanie and Kaitlin did. In a manner of speaking.' I shut my eyes and tell him the rest, quickly and concisely. I am glad I practised it.

'Wow. That's some heavy stuff. Jesus, if I'd known, I'd never have sent her to Dubai.'

'It worked out. I got to see Freddy.'

'And you're not regretting that?'

'Why would I be?' I don't always understand Ashok.

'Forget it. I need more coffee. Hang on in there.' Ashok moves the laptop and I get to see the vast kitchen of his apartment, full of high-sided pots, cast-iron skillets, bamboo steamers, stainless-steel tongs, sieves, colanders and industrial-looking scales. I watch him load his espresso machine. 'You heard about that plane crash in France this morning? Sabotage. It's everywhere. It's being played down. But it's happening. You've seen the news. If you and Old Man Whybray are right, and this is one epidemic and not two, then we're dealing with a whole new world out there. I mean, can you believe what those kids did? My own flesh and blood, for fuck's sake!' Manju walks in to say dinner's ready and finds Amit bleeding to death on the carpet. The kids are just sitting on the sofa, watching, like he's the TV. They're drinking Coke and snacking on those mini-poppadoms. He's gasping and then he's dead. *Snacking* for Christ's sake, like nothing's wrong!' A jet of steam shoots from his machine: he removes the coffee cup with a yell of irritation. 'He wasn't a bad dad. He took them on great holidays, bought them all the expensive crap they wanted. There's no way he deserved having his throat cut with a fucking kitchen knife.'

'It's random. You know that.'

'I know that. Fuck, fuck, fuck.' He's spilled his coffee and burned himself. He jumps about, yelling and flapping his hand. 'Look at me. Jeez. This is nothing. Nothing! You think I'm manic? You should see Manju. She's climbing the walls.' He starts mopping up the coffee. 'I took the kids to the Hendon Care Unit last night and handed them in. They're keeping them full-time. Turns out they do special deals on what they call *multiples*. Manju won't go visit them. Older kids say they never want to see them again. Our parents have this crazy idea about taking them abroad and starting over. But I'm telling you, they'll feel differently when they see them in that Care Unit. Those places, Jeez man. Imagine a trip to a fucking zoo.'

'What do you mean?'

He hunches his shoulders and swings his arms. 'Picture the monkey cage. *Hoo-hoo-hoo.* These aren't kids any more. They're freaks from some other planet. Good luck working with Whybray. But any meetings, we're holding them here at HQ. There's no way I'm setting foot in one of those places again.'

Although Ashok has a tendency to exaggerate, I do recall Naomi Benjamin referring to the unit environment as 'distressing'. Now

I'm more keen than ever to observe the children for myself. The sight I caught of them on the screen in Dubai, milling about in their red uniforms, intrigued me.

If Freddy and I were going on a trip to the zoo, which is what Ashok has suggested I prepare for, I would take a bottle of water and my camera and a book about fauna in case the zoo's labelling system was sub-standard or inadequately informative, as is so often the case.

'Anyway what is this place?' he asks.

I look up from the map: I can't rely on my mobile's GPS so I've been planning and memorising routes. 'It's called a Care Unit. It's a place for kids who have to stay off school for a while. The ones whose parents or friends or family have had accidents like Mum did.'

'Cool!' When Freddy grins he sometimes looks like the Cornish pixie on page 392 of my illustrated compendium of supernatural traditions. Now is one of those times. There's no repeat of his earlier, brief distress about Kaitlin. But I suspect it will come.

I can't raise a taxi, so the only option is for me to walk and for Freddy to ride his small red bike. I took off the stabilisers and got him up and running as a cyclist just before I left. He got the hang of it very fast.

It's a dull day, with thick wads of stratus cloud on the horizon, layered like insulation material. Apart from birdsong, it's very quiet, with no planes overhead and very little traffic on the roads. Many cars are parked at skewed angles, as if abandoned in a hurry. On eight occasions a driver honks his horn at us. As we skirt the vast orange ziggurat of Sainsbury's, a man behind the wheel of a huge lorry waves his arms angrily, as if to sweep us out of his line of vision. From a pedestrian point of view, the A308 is an unappealing stretch of road. Things improve on the A3220, but by the time Battersea Bridge comes into view, we are getting tired and Freddy starts to complain that his legs hurt, so I take the handlebars and stoop down to push him from behind. The rucksack weight of his comatose mother – my psychosomatic grief symptom – is still there. I would like to have a discussion with Elisabeth Kübler-Ross about the significance of this, and how she envisages it developing.

On Battersea Bridge we stop on the pedestrian walkway to sample the panorama. Freddy rests on his bike and stares, but makes no comment when I point out Albert Bridge to our left, downriver, the Physic Garden, and the Victorian lamp-posts that stud the bridge itself. The Thames is a dull brown, flecked with silver. I see a man on a roof scanning the horizon with binoculars, and make a mental note to start carrying my own. I estimate we are still 1.2 miles from our destination. No vehicles pass us, but there's a cluster of human figures on the far side of the bridge, on the opposite walkway, heading for the north side of the river. As they come closer I make out three adults and a child. Two men, one woman. The child is a girl. I guess that like Freddy, she is being escorted. She is taller, but not much older. Ten perhaps.

Just as they are about to pass us, the child stops. She looks up and her hand flies to her brow, as if she is about to give a soldier's salute. But it's a fist she forms. Then quickly she opens up her hand like a stretched starfish with fingers splayed, then closes it again just as rapidly. Two seconds is all it takes. But it's long enough for me to make a connection that tightens my throat and precipitates an intense storm of thought.

When I glance at Freddy he's already returning the salute, closing his fist at eye level and then opening it.

Within seconds, the little group has passed us. I turn and stare at them. The girl doesn't turn to look back, and Freddy is gazing at the river again.

'Freddy K. That signal she gave you. That girl. You gave it back. What does it mean? What were you saying to each other?'

'What are you talking about?' I think of the 'all-seeing eye' on Sunny Chen's drawings: an eye with rays emerging from it.

'She signalled to you and you signalled back. Like this.' I show him. Again and then again. My excitement is turning to agitation. I need an answer. Right now. 'What does this mean, Freddy K? What does this signal mean?' I may be shouting.

He shouts back. 'You're a freakman, Hesketh. I don't know what you're talking about.'

'She made a sign at you and you made a sign back, I saw it! Like this!' I imitate the signal again. The sign of the eye.

'NO!' he shouts. 'I didn't do anything! She didn't do anything! I don't even know her!' His face is pink and hot-looking with rage.

I can't tolerate lying. But I can't prove he isn't telling the truth.

'Come on.' I start walking fast, folding paper mentally in an angry rhythm: a single sheet that gets smaller and smaller and smaller, beyond the nine folds that are physically possible, until it is a dense cube. By the time I turn left on to the B305, Freddy's whimpering. I don't want him to cry.

'All right, Freddy K?'

I reach down and hug him. The bike wobbles as he clings to me. I close my eyes. 'It's OK, Freddy K. I'm sorry I shouted.'

For the remainder of the journey, I push him on the bike.

Apart from a very small sign on the outer gate, Battersea Care Unit does not draw attention to itself. We park the bike under a fire escape. The building, set back from the road on an industrial estate, is a warehouse conversion spread over three floors. The reception area is unmanned, but there's a computer and clear instructions regarding the electronic registration system. The names Hesketh Lock and Frederick Kalifakidis are already on a list marked SIGNING IN TODAY. I tick the box to confirm our arrival and scan in our identification documents as prompted. I notice a CCTV camera angled at us from the corner of the ceiling. A message saying CLEARED appears on the screen with a code number: 5672. I am to use it to open the red door and proceed with the child to the third-floor reception facility. We take the stairs. The walls are either bare brick or a milky yellow that Dulux calls Sundance. The third floor is a large, airy space overlooking an internal courtyard below, dominated by a spacious sandpit filled with children.

The swirl of cochineal bodies makes me think of swarming blood cells.

Freddy is instantly galvanised.

'Hey, cool!' He points at them and grins and I see the dark-haired pixie from page 392 again.

There's a lot of noise down there. The red uniforms consist of loose elasticated trousers and jackets that zip at the front. The children's first names are stencilled on the back of the jackets in large black letters. Many of them are much younger than Freddy. There is the usual racial mix, for London, with skin colours ranging from Ecru to Burnt Ebony. Many – the fair-haired kids especially – are wearing sunglasses. There is a slide and a set of swings, but the kids aren't using them. Those in the sandpit are digging industriously, raking its surface with their bare hands, or just sitting and sifting sand through their fingers. Elsewhere, there are groups clustered around the five rowan trees.

'And hey, look in there!' Freddy has turned, and he's pointing to a room to our left with a glass door, through which we can see more red-clad kids circling, some at a run, others sauntering. When fish shoal, or birds flock, their movements are simple to model mathematically. I can imagine the same models applying here. Elias Canetti's classification of crowds comes to mind too: *the crowd always wants to grow; within the crowd there is equality; the crowd loves density; the crowd needs direction.* Two female staff in white jackets stand at the edge, supervising what is effectively a bio-mass in a state of dynamic flux.

'Hello, Hesketh. And you must be Freddy Kalifakidis.' We both turn. Naomi Benjamin is just as striking in the flesh as she was on the screen. We shake hands. You couldn't tell on Skype, but she's a few years older than me – perhaps early forties. Big dark eyes. Short, dark hair and freckles. A short white jacket – it must be the staff uniform – over a Coral Sunset sweater and Charcoal jeans. 'Freddy.' She squats to greet him at eye level, giving me a view of her impressive cleavage. I will inevitably stare at her breasts in an inappropriate manner. I may even be doing so now. Kaitlin always accused me of being prone to this. 'I'm Naomi. Welcome.' She smiles and grooves form around her mouth, which means she must smile a lot. But unlike me, Freddy isn't interested in Naomi Benjamin: he's manoeuvring himself sideways in order to get a better look at the kids in the gym room. 'I'm going to take you to the nurse. She'll ask you some questions and then you can join the others. OK?'

'Yeah!' He punches the air with his small fist. 'Bye then, Hesketh.' He doesn't seem at all fazed. I feel a pang. Am I going to lose him to this milling tribe so soon?

'In a while, Crocodile,' I tell him.

'See you later, Constipator,' he says. He changed the Alligator a year ago, after a visit to the doctor.

I turn and watch them walking off together.

Naomi has a very firm-looking bottom.

'Can I let you in on something?' says a voice in my ear. I whirl around. 'There are advantages to being my age. Fewer distractions.'

'Professor!'

'Hesketh!'

He clasps my hand. We shake long and hard, and then he hugs me. He's wearing a white jacket like Naomi's. I am very happy to see him.

'Delighted to see you, boy. Are you still very keen on justice?'

'Is it something you turn your back on?'

'Then you'll agree it's not fair that you're still looking like a

pin-up while I've turned into an old crock with angina and vari-
cose veins.'

I can see that he has aged. But when he smiles, he's like a crin-
kled child. 'Let me give you a quick tour.' He drapes his arm across
my shoulders just as he always used to, and together we walk down
the stairs. The Unit has been running for a month, he explains. 'But
since Sunday, it's been crisis management. There's no telling if it's
peaked. And there's certainly no keeping a lid on it any more. We
figure that if we can understand the syndrome, we can work out
how to reverse it. But it's a race against time and right now, we're
losing.' He glances at me sideways. 'In fact, I'll be frank and tell you
I'm not hopeful. Some of the other units are experimenting with
drugs. They've found they can suppress some of the symptoms.
But these are strong medications with unpleasant side effects. They
can't be used in the long term. And they don't address the underly-
ing cause. Whatever that is.'

Freddy's not having drugs, I think. Full stop.

At the bottom of the stairs he unlocks the door with a card-swipe.

'Like a prison,' I say. It's just an observation of fact, but the
professor turns and looks at me. His eyes are like they were
when Helena was dying: wild, with dilated irises. Have I made
a gaffe?

'It *is* a prison. A very necessary one. From which, as you can
see, they can't escape.' I nod. It's not quite sinking in that Freddy's
becoming a prisoner. But I realise it needs to, and that I must adjust
my perceptions accordingly. 'We have army backup if we need it.
But believe me, your boy's safer in here than on the outside. There's
quite a crackpot movement developing. We've had staff targeted

too.' His smile is a small joyless wince. 'For aiding and abetting extra-terrestrials in their nefarious bid to rule the world.'

We enter the outdoor playground area, where he waves at the three supervising staff: a thin, muscular young man – I saw him before, on Skype – a girl of about eighteen with one arm in a sling, a semi-shaved head and a big red scar on her scalp and an older woman sitting on a bench. All three have the same alert, flitting look you see on the faces of bodyguards. 'We have twenty medics but it's nowhere near enough. The staff you see here are volunteers. The young one there: Hannah. She joined us straight from hospital. Her sister Jodie killed both their parents. They were all in the car. Kid grabbed the wheel and forced them off the road. You'd never guess she was a murderer, would you?' He nods at a small girl with an angelic face and wildly matted hair, sitting with a group of others sifting sand through their fingers. 'Not everyone's up to it. Some'll stay a day and decide they can't handle it. Others don't even last that long. Most parents who leave their kids here can't seem to get away fast enough. They get emotional when they see them like this.' He stops and chuckles suddenly. 'Naomi let some nuns in yesterday. But it turned out they were here to try out some sort of exorcism. So that was the end of that.'

He stops and puts up a finger: we stand and listen for a moment. Some of the children are making low hooting noises. Others are clicking their tongues. *Picture the monkey cage.* 'Their language degrades very fast in here. You'll hear snatches of speech, but it's pretty minimal.'

'Glossolalia?'

'Except that I'm sure the sounds actually mean something. They're communicating. That's one of the things I'd like you to investigate.'

'Freddy used a Cantonese word yesterday,' I tell him. 'He said *lap-sap*. It means rubbish. It's possible he heard it from me. But I was surprised. One of the saboteurs used it too.' I wonder: How long before Freddy starts hooting and clicking like the others?

Suddenly, the muscular man shouts, 'Hey, stop!' and charges up to a small boy who has wandered over to the corner of the sandpit where he has lowered his trousers, apparently to defecate.

'That's Flynn,' says Professor Whybray. 'He's ex-army. Useful.' Flynn grabs the boy around the chest, hauls him up, and marches over to a door marked TOILETS. 'We get a lot of that. In the dissociative state basic knowledge is absent. Hygiene. Literacy. Speech. Take that one there.' He's referring to a blonde, skinny girl aged about eight. She's standing still, with an alert and watchful look, both hands poised in mid-air, her line of vision constantly shifting. Suddenly, she makes a swift grab into the air and closes her fist. 'Hattie's our number-one insect-catcher.'

I think of Freddy eating woodlice.

'Does she—' Just then the girl slams her hand to her mouth and licks her palm.

'Strange, how when you spend time around something, it comes to seem quite normal. Excuse me,' says the professor, reaching in his pocket. 'Phone call.' He walks off to take it, stuffing a finger in his other ear. On the other side of the playground a door opens and a small figure enters.

'Freddy K!' I call out. Naomi's following.

He's clad in a red suit too big for him. I'm expecting him to run up and greet me, but instead he peels away and heads for some children squatting in a circle, all evidently focused on something. Within seconds he has been absorbed into the cluster. Naomi joins me and we stand watching them. The clucking and hooting reminds me of the soft babble of hens. A small blonde girl seems to be the ringleader of Freddy's group: she's clearly giving orders. Freddy looks anxious, then joins the others in an odd miming act involving furious digging movements.

'You'll see a lot of role-play like that in here,' says Naomi. 'Victor thinks it involves food. Hunter-gatherer stuff. By the way, Hesketh. I just wanted to say, I'm so sorry about Kaitlin. Poor Steph. She's devastated.'

'They're lovers.' I wasn't planning to say this. It just came out.

'I know.'

'So you're a lesbian too?'

She laughs. 'I don't see how that follows. As it happens, I'm not, no. As if it's your business.'

Next I want to know if she has a boyfriend, but since this might be perceived as not being *my business* either I ask, 'Do you have children?'

She shakes her head and makes a face that might be either rueful or humorous: I am not sure which. 'Nope. And you know what? Lately I've been pretty happy about that.' Is this what Freud called *gallows humour*? 'Look at them.' She gestures at them in a broad arc. 'A new generation of unhygienic, insect-eating murderers. That's the population crisis sorted. Did you know that condom sales have gone through the roof? And people are queuing up to get sterilised?'

I do a mental flow chart. 'Well it would certainly be good for sustainability,' I say, remembering some of my conversation with the Swiss demographer. 'But it would be bad for the economy in the short term.'

She laughs. 'A passion-killer on every front then.'

I take another sideways look at her breasts. D. D is good. 'I haven't lost the sexual urge myself.'

'So I see. Victor told me about your unique skill set, as he called it. But we need good staff and beggars can't be choosers.' The grooves on either side of her mouth reappear. I can't fathom her. But I'd like to try kissing her. Professor Whybray comes back from his phone call.

'Some new data's come in,' he says. 'I need to go and check it. Let's meet in the Observation Room. Naomi, can you finish off the tour? You can skip the staff room and the dorms.' And he is gone.

I like Naomi. I also like what is inside her Coral Sunset sweater. Though if we became intimate, we would have to have a discussion about the palette of her wardrobe.

'The canteen.' She points to a door on the other side of the play-ground. Inside, about forty children are congregated at long trestle tables, grabbing and jostling. They are wearing beige overalls over their uniforms, and scooping food directly from unmarked tins into their mouths. 'They won't use knives or forks,' she explains.

'What's in the tins?'

'A fresh, nutritious balanced diet in recyclable ring-pull contain-ers. The kids inspect them quite thoroughly first. If one's dented, they won't touch it. They seem to know you can get botulism from damaged cans. Almost like an instinct.'

'So on the one hand they're anxious about food contamination. But on the other they're happy to eat live, unwashed grubs?'

'Welcome to our world,' says Naomi. Her phone rings. She listens, then says, 'Christ. OK, I'm on my way.' She finishes the call. 'Sorry, Hesketh. There's been an incident.'

'You get a lot of those?'

'Too many to count. The Observation Room's on the third floor. Catch you later.'

It's spacious, with rows of seats facing a mirrored window through which you can see a roomful of twenty children. Microphones hang from the ceilings.

'You'll find their interactions remarkable,' says Professor Whybray, turning from the control desk to greet me. He adjusts the volume and immediately there's a cacophony of grunting, humming, tongue-clicking and hooting. Here and there is what sounds like a word. 'Record as much as you like. You'll be seeing groups of twenty on a half-hour rota system.'

'What are the non-English languages of this cohort?'

'Arabic, Urdu, Gujarati, Polish, etcetera. I hereby appoint you Battersea Care Unit's Chief Linguistic Consultant. Among your other duties. Get started, boy.'

I spend the rest of the day alone in Observation, taking notes. The staff supervising the kids I'm observing have a desperate look, as if constantly aware of the menace the children represent. I wonder how many of these youngsters are killers. The atmosphere is one of barely controlled chaos. Freddy is in the last group to occupy the room. It's four o'clock: he's looking listless and is beginning to yawn. Other parents are already showing up to fetch day children. When the numbers thin further, I put my head around the door of Professor Whybray's office.

'I'm taking Freddy home now. He's wiped out.'

'Of course. Miranda's got a car and she lives near Fulham. You'll find her in the playground. Ask her for a lift. First impressions?' He signals me to sit.

I pull up a seat and glance through my notes. 'Linguistically, the grammar's very crude. There's no comprehension problem. In English I've heard *over there, this way* and *fuck you. Lap-sap*'s common as a term of abuse. I heard *dupek*, which means arsehole in Polish. I heard *yallah* three times. It's Arabic for hurry up, or go, or come on. Also *ikenie*. It's Japanese. It means sacrifice. I couldn't work out the context. So we have a mish-mash of up to fifteen different languages. There'll be a whole phrase here and there, but never a whole sentence. There's a lot of signing. I'm trying to map it. But I've seen the eye gesture repeatedly, used as a greeting. Take a look at this.' I open my laptop and show him Sunny Chen's suicide drawings.

He points to the hand-print. 'We see a lot of kids making that mark,' he says. 'In the sand or on the walls. I hear from the Home Office that the police say it's been popping up as graffiti in the last few weeks. Always at child height.'

'And look at this eye.' I point. 'See the similarity to the eye gesture the kids make? Originally I thought it was an all-seeing eye. Maybe a deity. But—'

Naomi comes in and takes a chair.

'We lost three volunteers,' she announces. 'One of them seemed headed for a full-blown breakdown.' She glances at the eye. 'Hey, that's interesting.'

'Why?' asks Professor Whybray, alert.

'Because I just saw the psychiatrist's report on the Spanish twins. It said they both had the same nightmare, the morning before they attacked. It was about infected eyes.'

I jump up. 'That fits!'

'How?'

'Because the ophthalmologist's report on Svensson raised the possibility of his eye condition being connected to food poisoning. Apparently, some bacterial infections that begin in the gut can compromise the nasal cavity and put pressure on the optic orb, causing it to swell. If that swelling process is aggravated by bright light, it would explain the sunglasses.'

Naomi says, 'So the signal denotes membership of a kind of trauma club. Involving eyes that get infected and swell and then – what?'

'The word Jonas Svensson used was *pop*. If the eye infection's untreated, and exacerbated by intense sunlight, the eye could effectively burst.'

There's silence as we consider this. Outside, the rain begins to fall, slamming against the picture window. Then Naomi says, 'Since we're into speculating, Victor. Have you tried out your Big Theory on Hesketh yet?'

He hesitates. 'I'd like to hear it,' I say.

'OK. Maybe you're quicker off the mark than I am, Hesketh. But wherever they think they're living, it isn't here. This behaviour belongs to a very specific place. A place they feel at home. The more time they spend together here, the more they tune in, and the more time they spend in the . . . other world.'

Yes, I think. Freddy's is another world. A parallel world with its own rules. A world with no adults, no toilets, no fresh food, a world with its own landscape and props, its minerals, its food sources, its rites and rituals, its gestural password, its hierarchies, its own unassailable imperatives.

Stephanie comes home late, exhausted. She heads straight for the kitchen, opens a bottle of wine, and pours herself a glass. She nods at me. 'Want one?'

'No. But there's some dinner if you want it.'

'I've brought you Kaitlin's car,' she says, tossing me the keys.

'How about checking on Freddy? He might still be awake.' He fell asleep on the way home. When Miranda dropped us off I woke him briefly to get him into the house, then took him straight upstairs.

'No.'

'Why not?'

'Because I'm human, Hesketh. This is hard for me. Don't expect miracles. Let's eat.'

I've defrosted one of Kaitlin's aubergine bakes from the big freezer in the cellar. I hand Stephanie a plate. We consume our food in silence, not looking at each other. But I can feel my anger building.

Finally I say. 'He's just a child. He was in a dissociative fugue state when he attacked Kaitlin. Being a psychologist you'll be familiar with that? As in, he was unaware of his own actions, and therefore not entirely responsible for them?' She toys with a fork-ful of food and doesn't answer. 'He's still Freddy. His DNA hasn't altered. He's the same boy.' She finishes her glass of wine and pours herself another. 'Take a brain scan and there'll be nothing new, nothing that wasn't there before. It's a new phase. He's talk-ing less, that's all.'

She slams down her glass. 'Christ, have you quite finished? Listen to yourself! He tries to kill his mother and your only observation is that he's *talking less*? I'm sorry Hesketh, but Freddy's not the same. None of them are. You know that. If anyone's deluding themselves here, it's you.'

'No. That's not in my nature.'

'Oh no?' her face is flushed from the wine. Or rage. Or both. 'Then how come you failed to include crucial information in your Dubai report?' She glares at me. 'Come on, Hesketh. The girl on the skyscraper site.' She is right. I committed what is called a *sin of omission*. But I knew I was doing it. I was fully aware. I don't speak. 'And you still have that bruise, don't you?' You'd think it would have faded by now. But it's as clear as a fresh tattoo. 'Which didn't go in your report either. Have you told Victor Whybray *that* yet?'

I look at the swirls of grease the aubergine has left on my plate and begin to rock.

Kaitlin used to call me 'waterproof', referring to the 'impenetrable skin' she claimed I had: a heavy rind that protected and distanced me not just from her, but from life itself. If I am 'waterproof' I am thankful for it now. But Stephanie's mention of Dubai unsettles me. She is right to imply I am guilty of evasiveness. Or worse.

I saw the child-sized figure.

But was she or wasn't she real? And if she scared de Vries and the others so much, why didn't she scare me?

My contract with the world holds that there are no secrets we can't unlock, with persistence and time, because everything has a precedent. But now it is beginning to seem that there are two worlds: the world I have known and inhabited all my life, and still cling to, and the world beneath it, which I have glimpsed through myth and legend, but never perceived as a whole and never believed to be anything other than one of the multiple explanations man gives to ascribe meaning to his existence. But now this shadow-world — vivid, irrational, primitive — has begun to take a grip. Not just on those around me, but now, in a way that defies all I know — on me.

Awareness of the dividing line between facts and conjecture, science and faith, is part of my hard-wiring. Or has been. I have seen and studied the titanic power of the human mind to create and give succour to monsters.

All I can conjecture is that whatever is shaking the foundations of the reality we know, it is something we have summoned.

CHAPTER 11

THE PRACTICAL SIDE of looking after Freddy was never my forte, but when he joins me in the bathroom the next morning, after I've emerged from the shower, it's clear he needs cleaning up. 'Freddy K, you'd better wash your hair. And then brush it. It's filthy. And it's getting all matted.'

'Mum does that.'

I stop drying my hair and look at him. Has he forgotten what I told him? That Kaitlin has brain damage and might not wake up again?

I crouch down to his height and observe his freckles. 'Well Freddy K, the thing is, Mum's not here.'

He shrugs and mutters, 'Mum does it.'

'Freddy Kalifakidis. Aged seven. Old enough to do it himself. Official.'

He shouts: 'I said Mum does it!'

'Freddy K, Freddy K, Freddy K. Why do you think Mum isn't here?'

He shrugs. Then his lip wobbles. 'I'm not washing it. Or brushing it either.' His voice is shaky. 'My mum does that. That's what my mum does. My mum. My mum.'

I finger the tangled black mass of hair on his head. 'Freddy K. Mum's in hospital. In fact, I'm going to visit her there this morning to say hello from both of us.' Stephanie wants me to see *the extent of the damage*. Last night, during our uncomfortable meal together, she insisted on it, and I acquiesced. 'Do you remember why she's there?'

'No!' His eyes open wide, then squeeze shut. Big tears burst from the corners and trickle down his cheeks. The slight curve of their surface magnifies the freckles. He wipes his face with his hand. It comes away covered in snot. 'I don't want you to tell me, OK? So don't tell me!' he shouts. 'Don't tell me, don't tell me, don't tell me!' He covers his ears with his hands and a shudder works its way through his small frame.

I hug him. 'OK. It's OK, Freddy K. We don't have to talk about it.'

We do, of course. If not now, then sometime soon. He buries his face in my stomach, his body still racked with sobs. But when he pulls away after a few moments, he's smiling.

'*Oom not whooshing moi hoor! Ooom not whooshing oot, oom not whooshing oot!*'

'Well I'm glad you stopped crying, Freddy K.'

He frowns. 'I wasn't crying. What are you talking about?'

'You were crying, Freddy K.' I lift him up, show him his face in the mirror and point out the tear tracks. They're still glistening. 'See? We were talking about Mum.' I sit him down on the tiled surface next to the basin. 'We were talking about how ill she is. And you cried.'

'That wasn't me.' He leans across to the basin, opens the tap, and splashes cold water on his face.

'Who was it then?' I ask, passing him a towel. He used to like applying the shaving foam to my face. I hand him the can. He presses out a squirt of foam and pats it over my face, then puts a blob on his own nose, just as he always used to. 'I said, who was it then?'

'Who was what? What are you talking about?'

I persist. 'Who was it? You said the person who got upset about Mum wasn't you.'

But he's adamant that he doesn't know what I'm talking about. A hole has formed in his memory. I have lost him.

I start to shave. I always start on the left side and work my way up. Left chin. Awkward place under left lower lip. Upper left lip. Awkward bit under left of nose. My father taught me to do this, just as I might one day teach Freddy.

'When do you start growing hair on your face?' he asks. 'Does it itch?'

And for a slice of time, it's a normal Saturday 29th September and we are back in the world of who we once were. I am rinsing off the stubble and watching it spiral down the plughole and providing Freddy with information, and he is sitting by the washstand pulling grotesque faces in the mirror and mucking about with foam. And then I am shampooing his hair and he is complaining about it stinging his eyes and it is as if the clock has rewound to five months ago and his mother is downstairs listening to *Any Answers* on Radio 4 with a fully functioning and uninsulted brain.

A light rain is falling. On the way to the Unit we pass a group of kids openly scavenging in some dustbins near a mini-roundabout on the A3304. Most are in T-shirts and jeans, but one stands out: she is clad in Battersea's distinctive Empire red uniform. I tilt the rear-view mirror to look at Freddy. He has a little DVD player in the back and he's been watching *The Dry World* again, but I can hear he has paused it: he's watching the group intensely, twisting his head to stare back after we have gone past. Some of the children have tilted their faces to the sky and stand with their mouths open, catching raindrops.

'What is it, Freddy K?'

'Some of us can go wherever they like. Outside.'

'But so can you. In the playground. And at home there's the garden.' He says nothing, but folds his arms and juts out his lower lip. 'Didn't you like it there yesterday? I saw you playing with Hattie.' The little insect-catcher.

'It wasn't playing.'

'What was it then?'

'I have to do stuff for her.'

'What sort of stuff?'

'Just whatever she wants, that's what she said. It's a *majd*.'

I tighten my grip on the steering wheel. 'Freddy K, do you know what *majd* means?'

I watch him in the rear-view mirror. He shrugs. 'Not really.'

'It's an Arabic word. It means honour.' I've heard other children using it too. It always has the ring of a threat. 'Does it feel like an honour, doing what Hattie says?' In the mirror, a look I don't recognise crosses his face. Nervousness? Fear? 'Freddy K? Do you know what an honour is?'

But he's turned the DVD back on, and he's off in a world of lizards and scorpions. When I drop him off in the playground, he doesn't even turn to wave goodbye.

Half an hour later I'm at St Thomas' Hospital. The Reception area is milling with people, most of them in what I interpret to be states of distress. Long queues for specialist departments line the corridors.

It is one thing to know something. But quite another to see it made flesh.

Vegetable: a vitamin- and fibre-rich edible plant product.

Kaitlin is in a ward on the fifth floor. She's lying on a high bed with railed sides, her head fastened in a padded clamp that forces her to look straight up. It is strange to see her in the daytime without make-up. Her expression is so blank that her face seems more like a photograph than the real thing. Or it would, were it not for the movement of her left eye, which has an energetic agenda of its own, its gaze wandering about as though looking for a place to settle. Her hair is no longer dark: it is five or six kinds of grey. This change must have occurred in the hospital. You hear about that, though mostly as a phenomenon in ghost stories about haunted mansions with creaking doors. *Her hair turned white overnight.* A single lock, lighter than the rest – Pale Ash – snakes back from her forehead. I am reminded of Indira Gandhi. Her skin shines clammily. It used to look like this just after she applied moisturiser.

But I don't think she has done that now. She'd be incapable, and anyway, I'd smell it. Before I officially became a cuckold, I used to like kissing her forehead, then her cheek and then her clavicle, before 'working my way down' to more erogenous areas. Nothing could tempt me to do such a thing now. A snail-trail of saliva to one side of her chin catches the light. Stephanie smiles stiffly and wipes it off with a tissue. Kaitlin doesn't react, though her left eye fastens on her briefly before veering off again. She is on a drip. Various other tubes snake away into plastic receptacles under the bed.

'Hello Kaitlin,' I say. My voice catches in my throat. Something's blocking it.

She doesn't reply. I wasn't expecting her to. But Stephanie has insisted I behave as though she can understand. It is quite clear to me that she can't because she is the human equivalent of a vitamin- and fibre-rich edible plant product.

'There darling,' says Stephanie. 'Look. It's Hesketh.' She strokes Kaitlin's hand. When I used to picture Kaitlin and Stephanie together, the images I conjured made me violent and ashamed and overloaded. Not now. Stephanie is much thinner than before, and there are new lines. She must have lost three kilos since this all began. We sit in silence for four and a half minutes. All in all, there is little to be had in the way of conversation. I don't feel anything. Maybe I will later. Maybe I won't. An ex-lover becoming a vegetable is not something you would think to factor in, when flow-charting the future. Churchill was once asked what he most feared, as Prime Minister. He replied: 'Events.'

I pull out some origami paper from my briefcase – a deep strong purple called Thai Orchid – and begin a lotus flower. They were always Kaitlin's favourite.

'Freddy's missing you,' I tell her, as I begin folding. 'I washed his hair this morning. He's fitting in well at the Unit. I think he's enjoying it.' I can't think what else to tell her, so I carry on folding for a while and when I have finished, I hold it up in front of her face to show her. 'This is for you. A gift. Look, I'll put it here, where you can see it. I'll make you some more at home, and Stephanie can bring them in.' Stephanie forces a smile. 'Freddy might make you something too.' But I do not say this with confidence, as I'd guess there's less than a 5 per cent chance of this happening.

I place the lotus flower on top of one of the machines she's attached to. Its lights are winking green.

'That's a nice gesture,' whispers Stephanie. 'Thank you, Hesketh.'

'Well, goodbye then, Kaitlin,' I say, when we have sat there another three minutes. 'Get plenty of rest. I'd better go now. See how Freddy's doing.'

I am hoping that will be the end of it, but Stephanie follows me out into the corridor.

'They're letting her out soon. She'll need round-the-clock care. My sister's going to help me. Ashok's agreed to give me leave. So you and I have to discuss where we go from here. My starting point is, I refuse to put her in any more danger. I meant what I said about Freddy. He can't stay in that house.'

I say, 'Freddy's a child. There's no—'

'No danger? Were you about to say Freddy's no danger?'

I say, 'Kaitlin won't be at risk. I'll be there.'

'She was at risk before. You were there then. The only thing that's changed is that she's now ten times more vulnerable. Christ, Hesketh. I thought if you saw her in this state, you'd realise that.' I watch her mouth as she speaks. Her lipstick is Plum and there is a little scrape of it on her left incisor. 'He nearly killed her. You've seen for yourself what he did. She's pretty much a vegetable, Hesketh. Her life is effectively over.' I don't say anything. 'And who's to say he doesn't go for you or me next?'

'He won't.' I turn to go. I have been in this hospital for twenty-four minutes in total and I am ready to leave.

As I walk down the hospital corridor she calls after me: 'I heard today that fifteen children have attacked a second time.'

Humans cling to their hopes, Professor Whybray told me, when his wife was dying. *They forget their nightmares, if they can. Or at least refuse to relive them. They tell themselves stories for comfort.*

Is that what I am doing? I wonder, as I drive back to Battersea through empty streets. Or is Stephanie simply in the wrong? She wants to be loyal to Kaitlin. This involves trying to honour what she would have wanted. But she has admitted herself that she is 'finding it hard'. Each time I see her the tendons of her neck fan out more sharply from the clavicle. She leaves early on her bike, long before Freddy wakes. She is still avoiding him, and doesn't bother to pretend otherwise. She must be trying her best to quell her distaste for the children, and not call them Creatures, like the public has begun to do.

But later that night I overhear her speaking to her sister on the phone. And that is the word she uses.

She is right. Our awkward domestic arrangement cannot last.

CHAPTER 12

'IT WAS A disgrace,' Professor Whybray fumes. 'Human beings at their panicking and ineffectual worst.' He's talking about the EU teleconference he participated in earlier this morning. He has another meeting later today at the Home Office. He looks tired: I wonder when he last slept. 'Posturing politicians, power-hungry bureaucrats, the press baying for blood, NATO doing some very shameful muscle-flexing, and scientific hubris levels that were off the scale. And everyone wanting funding. Christ, Hesketh. Look at our species. Seven billion of us living in a fouled nest. And now this. If it is an anarchist uprising, it's succeeding. No wonder Better Without Us is doing so well.'

He flicks on the news. Acute gastroenteritis in Venezuela has claimed up to a thousand lives. It's been linked to 'organic substances' traced to a bread factory. The mass poisoning is being treated as an act of terrorism. A plane has crashed in the United States, killing over three hundred people. The disaster is 'believed to be the work of anarchist sympathisers'. The wave of sabotages which has hit industry worldwide is condemned by world leaders as 'an obscene terror campaign'. In view of the increasing disruptions, supermarkets will be limiting sales of certain commodities to prevent a run on goods. A rationing system is likely to be announced in the near future. Meanwhile, a decrease in attacks by children in Britain, which mirrors a marked decline worldwide, has led to speculation that that particular aspect of the pandemic has peaked. However, there are new reports of violent children running wild and forming gangs of up to fifty strong.

He sighs. 'OK. The world these kids are living in. What characterises it?'

'They sleep a lot. Which perhaps indicates it's a relatively safe place, in which they don't fear being attacked by wild animals, or another tribe. They fear food poisoning and eye infection. We know the wild groups on the coasts are eating seaweed and small soft-shelled crabs. Ours are eating insects. They're familiar with tins. They have a salt craving. Socially, there's a strong hierarchical system. I'm hearing references to sacrifice and honour. Usually in a threatening context. The merging of different languages is something you might find if many cultures were thrown together haphazardly. Freddy talks about the Old World. It's the world we know, but the kids behave as if they've left it behind them. They also seem to have a distaste for it. Contempt, even. The fact that they're stockpiling food makes me think their mythology's built around a survival story of some kind. They're very conscious of being a community. An *Us*.'

'A Freudian interpretation would suggest that they fled the Old

World because on some level they felt they'd sinned and needed punishment,' Professor Whybray proposes. 'Perhaps it's linked to growing up: the fear of it. Or the urge to. They're all pre-pubescent. Let's say the family represents Eden. In destroying it, by attacking their relatives, they've cast themselves out and left the Old World behind. Their freedom from adults is their punishment. Or reward, depending on how you see it. So the question is, Heaven or Hell?'

I say, 'Pyjama Girl dreamed about a *beautiful white desert that sparkled*. She said it looked like Heaven.'

'If it is, it's a salty one. What have you come up with on that front?'

I glance at my notes. 'The fact that salt's been very dynamic of late. Salt levels in most oceans have increased dramatically over the last fifty years. But even more so in the last three or four. There are many countries that are reporting massive crystal deposits inland because much of the water table is salt-laden. Farmers have been battling it for years. It comes to the surface by capillary transport and when it evaporates, you have whole deserts of it. In South Australia there are already millions of hectares where nothing will grow. They call it the White Death.' The professor shifts in his chair and winces in pain. He slipped a disc after Helena died. It must have left a legacy. I think for a moment. 'According to the renal specialist who looked at Svensson's autopsy, supernumerary kidneys are increasingly common in coastal regions. Freddy said something about having a different kind of blood. That makes me wonder if he's sensing a physical anomaly in himself which he interprets as haematological. Or if he's imagining it so vividly that it feels real. So let's hypothesise that the two affected groups believe they belong in a highly saline environment. Meaning they crave salt, and express a psychosomatic withdrawal reflex when it's absent.'

'It's not altogether outlandish,' says Professor Whybray. 'We're talking about dramatically altered states, after all. You just have to look at them to see something radical has occurred to their whole mental landscape. No reason why that shouldn't have repercussions on the whole system. In fact, it might even be odd if it didn't. My feeling is, if we can work out *where* these children believe they are, we'll get to the bottom of *who* they are. Or rather, who they *think* they are. And who they think *we* are. Because it's quite clear we're two quite different tribes.' One side of his mouth twists upward. 'Each of which believes its own reality to be the supreme one. Quite a metaphysical conundrum.'

'When Freddy talked about Jonas Svensson's death, he said, *You made us be born and then you made us live like that,*' I say.

'So who was the *you* referring to?'

'I don't know. That's just the—' I stop and blink. And then I see it. Of course. I open my laptop and pull up the Venn in which I've attempted to connect the sabotage cases. 'This diagram. It's a maelstrom. Too many overlaps.' I point to the jumble of circles. 'The world of industry, the world of economics, the world of work. *Everything's* interconnected. So any one of them might be the universal. But if you look at it from a child's point of view, it's obvious.' I pause as the realisation blossoms and spreads. I should have seen it before. 'It's the world of adults. Grown-ups. They're Us. And we're Them. Sunny Chen said *they hate us.* When he said *they,* I think he meant children.'

236

'Which leads us to what conclusion?' asks Professor Whybray.

I think for a moment. 'That an unknown proportion of the world's pre-teens have developed not just a group consciousness, but a cultural narrative in which they see their own survival as dependent on the destruction of a contemporary adult world.'

'And that this collective will is trying to force some monumental paradigm shift in mankind's relationship to itself. As a species?'

There's a shift in the atmosphere between us. A tightening. A recognition.

On the way out Professor Whybray claps a hand on my shoulder. 'Good work, boy.'

I smile. 'I'm thirty-six.'

'Well has the thirty-six-year-old boy got his car keys?'

'Isn't it too early for your meeting?' It isn't until two. Afterwards he'll be joining me and Ashok at Phipps & Wexman.

'Yes. But there's something I want to show you. Call it fieldwork.'

Ten minutes later I'm at the wheel, and he's strapping himself in.

'Just like the old days, eh?' he says.

I don't reply. It isn't like the old days at all. We never did any fieldwork together. If, on the other hand, he is referring to our visits to the hospital all those years ago, the analogy is wide of the mark. Helena is dead and the professor has a new life in Toronto and the world we once knew has changed beyond all recognition. I start the ignition. We drive in silence. After 1.3 miles I break it by asking Professor Whybray if Toronto is still a city after his own heart.

He slaps his knees. 'Excellent: a personal question. Unprompted. Yes, son. I enjoy Toronto more than ever.' Fired up, he enthuses about the metro system, the parks, the rich cultural life, the wide mix of races. And a 'charming, elegant and extremely well-read' lady auctioneer, whom he regularly meets for lunch at the Art Gallery of Ontario. 'I know what I said when Helena died,' he says. 'And it remains true. But I didn't bank on new things happening. Different, but just as enriching in their way.' He smiles. 'But then that's life, is it not, Hesketh? Expect the unexpected. And then adapt. It would seem a wise adage under the circumstances. Yet I note that in the midst of all this, you are still the same Hesketh.'

'What do you mean?'

'You're obeying the speed limit.'

'It's the law.' But he has a valid point. Apart from army trucks, police cars, cyclists and the odd taxi, the streets we're driving on are empty. Speeding cars will not be a high priority for the police. 'Force of habit,' I say.

'But are you really still the same Hesketh?' he asks. 'I'm talking about how life has treated you on the personal front.'

'I thought Ashok filled you in.'

'You know how I feel about secondary reports.'

The rain starts up again and I turn on the windscreen wipers. Their rhythm and the fact that we are not face to face helps me to tell him the story of the last three years. About meeting Kaitlin, and our life together, and how it ended. How I never planned on being a father. Or technically speaking a common-law stepfather. Or to be even more precise, a common-law ex-stepfather. If such a thing exists. If her legally trained brain were still functional, Kaitlin would be able to offer clarification.

How Freddy changed my life, and how I fear losing him.

'These times are a true test of parenthood,' he says, when I have finished. 'And also of all the other bonds that link the generations. Not many are up to it. I think you're probably one of the few, Hesketh. Hold on to that.'

We've reached the centre now. It's as deserted as the rest of London. The rain has eased off, and the sky is both bright and dark. There's a double rainbow ahead, with one foot in Covent Garden, the other to the west. The colours pulse, as if breathing. Near Waterloo Bridge Professor Whybray touches me on the arm and points.

'Over there.'

On the other side of the river is a muddy sandbank dotted with the small figures of children. I count fifteen, but there may be more hidden in the shadows of the bridge. Some are up to their thighs in the river, peering into its brown water, as if searching for something. Others squat near the river's edge, their bare hands thrust deep into the muddy sand. Some can't be older than six. Their clothes are soaked through and streaked with mud. Two are stark naked. It's low tide. You can smell the river's heavy organic stench.

He says, 'Cross the bridge and we'll take a closer look.' I hesitate. I can see six more children now. Twenty-one.

'You knew they'd be here?'

He smiles. 'I work for the Home Office, remember. We're tracking hundreds of groups. As are other . . . organisations. This group's being picked up later this afternoon. Come on, boy. Time for some fieldwork. The real thing.'

I park on the bridge, which is deserted except for an empty bus. Together we descend the steps. The rain is coming down harder now.

'Hey!' calls a male voice. I glance up: a bulky cagouled figure is standing on the broad concrete walkway above us.

'Watch out, there's Creatures down there!' he calls, pointing.

'That's why we're here. We're doing a government survey in this area,' the professor calls back. 'Thanks for the warning, but it's fine. We're armed.' Armed? I am always amazed at how people I respect can become skilled liars at the drop of a hat.

'We've got our own information if you want to take a look,' calls the man. He's waving a map.

'Best keep it separate,' says the professor. 'But thanks for the offer.'

'Well you take care there. I'll keep an eye,' says the man. 'There's backup if you need it.'

'That's most kind. Much appreciated!' calls the professor. When we are out of earshot he murmurs, 'Like I said. They're getting organised.'

'Vigilantes?'

He shrugs. 'You can call them that. But they tend to call themselves the public.'

'Why don't they leave it to the army?'

'Would you, if you knew that the Forces aren't any less vulnerable to sabotage than the rest of the community? All it takes is for one soldier to run amok with a gun. There was an incident yesterday. An officer with a stack of hand grenades. Five people killed. It's impossible to keep a lid on these things. I'm afraid word's already spread. In these circumstances social networking's more a curse than a blessing.'

As we approach, a couple of the children glance up at us, then turn back to their activities, in the same way that grazing cows do when you enter a field. Engrossed in the business of food-gathering, they display neither fear nor interest. It's no more than ten degrees centigrade, but they don't seem to feel the cold. Every now and then, one of them starts humming, and there's an occasional cry or grunt, but otherwise they are a silent group. They look peaceful and peaceable. To describe them as 'happy' or 'contented' might be going too far. But they give an impression of innocence. Not childhood innocence, but the innocence of wildlife.

We've descended the concrete steps and now we're level with them. We are only a couple of metres away from the closest child, a little girl of about nine with red curls and freckles. She's squatting in the sand in front of a deep hole she has dug. With a pleased little squeak she pulls out a sand-worm and shoves it in her mouth. You can hear the grit crunch between her teeth as she chews.

'Fascinating parallels,' murmurs the professor. A boy a little further off snatches something from the air and slams it to his mouth. The rain sets up harder, plastering his hair to his face. He tips his head back and opens his mouth, drinking the rainwater as it falls. We're getting soaked. I pull up the collar of my jacket. Suddenly, I have a clear picture of how two worlds can occupy the same space. Parallel existences. Minimal awareness. I glance up at the South Bank walkway: the cagouled sentry nods back. He's been joined by a second man, who also nods. *Keeping an eye.* I am not ungrateful for their presence.

'I'm curious about their speech capability,' murmurs the professor. 'Let's find out. Come on.' We approach the group with small steps, and soon we are right in the midst of them. The rain continues to pour down. They pay it no heed, except to occasionally tip back their heads to drink, like the first boy we observed. Our height is a hindrance: on a signal from the professor, we crouch down so we are at their eye level. I notice that the little girl with red hair has turned to look at him. I nudge him and he takes a look. He catches the girl's eye and smiles.

'What's your name?' he asks. But she makes no answer and goes back to her digging.

'Fuck off, *lap-sap*,' says a boy quietly. We swing round. He's skinny and dark-haired. The professor's face changes. Another boy, who is standing knee-deep in the water, looks up. 'Fuck off, *lap-sap*,' the first boy repeats. The second boy copies him. The intonation is exactly the same, almost like something uttered automatically in response to an adult presence. Then from all around, a low humming sets up. First one voice, then another, then a whole chorus. A throaty, tuneless wall of sound. I remember the girl on the skyscraper in Dubai, before de Vries jumped. I say urgently, 'Professor Whybray. We should go. Now.'

He sighs. 'Frustrating. But I suppose you're right. Let's take it slow and easy.'

That's when I see that the red-haired girl is right next to him. Suddenly, she reaches out her small mud-flecked hand and slips it into his. He stops, clearly astonished. 'Well look at this!' he smiles, swinging their joined hands in delight. But within seconds it becomes clear that it's not companionship she's after. It's something else. With her other hand, she starts fingering the cuff of his shirt, as if trying to roll up his sleeve. 'What do you want?' he asks her. 'Do you want to come along with us? You can come and stay at the Unit. And your friends too.'

She has undone the button, pushed up his sleeve and is now examining his forearm. It's not clear why it's of such interest to her. Then she lowers her face to it and sniffs.

'Let's go,' I urge. 'This is a potentially volatile situation.'

But the professor doesn't move. He's fascinated. Or enchanted. The little girl opens her mouth to reveal her small tongue and gently, but insistently, she begins to lick his skin. Still no movement from the professor. He's watching her intently. 'She's after the salt,' he whispers.

'Fuck off *lap-sap,*' says one of the boys who spoke earlier. The humming around us intensifies, punctuated with throaty clicking. The girl is still licking the professor's arm, but now he stands up and gently tries to prise her off. But she hangs on, still licking.

'Fuck off *lap-sap,*' the boy says again, and other voices join in, until it's a mounting chorus: '*Fuck off lap-sap, fuck off lap-sap, fuck off lap-sap.*'

Then, as if on an unspoken signal, they are upon us, grabbing our arms and licking our hands like little nuzzling animals. The humming is now a fierce, intense buzz. We are bigger and taller and stronger than them, but they are all over us. Until now I haven't felt vulnerable. But now I do. Just then there's a cry from somewhere above us. 'Stand right back, sir!' yells the man in the cagoule. 'And you! Both of you, get clear of them!'

'Come on!' I call out to the professor. I have disencumbered myself and am halfway to the steps. I see that he's largely succeeded in shaking off his own cluster, but when he kicks out to free himself from the last small hand he stumbles and falls to the ground with a groan. I shoot forward, haul him up from the sand and drag him with me towards the steps.

'Cover your faces and don't inhale!' calls the cagouled man from above. We're almost at the top of the steps when something hurtles past us and lands on the sandbank below. The children shriek and scatter. When we get to the top I see vapour spreading out from a canister.

Tear gas.

Below, the children are screaming. 'Best clear right off!' calls the cagouled man, as we rush towards the safety of the car. He's with his companion: both are donning face masks. I call out a breathless thank you.

As we drive off, in the rear mirror I see the chemical vapour rising from the shore.

I glance at the professor. His face is crumpled and drained of colour. 'I'd better get myself cleaned up,' he murmurs, checking his watch. He turns and grins valiantly. 'So. How did you enjoy your first bit of fieldwork?'

'I didn't. You could have been killed, Professor. I'm not a body-guard.' I drive on. Five minutes later I'm parking in front of a face-less building off Parliament Square. 'And you're wrong,' I tell him. 'It's not like the old days.'

Birds are hopping about on the pavement. Blackbirds, pigeons, a sparrow.

He sighs and stares out at the sky. It's still raining.

'No,' he says. 'I'm sorry, Hesketh. It was an absurd thing to say. It was wishful thinking, that's all. To which, as you know, I am highly prone.' He looks at his hands. 'I want you to think very hard about this phenomenon, Hesketh. I want your ideas, however off-the-wall they may seem.' It's time for his meeting. But he seems reluctant to leave the car.

I'm still angry with him. I ask, 'Why did you want me working on this?'

He takes a deep breath and exhales slowly. 'Because you understand the difference between fairy stories and facts. Because you are a materialist who will never be vulnerable to superstitious belief,' he says.

'The reason for that is that superstitious belief is extremely fanciful, Professor. And there's no evidence to back it up.'

'You could say the same about the notion of time travel, until Einstein's theory of special relativity was thrown into question. For years, no one believed that the dinosaurs became extinct because of a meteor. The idea was ridiculed. Anti-matter was derided when it was first posited. So what if other theories now have to be reassessed?' I glance sideways: he has covered his face with his hands. When he speaks again, it is through the lattice of his fingers. 'Not just time, Hesketh, but space, and mankind's place in both?'

CHAPTER 13

'MAKE ME SOMETHING I can hurl, man,' says Ashok. 'One of those water-bombs.'

We're in his office on the eighteenth floor. Normally he's proud of his panoramic view, but when I came in he said, 'Welcome to my aerial goddam bunker.'

I slide some origami paper from the front pocket of my briefcase and begin folding. Through the picture window opposite me, the familiar ancient–modern geometry of London sprawls as far as the eye can see.

'I just heard from Belinda an hour ago. That fire back there.' Ashok jerks his thumb back at the horizon, where a billowing discolouration of air in fifteen shades of black and grey indicates a colossal conflagration. The smoke expands in the same way as a fast-growing fungus, sprouting new growth as it rises. It has great beauty. 'Postal-sorting station. And someone's sabotaged the water supply in Manchester. So now there's another scare. And who knows how long the oil stocks will last.'

I look out at the middle distance. Grubby skyscrapers. Domes and bridges and riverboats and spires. The rigid cobweb of the London Eye.

'*Earth hath not anything to show more fair,*' I quote for Ashok, making more folds. Sometimes a line or two can cheer him. '*Dull would he be of soul who could pass by a sight more touching in its majesty.* Wordsworth.'

I pass him the completed water-bomb.

'Huh.' Ashok does not care for poetry today. 'This thing. It's worldwide, right? You see the implications? What you see on the news, that's just the tip of the iceberg. Factories at a standstill. Public transport all but halted. Utilities operating on red alert. Bang go imports, bang go exports, bang goes what remains of the global economy, bang goes capitalism itself for Christ's sake! We'll be growing potatoes on the rooftops next. Bartering. Keeping goats on balconies. Filtering rainwater and darning socks, like we're all living in some wrist-slitting documentary about Ceaușescu's Romania. This is turning into a fucking war, man. The world's most highly developed nations watch like dorks as their infrastructures are trashed from within. By a bunch of . . . random people claiming they've been hijacked by supernatural beings. Who also happen to be kids.'

Professor Whybray insisted he will still be joining us after his Home Office meeting. And rather to my surprise, Stephanie has texted to say she is on her way.

'I still wonder how random it really is,' I say.

'Come on. If the saboteurs all shared some weakness that made them vulnerable to this shit, someone would've spotted it by now.

You and Whybray, for example. Or some other team some other place. But that hasn't happened.'

For a while, as I fold more water-bombs, we argue to and fro about the term 'grassroots terrorism' that has become the media term for the upheavals. I object to it on scientific and linguistic grounds.

'Sure,' counters Ashok. 'You can split hairs. But I say it's looking and behaving like a terror campaign, so we might as well call it one. Ten plane crashes now. Fifteen trains. Food poisonings. Factories producing fucked-up stuff, everything on its knees. You heard about the arrests: all those anarchist so-called ringleaders? Turns out they're in the clear. As confused as the rest of us. You and Whybray have flow-charted this thing, right? Give me the worst-case.'

I run through the more drastic possibilities: restricted agriculture and manufacture, diminished utilities, minimal transport, little reliable news. With foreign imports halted, Britain's island status will come into stark focus. Limited and dwindling food supplies will lead to further looting, lawlessness, gang warfare, black marketeering and regionalism. When the pandemic has run its course, daily life will eventually stabilise. But there will be fundamental changes. Enforced curfews. Draconian laws. New safeguards for industry. The opportunistic restructuring of institutions. Reinvented forms of government. A massive drop in the birth rate. A new focus on agricultural self-sufficiency and more transparent forms of corporatism are also possible. Either way, the world will never be the same again. I turn the origami paper and confirm the first set of creases. 'But if it's terrorism, that implies it's co-ordinated,' I finish.

'In which case, where's the strategy, where's the communication, where's the coherence?'

'And what the hell's the message?' storms Ashok. 'Unless the aim is simply to bring civilisation to a halt and stop everything in its tracks and ... reverse all the goddam progress man has ever made since the Industrial Revolution. We're heading back to the Stone Age. At least with Iraq, or the Pacific rim after the tsunami, there were reconstruction opportunities.'

'We've got the Home Office contract.'

'Whoop-dee-do. Followed by what? The Transition to Planet Fucked contract? It's not the kids that matter. It's the factory workers, the farmers, the managers. The adults, for Christ's sake! Look what's happening to growth! How can anything be rebuilt, or even survive when industry's being sabotaged on this kind of scale?'

'Anyone who believes in indefinite growth in anything physical, on a physically finite planet, is either mad – or an economist.'

'Uh?'

'You asked a question. I replied with a quotation. From one of JFK's advisers. Kenneth Boulder. A wise man.'

Stephanie arrives looking raddled, her hair wet from the rain.

'Half the roads are shut off. So what have I missed?' She's shaking her hair and taking off her raincoat, which is a green that Dulux calls Autumn Fern. She's even thinner than ever.

She called Freddy K a *creature*.

'Oh, just the usual discussion of the disintegration of the world as we know it,' mutters Ashok, bouncing my newly finished water-bomb in his palm, 'and how everything we thought we knew is bullshit because the rules have changed. Adapt or get screwed in the ass.'

There's a knock at the door: it opens and Professor Whybray appears.

Ashok waves him into a seat and asks, 'What's new at the Home Office?'

The lines on his forehead deepen as he settles into a chair. 'We had a briefing from the army. The ones running wild are moving out of urban areas and into the countryside. They're going for woodland, mostly, where they can hide. In coastal regions they're finding caves. A lot of them are living directly on the beaches. It's unofficial for now. But the strategy is to house as many children as possible in one place. Other cities are taking a similar line. They're converting the O2 building.'

'The Dome?' asks Ashok. He grins. 'I saw Leonard Cohen play there. It has the capacity, I guess. Ha. Britain's biggest playpen.'

'I advised against it. I don't like the way they're headed with this. But there've been some developments. In view of which they feel they're justified in rounding them up and keeping them locked in.'

'What developments?'

He waves some papers. 'Firstly, some autopsies. Three children have now died in British Units. Various natural causes. Nothing untoward for a cohort this size. Two had epileptic fits, one had an undiagnosed heart condition. And we've recovered the corpses of seven children who were probably murdered by vigilantes. I am sorry to say they were mutilated. But the autopsies of all of them – and there are similar cases documented abroad – also show an anomaly of the kidneys.' I look at him. 'Yes. Similar to what Svensson's autopsy showed. In many cases the kidneys are simply larger. But in a surprisingly high number, there are multiple organs. It's too rare a phenomenon to be pure coincidence. Alongside that—' he stops and frowns. 'I'll show you.' He flips open a folder. 'It's utterly baffling. There's just no way to explain it.' They are medical records. Names of children. Their birth dates. Their height and weight measurements. Various dates. And in each case, a graph that defies logic. 'We've been tracking them.'

I run my eyes across the charts again, one by one, then hand them to Stephanie. She takes a moment to absorb them, then asks, 'And these are otherwise healthy children?' He nods. 'Could there be a mistake?'

'No. Staff at sixteen other UK Units confirm it. Others do worldwide. It's not been made public yet, but it will be out there soon enough.' He puts his head in his hands.

I ask, 'Why aren't they growing?'

'Not growing?' asks Ashok. 'What, none of them?'

'That's what these figures show. They're all exactly the same height and weight they were a month ago. In many cases longer than that.'

'But if that's the case—' I stop. 'Then what?'

'Arrested development?' asks Stephanie.

'But that's crazy!' says Ashok. 'So what happens, they just . . . stay this size? They're children for ever, like Peter fucking Pan?'

The professor shakes his head. 'They could start growing again any time. Or have a sudden spurt. I'm getting some nutritionists on to the team at Battersea. Let's see what they can do. But in the meantime, we have a problem that goes beyond health. As in, ethical. Political. Moral.'

Stephanie says, 'I don't see how a medical oddity can alter policy.'

'Me neither,' says Ashok.

Professor Whybray sighs heavily and looks at me. 'You'd better explain.'

'It's cultural. Anthropologically, the children already fit into the barbarian category. The unknown and feared outsiders. They're seen as dirty and diseased and backward. This medical evidence – the kidney anomalies and the fact they're not developing normally – suggests they might actually be different biologically. It's not a small step from there to argue that they're not strictly human.' I address Stephanie. 'Intelligent people are already calling them mutants.' I pause. 'Or *creatures*.' She flushes. 'If they're in a separate species category, they don't have the same rights.'

Ashok says, 'Shit.'

Stephanie has been very quiet. Now she sends me a look, and makes the small distinctive head movement – a raising of the chin, a widening of the eyes – which I have come to recognise as her version of a silent command.

But I don't respond.

'Hesketh,' she says evenly, 'I think this might be the moment to tell them what you've been holding back.' I reach for a sheet of paper. I feel ambushed. But I can't lie. Nor can I even try. Stephanie is still looking at me.

'What's going on here?' says Ashok. 'If this is some personal bullshit between you two over Kaitlin—'

'No,' says Stephanie. 'It's not personal, Ashok.'

Professor Whybray says, 'Is there something bothering you, Hesketh?'

I start folding. A cockroach. Their wings are elaborate. I say, 'The facts. The facts are bothering me.'

'Go on,' urges Stephanie. Her eyes are glittering. 'Tell them. Tell them now.'

I stand up, take off my jacket and roll up my sleeve to reveal the bruise. It's finally beginning to fade but the finger-marks remain distinct.

Professor Whybray says 'May I?' I go over to him and he inspects it with interest. 'I presume this was Freddy.'

'No. It was Jonas Svensson. In Sweden.'

'Hmmm. He must have had very small hands.'

'No. That's the point. He was big. But when he grabbed me, this is the bruising he left.'

I go back and sit down again and continue the cockroach and wait. Nobody says anything for a while. Then finally Stephanie clears her throat. 'Hesketh also saw something in Dubai that you should know about.'

I give the short version.

'So I and twenty-seven other men saw the figure that de Vries called a *tokoloshi*,' I finish. I'm aware of them looking at me. The silence lasts long enough for me to complete the cockroach.

Professor Whybray shifts painfully in his chair, then rises and goes over to the window. The silence continues as he stands there staring out at the cumulus of smoke on the horizon.

Ashok has had his head in his hands, but finally he looks up and says, 'Why the hell didn't you tell us this before?'

'Because you very specifically said, *no little people.*' Ashok lets a rush of air out of his nose and drums his fingers on the table in a way that indicates aggressiveness. He can't deny it. 'But Jonas made the bruises on my arm and I saw a little girl.'

He chucks a water-bomb up into the air. It lands on the desk, then bounces off on to the floor by my feet. I pick it up and cup it in my palm. It's an admirable specimen.

Professor Whybray turns. His face is very pale. He looks old.

'Hesketh. If it came from anyone but you, I'd be sceptical. But I can't doubt that you saw what you saw.' I shut my eyes and mentally send my little cockroach fluttering up to the ceiling. 'People with your kind of wiring don't lie.' He eases himself back into his chair, apparently in pain. The skin of his face resembles ancient papyrus. I am sure he is not sleeping properly. 'You should have told us earlier, that's all. We'll have to work out what impact this has on our other findings.'

'It'll be a very unscientific one,' I say. 'Because it appears to make no sense.'

He looks up. 'New parameters,' he says bluntly.

'What do you mean?'

'He means blue skies. Out of the box,' says Ashok. 'As if this whole goddam thing isn't. Right?'

The professor nods. 'So to begin with, let's hypothesise that we're looking at a generation whose DNA has been somehow altered.'

'By what? And when? It can't change once you're born.'

'Not yet it can't,' he says.

'What do you mean?' asks Stephanie.

Ashok says, 'Are we talking about genetic engineering here or what?'

255

Stephanie says, 'Or evolution. But mutation takes centuries.'

'No. D'you hear about those worms they've found thriving in old arsenic mines?' asks Ashok. 'Took them just fifty years to adapt to eating one of the world's most vicious poisons. Or the Nepalese. Extra blood vessels, so they don't get altitude sickness. A survival mutation.'

I say, 'And according to our renal expert, congenital kidney abnormalities are already occurring regularly in some parts of the world.'

'Which means that theoretically in a couple of hundred years' time it could be the norm,' says Professor Whybray. His eyes are shining oddly. As if he has a fever.

'Stop,' I say. 'This is now. This is the world we're in. We're not talking about some . . . future scenario.'

'So the idea of a hypothetical world paying us a visit would be philosophically interesting, but quite irrational, according to you, Hesketh?'

I nod. 'Completely and utterly.' I wonder why he even needs to ask.

'So you see no room for metaphysics?'

'If there's rationalism and scientifically verifiable data involved, I see room for everything and anything. But if it's just fanciful speculation, I don't.'

'Even after our discussion about CERN?'

'Whoa there,' says Ashok. 'You're losing me, guys. Why are we even discussing this, this . . . what is it anyway?'

'A theoretical eventuality,' says Professor Whybray. 'Involving a paradigm shift.'

'Bring it on,' says Stephanie. Her face is pale and grim. 'If this paradigm shift involves waking up tomorrow morning and finding out it's all been a bad dream, I'm in favour.' Her phone rings. 'Excuse me a moment.' She pulls out her mobile, gets up and walks towards the door and faces the wall for privacy.

'Well I suggest we drop the blue-skies stuff and stick to the facts,' mutters Ashok. 'Now who's for a drink? I sure as hell need one. I've got vodka or whisky. Any takers?'

But Professor Whybray isn't listening: he has perched his notebook on his knee and started writing very fast. So I tell Ashok we'll both have whisky and watch the old man write. He doesn't do diagrams: instead, he sets out his ideas in the form of sentences, paragraphs, headings and lists of questions. Often, they are very elegantly phrased. I am a diagram-and-symbol man. But what diagram, and what symbols, can describe a breed of vengeful human child that brings the world as we know it to its knees?

I must've swallowed one, said Jonas Svensson.

You can't come in, said de Vries.

Complex organisms like tapeworms can live inside the body for decades. They make huge demands. They are in control. Like puppet masters, they call the shots. The host and the parasite become inseparable. They form a 'we'.

'Human history is a juggernaut,' murmurs the professor. Ashok shoots me a questioning look. I take a deep swig of whisky. A light rain starts falling in wires of silver outside as my mentor's pen travels across the page, line after line. I fold more paper. Another water-bomb for Ashok. I chuck it over to him and he catches it in one hand. Stephanie's conversation hasn't lasted long: she has already said 'thank you', sat down again and put the phone back in her handbag. But her movements are a little clumsy.

'Drink, Steph?' asks Ashok.

By way of an answer she stands up very suddenly, then staggers and sinks to her knees. Her face is not its usual shape. Professor Whybray drops his notebook, jumps up and grabs her under the arms, just as she's about to collapse against the desk. He settles her back in her chair and forces her head between her knees.

'Deep breaths,' he says, a finger on her pulse. 'That's good. That's good.'

Stephanie groans. It has all happened so quickly I can barely take it in. Ashok is staring wide-eyed. 'Oh boy,' he says. 'Oh Jesus. Oh no.'

I can be slow on the uptake.

It will take some time, therefore, for me to register the news that at 3.15pm the female patient in Bed 67 of the Brown Ward on the fifth floor of St Thomas' hospital suffered a catastrophic brain haemorrhage, and that due to severe staff shortages, lack of resources and patient overload, no medical staff were able to apply the necessary procedures, and that very regrettably, therefore, the thirty-seven-year-old patient Kaitlin Kalifakidis, mother of one, tragically expired.

CHAPTER 14

KAITLIN KALIFAKIDIS IS dead, Kaitlin Kalifakidis is dead, Kaitlin Kalifakidis is dead.

When I told Freddy, he just nodded. That was three days ago. Since then he has asked no questions. I haven't pursued it. He has approximately 90 per cent of his life ahead of him. I may have 60 per cent of mine. One day, perhaps, it will sink in for both of us.

But not today.

I have seen nothing of Stephanie since she received the call. She went straight from Phipps & Wexman to the hospital, then to her sister's. When I spoke to this sister to discuss the funeral arrangements, she did not sound like the happy person conjured by her name, Felicity. Felicity described Stephanie as being 'utterly distraught'. She also conveyed Stephanie's hope that attending his mother's funeral might 'bring it home' to Freddy.

I consider this to be highly unlikely.

In my workroom, I locate the box that contains my origami supplies. I find the Kawasaki rose in an envelope marked HL. I knew she wouldn't throw it away. She knew how hard it was to make. How much pre-creasing was involved, how much crimping, how many mountain, valley, squash, reverse and petal folds. It has faded a little. But it is still viable, and a thing of beauty.

It's mid-morning on Wednesday 3rd October. The cemetery is in Wimbledon. The pony-tailed Flynn drives Freddy, me and Naomi there in a six-seater. Professor Whybray pulled some strings to book Kaitlin's family an early funeral slot. Care Unit children are only allowed in public places with official Home Office authorisation – this the professor has also seen to – and must be accompanied by three adult minders. Naomi looks beautiful in a cream silk shirt and black skirt. Freddy is in a black school tracksuit which was all I could find that seemed suitable: his red uniform would arouse too much attention. He's curled up on the back seat, quietly clicking and humming to himself. Since I don't have a dark jacket with me, I have borrowed one from Professor Whybray. But I don't feel at home in it because it's too short, and tight across my shoulders. For this and other more obvious reasons, I feel *mal dans ma peau*.

We drive through largely empty streets, the surreal quiet broken occasionally by the wail of a siren. There are no traffic lights working. In Wandsworth we are forced into a wide detour: a burst water main has turned a whole section of road into a lake. It's dotted with half-submerged black rubbish bags. Clouds of flies vibrate above them. The smell in this sector is overpowering. Freddy is blank-faced in the back seat.

The cemetery spreads across a couple of acres, a dusty, layered oasis in an urban hinterland of warehouses, high-rise tenements and 1980s retail parks. Subsidence has skewed the gravestones so that barely any stand at right angles. Some are deeply sunk, as though into quicksand. At one end, a piebald horse stands tethered to the gate, grazing on the dry grass that's worn away in patches, like old carpeting. The car park – crazed tarmac with worn space-markings and weeds soaring through cracks – is ringed by straggling wood-land and rhododendron bushes. From here there's a path into the centre of the cemetery, through an alleyway of desiccated beech trees. On one side there's a drop to a railway line. A train rumbles past, a flash of blue and red behind the tall banks of Japanese knot-weed and rosebay willowherb. Flynn locks the car and we stand for a moment, recalibrating.

Ashok and Stephanie are already waiting in the car park, where the mourners of an earlier funeral are preparing to leave. An older and even paler version of Stephanie is with them: she introduces herself as Stephanie's sister Felicity. I guess that since she organ-ised this event, she is in charge of the flowers, so I hand her the Kawasaki rose and tell her it's for the coffin. She accepts it distract-edly. Stephanie doesn't acknowledge Freddy. Nor will she look at him. This doesn't seem to bother him. Ashok, in dark pinstripe, says, 'Hi kiddo', but he keeps his distance and offers none of the hair-ruffling, shoulder-punching or high-fiving with which he's greeted

Freddy in the past. He looks exhausted and tense and his skin has the yellowed tinge of a fading Polaroid snap.

'The others are over there,' says Stephanie, pointing. 'But keep Freddy right away from us, if you don't mind.' She points out a straggle of black-clad figures heading towards a low red-brick building that must be the chapel. The women tread carefully on the uneven paving stones. The building is very small in relation to the cemetery, and unambitious in its construction: it could be one of Freddy's Lego models, scaled up.

I am not good with faces. I didn't meet Kaitlin's family that often, and I haven't seen her brother Alex in a year. He never liked me. Their mother is still in the hospice. Stephanie has told me they took a joint decision not to tell her about Kaitlin's death.

Without warning, Stephanie starts crying, and Felicity embraces her tightly. Naomi addresses me and Flynn. 'Bring Freddy in once the service has started. I'll go with Steph.'

'I'll join you,' says Ashok.

While the others head for the group of mourners at the chapel entrance, Flynn lights a cigarette and I read some of the headstones. Most are crusted with lichen, the edges like the frilled coastline on a map. *Kenneth Melhuish fell gently asleep in 1922.* Freddy has turned his attention to a mottled yellow and white butterfly high-stepping between the petals of a rose. He grabs the insect so fast that by the time I fully register it, he's swallowed it down and has turned his attention to a knobbled stick, whose bark he begins to peel off like 'dead pirate skin'. *Connie Anne Kenderick passed into a fuller life aged 93.* There are many euphemisms for dying. *At rest. Left this world.*

After ten minutes, the chapel doors close; a little later some music strikes up inside: I recognise the opening chords of 'Abide with Me'.

'OK, Freddy,' says Flynn, after the second verse. 'Me and Hesketh are taking you in now. You can bring your stick.'

We walk him between us – one arm each – and enter quietly through the heavy door. He doesn't resist. Everyone is standing for the hymn, and too busy singing to look at us.

'First empty pew on the right,' says Flynn. We slide into the empty back row and sit with Freddy between us. I am right next to the aisle.

I haven't been to many funerals. My grandfather's, when I was a boy. My father's and then my mother's, at both of which I read Herbert's poem 'The Flower', which I quoted for Detective Mazoor. Mrs Helena Whybray's. She had a humanist service, followed by a cremation. When the hymn comes to an end, we sit and after a great deal of rustling, the chapel falls silent. Naomi half-turns her head, spots us and gives a small nod.

Kaitlin's coffin stands on a trestle near the pulpit. It's white, and bears a simple bouquet that looks home-made. My rose is tucked into it, towards the centre. I am relieved that Felicity was not too distracted to engineer this because there is a symmetry – which I think Kaitlin would have appreciated – in the paper flower being my goodbye to her, as well as my hello.

Among the mourners there are several women wearing hats. There are a couple of teenagers, but no young children. I get a glimpse of Ashok in the row behind Stephanie, who is seated at the front with the family.

The vicar, small and bald-headed, looks sober against the vibrancy of the stained glass, which depicts the Crucifixion. He begins to speak ponderously. It's a speech about the nature and function of grief, and the value of memory, and about how the life of Kaitlin was tragically cut short, in a painful and inexplicable way, and yet she will remain a cherished and beloved fixture in the hearts of all of us gathered here.

'As long as that love is felt among us, she is immortal, and present still.' *Departed this life. Left this world. Fell asleep.*

My belief is that when you die, that's it. As a mature person, one should accept that. But despite the total absence of concrete evidence, billions on this planet are convinced there is more. Most curious.

Freddy shows no interest in the proceedings. He sits next to me, concentrating on picking the bark off his stick. After the Lord's Prayer, the vicar nods and Kaitlin's brother Alex gets to his feet. He's naturally thickset, but fatter than last time I saw him. With obvious effort, he straightens up his body. He has a piece of paper in his hand, which he isn't in complete control of: he holds it some distance from his face, then shakes his head. Someone in the front pew hands him a pair of reading glasses and he grunts his thanks. His face is streaked with sweat. He says that it hasn't been an easy journey for many of the people here today and those who are absent convey their apologies.

'We all know how hard it is nowadays to travel, especially from a distance. Kaitlin would have appreciated your presence here today. In these tragic circumstances. Knowing that her death was part of an unexplained epidemic doesn't make it easier for any of us. It makes it harder.' He takes off the glasses and rubs at his face, then loosens his tie. He is breathing heavily. He gazes, apparently lost, at the piece of paper in front of him. It's still shaking. 'We all remember a lovely mother and son. Kaitlin and—'

Freddy starts clicking his tongue. Gently at first, then louder. I nudge him to stop. Flynn leans over and makes a mouth-zipping sign. But Freddy keeps it up. The woman in the broad hat turns, sees the boy and sucks in her breath. People shift in their seats. As he clicks, he's still peeling the bark off his stick, quite oblivious to his surroundings. There are crescents of grime beneath his fingernails. Alex continues. 'Kaitlin and Freddy. This has been very hard for all of us—'

'What is this place?' Freddy asks me suddenly. His voice is loud enough to cause a ripple of attention.

Alex hesitates, then resumes his speech falteringly: 'Harder than anything we could have imagined.'

Freddy again: 'What are we doing here?'

'It's your mum's funeral,' I whisper.

'Her what?'

'We need to talk quietly Freddy K. Mum died. In hospital.'

His eyes flare wide. 'She died?' he whispers. 'How? Why?'

'She fell down the stairs at home,' I whisper. 'The fall damaged her brain and it bled into her skull and nobody could save her. I'm sorry Freddy K.'

His eyes gleam with clear, bright tears. Maybe Stephanie was right after all, about the funeral 'bringing it home'.

'But why did she fall down the stairs?'

'You were there, Freddy K. When we found her she was near the bottom of the stairs and . . . you were at the top.'

His lip wobbles. The tears are spilling. 'No,' he whispers. Then he stands up and shouts: 'NO!'

The effect is electric. People turn and look. Alex stops speaking mid-sentence and stands staring at us with his mouth open. An agitated murmur ripples across the chapel.

'What's he doing here?' says a bulky man two rows ahead. 'What's he, I mean what the hell's he—' he stops. 'Just get that creature out of here!'

'No!' Freddy shouts again. 'Stop it! Stop it! She's not dead!'

The vicar signals for calm with an air-patting movement. 'May I ask you all please to—'

Flynn mutters, 'Hesketh. This is going to get ugly. Let's go. Now.'

Alex seems confused. Dropping the piece of paper to the floor, he sits down heavily on the steps of the altar. The priest signals to the organist to play, and some mellow chords strike up.

Shooting up from her seat, Naomi walks towards us fast. I grab one of Freddy's arms and Flynn takes the other. He gives a sharp cry as we pull him to his feet. He drops his stick and starts shrieking wildly, trying to corkscrew his way out of our grip.

We hold on tight and keep heading out. But Freddy squirms: Flynn makes a sudden gasp and stops in his tracks. Something's happened: Flynn has lost hold of Freddy. He's doubled up in pain, clutching his wrist. There's blood. A lot of it, dramatic against his white shirt.

'He bit me,' he mutters. 'Go,' he says, nodding at the door. 'Go now.'

A man yells: 'Get him!' and there is a rising and rush of bodies. I charge to the exit, dragging Freddy. Naomi's up ahead, pushing open the door.

'Now you all sit down!' shouts a commanding voice. The accent is American. It's Ashok. 'Sit the fuck down! Immediately! This is a funeral! The boy is leaving! He's distressed. We all are. But he's a kid. Let's have some dignity here, guys!'

People hesitate. The music continues, waveringly. The vicar chimes in with his own more diluted appeal for calm, but panic has taken over. Lifting Freddy bodily, I barge out of the door. As Naomi closes it behind me she calls out: 'We'll meet you at the car!'

The daylight is dazzling after the gloom of the chapel. Freddy's writhing furiously, but I keep my grip as I run, half-tripping, my arms round his chest, his legs flailing beneath. I'm heading for the car park when a searing pain shoots through my groin. Somehow or other, he has freed a hand and rammed me in the testicles. I crash to the ground and for a moment everything collapses into blackness. There's movement in it: a smooth sickening shift of mass.

When I regain control of myself, Freddy's hurtling across the cemetery towards the railway line, leaping over skewed graves, screaming as he runs, his black curls bouncing. My heart bangs.

'Freddy! Stop!' But I choke: my voice has no power in it. My groin is thumping with the worst pain I have ever felt. Behind me Flynn and Naomi are charging up, followed by Ashok. Stephanie emerges and a cluster of women forms around her. Several are in tears. A small crowd of angry mourners congregates at the chapel entrance. Struggling to my feet I sprint off in the direction Freddy went. Every footfall brings more piercing pain – but I've seen him and I know where I'm going. He charges down the railway cutting and across the tracks, then flits into the thicket on the other side, a few metres from a vast copper beech. Using the tree as a marker, I scrabble down the steep cutting in Freddy's footsteps, through a mass of nettles, thistles, knotweed and willowherb. The voices from the cemetery grow fainter as I plunge into the woodland, shucking off Professor Whybray's jacket as I go. No sign of Freddy.

I need a system. Trackers look for damaged foliage. I get to my knees. At the boy's eye level, I spot a tunnel-like entrance in the bushes to my left. The stalks have been trampled. I enter and stumble through, my sleeves catching on briars. After a few metres I am standing at normal height again, scratched and bloody, in a waste tip. A rusted car, black plastic bags, old washing machines, a punctured Spacehopper. Nearby is a stagnant pool rainbowed with oil, full of half-submerged shopping trolleys and swathes of sooty bulrushes. My phone vibrates: it's Ashok.

'Where are you?' I keep my voice low as I explain. 'Flynn's on his way, and I'm joining you as soon as we've got them back inside,' he tells me. 'They're going to resume the service. Closure and all that shit.'

This is a relief. Just then, a small dark shape scurries through the trees towards a fence. 'He's here. I've got to go.'

I duck as Freddy darts through the scrub. I want to catch him on open ground. At the base of a huge pylon he halts and cocks his head, as though listening for something. There's a rustle of vegetation. I hold my breath, keeping myself hidden. Something grinds in my chest. *I can't lose him, I can't lose him, I can't lose him.*

Then, through the branches – five metres away at the most – I see them.

They're behind the tall rusty fence, packed in a huddle, their small fingers clinging to the wire, which rattles as they shift from foot to foot. They are making a soft clicking noise. I count eleven. Several are wearing adult sunglasses that are far too big. There's a smell. Urine and something else. Something rotten. One of them – a black-skinned boy with a broken front tooth – puts a filthy fist to his eye and opens his hand in a salute. Freddy returns it, then runs towards them, hopping over the detritus in his path. Their hair is matted. Their legs and feet are bare and they're wearing a minimum of clothing: T-shirts, underwear. One girl is in a torn dress, another wears just a swimsuit. Their flesh is scratched and soiled. Squinting to focus, I see that one boy is wearing a necklace like the one Freddy made for Stephanie. It's rotten-looking. Then I see why. It's made of bits of meat.

It takes a moment to absorb what kind of meat it's made of.

I shouldn't be surprised.

I have seen footage of the feral tribes. So I have to some extent already deduced the content of their more brutal rites. If Professor Whybray were here, it would prompt an energetic discussion. But this is not the time to be an anthropologist. It's time to get Freddy back.

I have no doubt that I can catch him. But I want to make sure Flynn and Ashok are ready to back me up when I make my move. Just then, the tallest boy points to a hole at the bottom of the fence. Freddy nods, makes the eye-salute, falls suddenly to his knees and wriggles through. Once among them he is a fish absorbed into a shoal. Wordlessly, they turn and start scrambling up a patch of higher ground which is divided into individual allotments dotted with garden sheds. Staying hidden, I keep up with them in parallel along the railway track below. None of them looks back. If they're worried about an adult presence, they don't show it. I have no doubt that the funeral has vanished from Freddy's mind, and me with it. He has entered a dimension in which our world is an irrelevance.

Once past the allotments, they turn and head for a parade of shops near the railway bridge. The street looks empty, with no sign of human life. I can intercept them higher up, if I climb the siding, and catch them unawares. When I reach the top, I get a clearer view of them from behind a lilac bush. I realise that more kids have joined them. Where from it's not clear. There must be more than twenty. It's hard to count, because they're more agitated and fluid now, hooting and clucking and stirring about. I'm much bigger than any of them. But now that the group has swelled to double its original size, I hesitate. Still crouching by the railway bridge, out of sight, I send Flynn a text telling him where I am.

I'll wait for you.

And that's what I do. It's intriguing to see them like this, in their feral state. An older boy and a younger girl in grubby goggles seem to be the ringleaders. They're grouped in a car park next to a parade of closed shops. It's a no man's land. They don't seem to have any particular focus, until almost idly, one of them picks a loose brick off the low wall of the Sainsbury's Local car park and hurls it at the window of the store. The glass fractures, but doesn't break. Apparently energised by his action, the kids begin loosening more bricks and joining in. Before long, they've smashed a hole large enough to get through, and they're pouring inside. Freddy's still with them, and as I lose sight of him my anxiety mounts: might there be a back door they'll all escape through, and disappear? But a minute later they start emerging, clutching tins of food. An argument starts up, with shouts, violent elbowing, shoving and snatching. I'm too far off to catch the words, if there are any. More kids come out of the shop, weighed down with consumables, some bleeding from glass cuts. Several are clad in new eyewear, the price-tags still attached. Freddy, clutching a tin in each hand, seems completely at home among them, as if this were just an extension of life at the Unit. Then, for no obvious reason, the squabbling tails off. One of the kids must have some chalk, because he starts drawing the burst eye on the end wall of a row of terraced houses, in white. A group of ten or so makes encouraging noises while passing round a bottle of ketchup. In turn, they upend the bottle into their palms and smear the paste on their hands before stamping their prints on the wall. Then they lick their fingers and punch the sky with their fists, clicking and hooting. A baying cheer goes up across the whole group.

Where is Flynn?

The sky is darkening. I remember that the forecast was for rain.

As soon as he comes, we must both rush in and grab Freddy. We may have to fight the others off, but they're small, and we're stronger. It will be a kidnap operation. He'll resist. I have no doubt of that.

I'm flow-charting the repercussions of this when it happens.

I don't have time to think.

Or move.

They come up from behind, silent. One grabs my wrist with a small hand. I swing round and face them: it's a new group, comprising ten or so kids. Then there's a squeal and suddenly the group I've been watching is rushing in towards me too. It's a pincer movement. Then they're all over me, pummelling as high as they can reach. I'm still trying to fight them off when I lose my balance and crash backwards down the slope. I take advantage of the momentum and roll at speed. This buys me some time, but when I stop I'm disoriented and my skin is buzzing with nettle stings. When I get my bearings I spot Freddy, at the front of a whole swarm of them beating down through the weeds towards me. His eyes are gleaming with a new light.

I don't know what his intentions are, but when he throws himself at me in a monkey leap, I know what to do. Grabbing him tight, I hurl us both further down the slope of the railway siding in a chaotic, desperate tumble. He's kicking and pummelling at me with his fists, but this time I'm not letting go. The others are closing in, hooting and clicking, when from the corner of my eye I spot Flynn and Ashok racing up the track, with Naomi following behind. Suddenly, Freddy gives a spasm, then flops like a rag doll, as if the breath has been shoved out of him. Rushing up, Flynn grabs him and hauls him off me. Then, handing him to Ashok, he rugby-tackles a boy with a stick who has launched himself at us like a missile. Just then, something hits me hard on the back of the neck. I fight the dizziness, but fail. I'm falling and I need to vomit. Bright lights bombard me.

Then the world shrinks to a pinprick and goes black.

★　　★　　★

When I wake up, I'm in the fragmenting relics of a dream about CERN. I am working there, looking after the ghostly sub-atomic particles known as neutrinos. They resemble airborne amoeba and my job is to feed them and ensure they stay in their cages. Far from travelling faster than the speed of light, as in the famous experiments, they move in sluggish slow motion. It's not clear why they can't just float through the bars and away. I find my role as their keeper stressful.

It takes some time before I realise I'm upstairs in the bed I once shared with Kaitlin. A woman is with me. But it's not Kaitlin Kalifakidis because Kaitlin Kalifakidis is dead. I don't know why I don't recognise her immediately. Perhaps because she's still in her funeral outfit.

She is beautiful.

'Hello Hesketh,' she says.

'I dreamed about particle physics.'

She laughs. 'I'd expect nothing less. We brought you back to Fulham. It seemed like the best idea. You need to rest up for a few days.'

'Did I lose him?' It hurts to speak. I must have cut my lip.

'No. He's here. Asleep in his room.' I'm aching all over. My ribs hurt. 'I've had a look at you. You probably have a cracked rib. Then there are a few flesh wounds and a lot of bruising.'

I am stark naked under the sheet. Realising this, I get an immediate erection which forms a little tent. I don't bother trying to hide it.

'I want to kiss you,' I say.

Naomi smiles. 'That would be impractical. You haven't seen

what your mouth looks like. You were lucky. They could have killed you.'

I reach out and take her hand. She doesn't pull away. Instead, she pats my arm with her free hand. I don't know how to interpret this. It's a gesture my mother might have made. But one gesture can lead to another. I'm about to experiment by bringing my other hand into the equation, and reaching for her face, when the door opens.

'My God, boy. You look terrible,' says a familiar voice. My erection vanishes as suddenly as it came. Naomi and I disengage as Professor Whybray approaches the bed. He takes my chin in his hand and looks into my eyes searchingly. 'Are you back in the land of the living?' I nod. 'Well thank God you're safe, boy. I came as soon as I could.'

I say, 'My apologies concerning the loss and possible destruction of your jacket.'

He waves his hand dismissively. 'You had a close shave.' He pauses. 'I caught the news on the way here. They found a dead child in the Forest of Dean. Butchered. Quite expertly it seems. The internal organs were missing. And so were the fingers. There was evidence that some parts of the body had been consumed.'

I sit up in bed, painfully. Naomi adjusts the pillows behind my head.

My mouth hurts when I speak. 'Out there, I saw a kid – he had that necklace. It's made of—' I can't continue. Something is stopping me. A blockage. I frown and clear my throat. 'It fits with the older kids expecting the younger ones to be their slaves. The idea of honour. And *ikenie*.'

'If this was a dismemberment,' says Professor Whybray quietly, 'it makes it harder to argue against rounding the children up and treating them with drugs. I feared something of this nature. I should perhaps have articulated it. But I couldn't bring myself to, er ...' He stops. When he speaks again, his voice cracks. 'I couldn't bring myself to find an appropriate term.'

He still can't. But I can. Ancient and primitive tribes were never my main field of study, but I have read the central texts. And so has he.

The term is ritual cannibalism.

'Let's see the news,' murmurs Naomi, switching on the small TV set that stands on the chest of drawers. Kaitlin and I used to lie here watching *Newsnight*. She flicks through the channels until she finds the BBC.

'*In Britain, the Home Office is stepping up work on the conversion of the O2 building into a holding centre for child terrorists in the southeast. Other cities are working on similar conversions in the wake of the startling new evidence of physical mutation. Medical findings just released indicate the pre-teen attackers share an unexplained anomaly of the kidneys. This has prompted urgent new discussions in governments worldwide about the best way to handle the escalating crisis.*'

'My God,' the professor chokes. 'They went public with it!' He bangs his fist on my bed with surprising force. I wince in pain. 'They've hijacked our work! I'd never have approved this, never.'

My heart starts banging. I am getting overloaded. I fold a mental *ozuru*.

'This will appeal to the worst in everyone,' says Naomi. 'They're sub-human. *Evil*. That's the message!'

'Hell,' storms Professor Whybray. 'Why does ignorance have to be so much more damned powerful than knowledge?'

I finish my *ozuru*. 'Because it's more dynamic,' I tell him. 'That's how it fills empty spaces faster. That's how it comes up with theories that knowledge can't.'

Freddy K, Freddy K, Freddy K.

'You know what'll happen when they get them into those facilities,' says Naomi, her face flushing red.

Professor Whybray looks as broken and miserable as he did the day Helena died. 'I fear the worst. It's an old story,' he says. 'But it's one I never thought we'd hear again. They're freaks now. It's official. They can do anything to them. Anything.'

I fold another *ozuru* in my head. A huge and beautiful one, in red.

I can't let 'anything' happen to Freddy K.

And I won't.

From now on, he's staying by my side.

CHAPTER 15

THE NEXT MORNING I wake in tremendous pain. It's Thursday 4th October. The forecast is for a high of thirteen degrees and a low of four. Naomi urged me to stay at home for the next couple of days: she could easily arrange for Miranda to ferry Freddy to Battersea. But I want to see her. I want to experiment with holding her hand again. I also need to get Professor Whybray's advice.

Freddy is in a truculent mood. He won't discuss the events of yesterday. When I suggest we stay at home for a while and work on the Lego model he thrusts out his lower lip.

'I want to go to Battersea.'

I do too.

It's eight minutes past eleven by the time we get in the car.

Despite the grey sky, Freddy insists on wearing his small sunglasses. Out of habit, I consider the structure of the clouds on the horizon.

'Cauliflower,' says the boy, out of the blue. Cauliflower is his version of 'cumulus'. 'And look over there,' he says, pointing upward. 'That's lasagne.' He means stratus. Because of this sudden and unprompted return to the normal Freddy, I'm smiling when I turn the corner into the Unit's access road.

But when I see the ambulance, my smile dies. There are also two police cars and an army jeep. A cluster of soldiers stands at the facility's entrance: one of them spots me and waves me away, indicating the diversion sign. Quickly, I reverse out, find a side road, and park. I don't think the soldier registered Freddy, but I'm not taking any chances. I tell the boy to lie down on the floor in the narrow space under the back seat. Now. Thankfully, his reaction is of instant alarm. He whips off his seatbelt and scrambles to the floor. I unhook the DVD player from the back of the seat, and hand it to him.

'Here. You stay lying down, and watch this.' I cover him with the blanket Kaitlin kept for picnics. 'Put your head right under. It's nice and dark. You have to stay hidden. Wait here like this till I get back. Don't move. If you do, they'll see you and they'll take you away. You won't like that. If you stay here I'll keep you safe. I promise.' I'm struggling to keep my voice level. 'Just watch the DVD, OK? I'll be back before the end of this episode. But if I'm not, keep watching. And if I'm still not back, just go to sleep.'

I hear a muffled 'OK.' He sounds scared. Good. He should be. Fear will keep him safe.

I lock Freddy in the car and walk around to the side entrance where there's another soldier on guard. I show him my pass. 'What's going on?'

'There was an incident here a couple of hours ago. Whole load of creatures escaped. We've got search parties out now; they can't have gone far. And no one's going to mistake them in that uniform.'

'Are you saying all of the children are gone?' He nods.

'None's left in there. As far as we know.'

'What about the staff?'

'They're taking the injured ones to hospital now. The rest are at the police station giving evidence.'

'How can so many children have escaped? This is a closed facility.'

'Sabotage I'm afraid, sir. Looks like one of your colleagues deactivated the door codes.'

I think fast. 'I came to pick up some documents. A report for the Home Secretary. She's expecting it today. I need to get in.'

He shrugs. 'The danger's past, but it's not charming in there, I'm warning you mate. It's a crime scene, so don't remove or touch anything.'

He waves me in. I want to run, but I force myself to walk. I take the thirty-six stairs two at a time. The place is deserted. No milling kids, no clucking or hooting or humming, no bright uniforms: just the hollow feel of a place suddenly and inexplicably deserted. I think of bees and Marie Celeste syndrome. The corridor leading to Professor Whybray's office has been cordoned off. Some soldiers are standing there, blocking my view.

'And you are, sir?' asks one of them as I approach.

'Authorised staff,' I say, brandishing my ID.

'Good,' she says briskly. 'You can identify your colleague for us, then.'

She signals to the others to step back. When they move to the edges of the corridor I see that there's a body on the floor, face down.

It is male and it belongs to someone tall. I am totally unprepared for this. I put my hand against the wall to steady myself. I recognise the high-quality leather shoes. The white hair. I start to rock.

'We'll turn him over for you, sir. Are you ready?' Two soldiers reach down.

No. I will never be ready. They roll him over gently. His shirt is wet with fresh blood. His eyes are open. The left one has been horribly damaged. There is blood under his nose and his mouth is crusted with vomit. The skin that is not red or purple – on his neck and his left hand – is papery and translucent white.

'Is he dead?' I don't know why I ask. I know the answer. I rock harder.

'Bit of a shock for you, sir,' says the female soldier. 'I'm sorry.'

I rock some more. 'It's OK. I don't feel anything. Maybe I will later.'

Or maybe I am a robot made of meat. Perhaps if I am, that is a good way to be, because it enables me to think and act rationally. I run a mental flow chart. It tells me to get hold of the professor's notebook and then find Naomi.

'How did he die?' I ask. It's important to know the facts.

'Trampled by the look of it,' says a man in a white suit and a face mask. 'They probably attacked him in a gang. Jumped up and down on him. Not difficult. He was elderly. Crushed out the life.'

Crushed out the life. He was seventy-three years and five months old. Young, in today's world. He might have lived to a hundred.

'Where's Naomi Benjamin? I need to talk to her.'

'She's at the police station.'

'Is she under suspicion?'

She shrugs. 'Can't say, sir. They're all being questioned.'

Professor Whybray is dead, Professor Whybray is dead, Professor Whybray is dead, I say to myself over and over as I head for his office. I find his notebook in his briefcase and pocket it. I can't risk taking anything else. *Professor Whybray is dead, Professor Whybray is dead, Professor Whybray is dead.* It doesn't help. It doesn't feel real. Another person would feel something. They might cry. Instead, I think about the escaped children. They'll catch some. But others will evade them. They'll live wild in forests and on beaches and in holes. They'll raid shops for tins, dig for bugs, mill about in their cochineal uniforms until they get discarded or fall apart and they are stinking and dressed in rags and eating insects. Killing, dismembering and devouring each other and making little hand-prints in human blood.

Freddy is asleep on the floor of the car. The *Dry World* DVD is still running. I don't bother waking him, but drive straight to the police station. If she isn't there, I'll go to the hospital. That is my strategy. It's the only one I can think of. I park and lock Freddy in. It's a risk. There is a 40 to 60 per cent chance that he'll wake up and panic. But I have no choice.

'I'm looking for Naomi Benjamin, from Battersea Care Unit. I gather she's here.' The policewoman at the reception desk scrolls through a file on the computer. I see Naomi's name before she does. I also register the context.

Charge: sabotage.

Can Naomi really have deactivated the door codes and let the children loose? If she succumbed to whatever madness overcame

Sunny and Jonas and Farooq and de Vries, then maybe the answer
to that question is yes. But it's none the less unthinkable. Or could
it be that she feared what would happen to them if they stayed? I
need to know.

The policewoman asks, 'Are you her lawyer?'

I'm not cut out for deception. But there aren't many options. I
select the best. I point to the folder I'm carrying. 'I need to speak
to her right away.'

'Interview room's second door on the right.'

I try not to run there. I am a lawyer now. Lawyers don't run. Not
in the course of duty. It's mostly a desk job.

The door has a small reinforced window through which I can
see the back of Naomi's head. She's sitting in a chair opposite a
female police officer who is writing notes. I knock. The WPC
looks up. She is freckle-faced and fair-haired and young. She can't
be more than twenty. She says, 'Come in'.

I enter and wave the folder. 'I'm representing Naomi Benjamin.'

'Well I hope you can get some sense out of her,' sighs the young
policewoman, getting to her feet. 'She's not exactly co-operating.'

Naomi hasn't turned. She is sitting very rigidly. There is something odd about her posture.

'Naomi,' I say. She doesn't react, so I move closer. She's looking straight ahead. No smile. I miss her smile, and the two shallow
brackets around it. I need to see them. I want to kiss her.

'Can I have a minute alone with her?'

'Sure. You can have five. She's all yours.'

When the WPC has gone I squat next to Naomi's chair and
take her hand, but immediately I drop it. It's cold. Far colder than

it should be. Can shock do that? I must look it up. I stroke her hair instead. Beautiful hair. Smooth and strong.

'Professor Whybray's dead,' I tell her. 'Trampled. The children did it. They crushed out his life.'

She nods and blinks.

'Did you let them escape?' She looks around the room and then slowly nods.

'Why?'

'Because there's one in here.' She whispers, pointing to her chest.

'What do you mean?'

'It got in,' she whispers. 'I did what it wanted. I had to.'

'What do you mean?' I whisper back, my mouth close to her ear, her silky hair in my face.

'Freddy was right. We belong to the Old World. Time doesn't work the way you think. They've come back to stop us.'

Slowly she pushes me back, raises her hand, and makes a fist next to her eye.

'No. Don't do that. Please Naomi. Don't.' I grab her head and clutch it to my chest.

But she keeps her hand there, fingers splayed. I can't stand this. I grab hold of her fingers and press them to my face. Her flesh feels well below thirty-seven degrees. It feels cold as stone. Suddenly, my breathing goes haywire and ugly noises start pouring out of me. My eyes fill with liquid that runs down my face. It's like another tear-gas attack. Naomi just looks at me with a very gentle smile. Both hands are on her lap now. It's a modest pose, the pose of the Madonna in Italian paintings. She doesn't say anything. I grab her around the waist. I want to carry her away from this place. I

283

bury my face in her stomach, her breasts. The terrible noises keep coming. I can't stop them.

I'm not aware of the door opening. The young policewoman takes my elbow. She pulls me to my feet and hands me a tissue. I blow my nose, then shove it to my eyes.

She puts a hand on my shoulder.

'You're not a lawyer, are you,' she says. 'I mean, you're not behaving like one.'

'No.'

'Then I think you'd better go.'

Back in the car, I try to get my breathing back to normal. But I can't stop the hiccuping, or the snot, or the tears that keep coming. Freddy wakes. I tell him to stay under the blanket until I say he can come out. He doesn't ask why I am crying. I sit there fighting it and losing.

We belong to the Old World. Time doesn't work the way you think. They've come back to stop us. What is that supposed to mean?

I start to drive. In the absence of traffic lights, I honk the horn at each crossing. But I don't obey the speed limit.

Fifteen minutes later, I let Freddy come out and sit on the back seat.

'Why can't we go to the Unit?'

'Because it's closed. There's been a problem.'

'Where are the others?'

'They left.'

'Where to?'

'I don't know.'

'Well we have to find them.'

'I'm sorry Freddy K. We can't.'

'Let me out!' He reaches for the door.

I slam down the child lock and keep driving.

He starts to cry.

I don't care. I don't care about anything. I am a robot made of meat.

I stop at a corner shop, get out and lock Freddy in the car again. They have supplies, the man says.

'I do boxes. With tins, if that's what you're after.' He looks at me sideways. 'But it'll cost.'

I give him all my cash.

I don't notice the figure on the roof of the tower block opposite right away. I'm too busy loading the boxes into the car.

But a distinctive noise makes me look up.

SCHTUKKK.

There is a connection I should be making, but I don't.

Then the noise comes again – *SCHTUKKK* – and I realise. There's a sniper. And his gun's aimed at Freddy. The boy hasn't noticed. He's still on the back seat, deep in his DVD, in the world of sand and snakes. I want to stay there and rock, gathering my thoughts. But that's not going to work. I can tell.

So I yell at Freddy to get down, hurl myself into the car and drive.

My heart is banging. I am overloaded. For once, mental origami is no help. The paper resists me, crumpling at the first touch.

★   ★   ★

Three hours and nineteen minutes later, when I stop for petrol on the M1, I manage to unclasp my fingers from the wheel. They are pale and stiff, as though they have been deep-frozen.

Half an hour later, eighteen army trucks pass us in the opposite direction.

And I know, definitively: a new phase of human history has begun.

CHAPTER 16

I USED TO imagine Freddy coming to live with me on Arran, in the cottage by the sea. I'd point out how the colours of the scrubland change by the minute, flashing their way through the spectrum according to the cast of the sun. He'd see how the salt sparkles on the sheer granite boulder after a storm. We'd walk beyond the cove as far as the wind turbines, and I'd explain their aerodynamics and engineering: he'd listen for a bit, then scramble up the hill by the ruined cairn, shrieking into the wind at the top of his lungs. We'd make kites, hunt for edible berries and fungi, construct driftwood boats to float in rock pools, identify bird-calls, build bonfires to grill the mackerel we'd caught, read books bursting with facts.

But nothing's as I thought.

A month has passed since we left London: soon winter will be setting in. My decision to move to the island after splitting up with Kaitlin was fuelled by an urge to be isolated and alone. But I see now that being encircled by sea gives us an advantage over main-landers at a time when containment is vital. Arraners have always known how to subsist on what there is. Once the fuel supplies have run out and the ferry to the mainland stops, they will have no choice but to resurrect the habits and lifestyle of their ancestors: hunting, fishing, trapping, sheep-shearing, planting and harvesting crops according to the season.

To the rear of the cottage, behind the jumble of rusted tractor parts there's an overgrown patch of land that was once cultivated. In the summer, the purple balls of onion heads and potato flow-ers stood tall among the weeds; now, they're flattened and rotting. Here's where I'll plant my amaranth, in honour of Jonas Svensson. Here's where I'll experiment with salt-resistant crops. I'm digging the soil over, a few square metres a day, before winter hardens it. Repetitive movements soothe me. While I dig, Freddy pulls out worms from the freshly turned earth, or wanders further off and rakes in the heather, returning with the bones and skulls of birds, voles, weasels, rats and mice. With his agile, filthy hands he assem-bles them into crude necklaces, adding twigs, berries and snail shells which he secures on nylon fishing string or horse hair he's picked from barbed wire. Other times, he likes to burrow about in the scrubland on the far side of the bluff, collecting beetles, spiders and larvae of all kinds. Or he'll scour the beach for crabs, shrimp, seaweed. It would be futile to try and stop him devour-ing what he forages. He knows what he needs, in the world he inhabits.

★   ★   ★

The morning after Freddy and I arrived, I showed him where the fish lived. Together we scooped the chickweed out of the bathtub and decanted the creature into a bucket. The rubber plug was still functional: I pulled it free, sluicing the stinking water on to the mud below so we could right the tub properly on its supporting stacks of bricks. We wiped the enamel down, replaced the plug and filled the tub with rainwater from the butt. Once the sediment had settled, we put the goldfish back. There was damage to one of its trailing fins and what looked like a tumour by its eye. But it held Freddy's attention – or seemed to, until I suggested we give it a name. He used to like christening things.

But he just looked at me blankly. I might have been from another planet.

Since then, communication has been minimal, as if he has moved to a realm where he simply has no need of the conversations I offer. But there are occasions when he'll be preoccupied with something – a dried-out jellyfish, a daddy-long-legs, a maggot – and I'll catch him unawares, and get a short flow of speech. It never lasts long.

The first time it happened was when I was digging. As I bashed flints out of clods of cold earth, I told him about the belief that if you make a thousand *ozuru*, your dream will come true. I recounted the story of the Japanese girl who got radiation cancer from Hiroshima.

'She folded and folded until she had a thousand cranes and then she made her wish. Which was to be cured. But when she found out that couldn't happen, she wished for world peace instead.'

That didn't materialise either. But I didn't tell him.

'I'm going to make a thousand *ozuru*,' said Freddy, pulling a worm from the soil. I wasn't expecting him to respond: my heart crashed about. The worm coiled and uncoiled between his finger and thumb. He wiped it clean.

'What will you wish for?'

No reply. I asked again. But he just stood there and chewed his worm.

Later, I asked myself why I hadn't pressed him further. Why I kept digging instead, harder and harder, working up a furious rhythm, concentrating on what I'd plant in the spring and summer: root vegetables, runner beans, tomatoes, aubergines, a few varieties of pumpkin, some soy.

The answer is that I get overloaded. I am slow to take things in. I know when I am not ready.

I wasn't ready. So I dug.

Soon I must acknowledge the thing he craves so badly. He is a child. He wants to be with others like him. According to all the books I have read by paediatricians, it is normal for them to seek the company of their peers.

But the thought of losing him again kills me. This is, of course, a figure of speech. I will remain alive. But I will not know happiness.

As for myself, I try to eliminate all but the useful memories of what life was like before. By which I mean those that can provide clues as to what has happened, and help me map out a future worthy of the name.

Routines help. So does planning.

I order supplies by phone. Seeds and tubers to plant, an array of animal traps, a gun for shooting rabbit and deer, some sacks of seed, a good stock of tins. A man who doesn't ask questions drops a box at the gate when I need him to. By springtime, I'll have no further need of his services. There are three feral groups on the island, he told me. All native kids. 'And we protect our own.' It was meant as a warning – he'd seen the gun – but it came as a relief. From the local adults at least, Freddy will be safe.

There's no internet any more, and little in the way of media coverage since the military took over on the mainland. Inevitably, things are far worse there. This is confirmed occasionally when there's a phone signal, and Ashok rings. His tone is angry and unsettled. He's frustrated that there's no role for the man who could once shine the hot light of a business idea through any prism. The fact that capitalism has become 'a dirty word' enrages him. He'll find his place, I am sure of it. But it may not lie where he hopes. He's doing 'a shit-load of figuring out' what he's got 'to put on the table', he reports. 'Things suck here, you did well to get away. Just keep your head down, keep Freddy safe and wait it out. The child attacks are dying off, but the sabotages, they're *rife*, man. And the kiddie-camps are full. Nobody asks what goes on inside them. Or what drug combination you use against so-called evil. Or what effect it has. And you don't even want to know what's happening in China. Anyway, take care of yourself, bud. Did you hear that Steph's taken over Old Man Whybray's post? Let's stay in touch.'

The professor's death has not sunk in. Perhaps it never will. The thought of his bloodied, open-mouthed corpse lying on the floor of the corridor at the Unit returns to me daily, sometimes hourly.

And it does so in such vivid detail that I could tell you the exact shade of every element of it.

In the drawer of my desk, on top of the sheets of origami paper I have pre-creased according to Robert J. Lang's instructions, lies the professor's notebook. Sometimes I need to read his words over and over again. Other times, I am not in the mood to, because his reflections are as demanding and as complex as Lang's folds. So I work with paper instead. I can get so absorbed that I don't notice the hours pass. This is good.

Later, I'll lie in bed trying to make sense of what he wrote, travelling miles on my restless legs.

Human history is a juggernaut. If it's to change direction, it must first come to a stop. If our visitors believe the destruction of the world we have built is a prerequisite of humankind's continued existence on the planet, no wonder their occupation is so brutal. It needs to be.

His handwriting is neat and precise: the handwriting of one uncorrupted by keyboard use.

People think ghosts are from the past, Sunny Chen said in his testimony to Hesketh. Quote: 'We think they are all dead. But they are alive. And some of them are not even born yet. They are travellers . . . They go wherever they like.'

So where is it transmitting from, this occupying force? And what is its mission?

Hesketh asks what mythology the afflicted ones are replicating. But that begs the question: why should we imagine they are replicating what has gone before? And why must we assume it is 'mythology' at all?

There is a lot more in this vein. Much of it is highly speculative and emotional. The idea of a 'hypothetical world' he posited that day in Ashok's office is taken much further. Like me, the professor was interested in the neutrino experiments – what scientist wouldn't be – but the conclusions he drew made me wonder whether he was ill when he wrote them. I don't like to consider the possibility that my mentor became unstable. Especially now that he is dead and I have no way of ascertaining precisely what he meant.

The idea that the children have indeed travelled – not forward in space, but backwards across time – is as heroic as it is unthinkable. But how else to explain their creeping occupation of our world?

What if they are indeed a manifestation of man's own possible future? And that they have come not to 'haunt' us (as superstitious minds might insist), but instead, to simply show us – in only part of its full horror – the legacy our era will leave them, if our despoliation of Earth continues unchecked? If so, one can see their arrival as a desperate attempt to avert that future, by stopping it in its tracks.

It seems counter-intuitive to salute the children for what they have done, given the destructiveness of their methods. But instinct has its imperatives. And so does DNA. Can we blame them for craving survival, when that survival is that of our own descendants too?

When he speculated about a new paradigm that day in Ashok's office, I dismissed it as 'fanciful'. It never struck me that I might be wrong to. The final entry in Professor Whybray's notebook is very short.

We are a species in crisis: a species on the brink of collapse. If this is crisis intervention, then I am glad to have seen the start of it, however appalling its immediate consequences. Yet I fear that of all the people on the planet, my beloved Hesketh will be the very last to understand: the last to make the leap of faith that's needed. His need for proof blinds him.

This is very painful for me to read. He always praised my cast of mind. Yet here, in black and white, he condemns it. If a 'leap of faith' is required, how does one go about taking one? And to where must one leap? I would like to show the contents of Professor Whybray's notebook to Einstein, or Plato, or some of the physicists from CERN or the High Energy Research Organisation in Japan, whose job is charting and assessing the unseen. But in their absence I must make do with the only expert I have access to: a boy of seven.

'Freddy K, go and fetch some old newspaper from that pile over there.' I point. He looks blank. I'm about to give up and try later when I see him give the little shudder I recognise: a sign that he is switching mode. 'Freddy K. We're going to make the world. Your world, not the old one.'

'OK.'

'Are there trees?'

'Just dead ones.'

'So get some twigs.'

Soon he's at work on a hawthorn branch. While he's busy, I fold half a dozen origami men, on the same model as the one I made for Sunny Chen. I remember there's a sack of sand among the rusted farm machinery. I haul it to the porch and spread it out by the doorstep, and sprinkle some coarse dishwasher salt on top.

There. A sparkling white desert that looks like Heaven. Freddy is immediately excited. He doesn't say anything, but he rushes to gather up the origami figures and the makeshift trees.

'So what next?' I ask.

He plants the twigs first, in clusters. 'Scissors,' he says.

When I hand them over he calmly begins snipping my origami figures into pieces.

'What are you doing?'

He digs a shallow hole and throws them in. 'They die.'

'Who?'

'People. They get sick. From poison and the sun. Their eyes pop. Then they die and we bury them in salt. And when they're ready we dig them up. For eating.' He throws a handful of sand and salt over the chopped pieces.

'That's a sad story, Freddy.'

'It's not a story.'

'But if it was, how would it go after that?' His face changes again. As if sleepwalking, he gets down from the table and opens the front door. 'Freddy K?' A blast of freezing air rushes in as he steps outside, still barefoot. He never wears shoes any more and I have stopped trying to make him. 'Freddy!' We were getting somewhere: I can't let him go now. 'So what happens next, Freddy?' He doesn't respond. 'How does the story go?'

It seems like an innocent question, but I have said the wrong thing, because he whips round and shouts: 'I told you, it's not a story! You're not listening! It happens!'

He runs around the back of the house, picks up a rock and smashes the ice on the bath tub, then starts hauling out the huge shards. They clatter to the ground, falling next to his red bare feet. I take a deep breath and shout back.

'*What* happens, Freddy. Tell me!'

Frenzied, he grabs the chain and pulls out the bath plug: instantly, the freezing liquid glugs down the plughole and waterfalls down on to the icy mud, leaving the goldfish flipping about on the white enamel base in a swirl of mud. Then, too fast for me to react, Freddy has reached in, grabbed the creature, stuffed it into his mouth and run off.

Indoors, freezing, I strip off and dry myself. Then I go upstairs and sit on my bed and rock.

It's not a story, Freddy said. It happens.

But when, and where, and why?

The soil is rock hard, but I dig it anyway because the fight of it soothes me. Darkness is closing in. You can see the dance of will-o'-the-wisp as the bog exhales its methane into the air, mixing with the distant froth of the shore. I stare at the silhouettes of clouds drifting across the horizon. I try to see the story Freddy is telling: the one he insists is not a story, but reality.

Once upon a time the Earth we know went amok: hurricanes crossing vast oceans; coasts drowned; lowlands steeped in salt; landscapes baked to desert; aquifers welling up and crystallising. *Salt is born of the purest parents.* Too much sun, too much sea. White Death. The Swiss demographer's conference: *The Perfect Storm: Climate, Hunger and Population.*

A species in crisis. The exponential growth phase giving way to the stationary and death phases. The curve's end: the collapse of humankind that Professor Whybray wrote of in his notebook. And the aftermath?

A place my boy knows well. A place he feels at home. A land of insects and dried seaweed, of stockpiled tins from a bygone era which this version of himself never even knew. Poison and sun-blindness. Mass death, mass graves of salted meat. And when the last food is gone, only one way to assuage the hunger.

Majd. Ikenie.

The eating of each other. And then fewer of them still.

Until – the opposite of a Creation myth: just one is left. And then none.

The children's story is the story of man's end on Earth.

An hour later he's standing next to me, peeling the bark off a stick. Barefoot, as usual, despite the cold.

'Freddy. The hand-print you make. What does it mean?'

'Stop. It means we want you to stop.'

'Stop what?'

He shrugs and throws down his stick. 'Everything grown-ups do. Everything you did, when you were alive. Everything you did before you died.'

'We're dead?'

'You're from the Old World. Same thing.'

'You say we want you to stop. Who's we?'

He shrugs. 'Me and the other kids. We have the same blood.'

'So where do you come from?'

'The place you are before you're born. And after you're dead.'

'But you're alive Freddy. You're here with me. We're both alive.'

He shakes his head. 'No. You're dead. This feels like now, for you. But it's a zillion years ago.'

. . . beloved Hesketh . . . the very last to understand: the last to make the leap of faith . . . His need for proof blinds . . .

The Venns erupt in my head. Circles within circles. Fairy rings. Neutrinos. I lean harder on my spade and start to rock. The CERN experiment represented a seismic breakthrough in our grasp of the universe. Can undreamed-of dimensions be fused, in times of crisis, to the dimensions we know? Can a child be in two realms of time at once? Quantum physics would say yes. When the professor spoke of an 'occupation' he was being serious. But I dismissed it.

We belong to the Old World, said Naomi. *Time doesn't work the way you think. They've come back to stop us.*

I remember a day in London, Ashok silhouetted against the sky, ranting.

Look what's happening to growth! How can anything be rebuilt or even survive, when industry's being sabotaged on this kind of scale?

Growth. Progress. More. Newer.

The Holy Grail.

Look behind and you shall be turned into a pillar of salt.

Beloved Hesketh, he called me. But it took Freddy to show me the thing I couldn't see. It is not a hypothetical world to them. It is as real as ours.

The question is not how they came. Let string theory work that out. The question is, how could they not?

After Freddy wanders off, I stay in the darkness for a long time, leaning on my spade.

A few days later we go for the walk I will come to think of as our last. There's a light rain.

The boy stops by the boulder that marks the sharp turn of the sheep-path and gazes up. The sunlight refracts in such a way that I don't see it at first. But then I do.

High at the top of the dark granite, the familiar image scrawled in white chalk.

The eye.

He has been summoned.

In the weeks that follow, there's a scenario I conjure as a comfort to myself. It comes to me when I sit at my desk, swivelling in my chair and watching the dancing shadows of the candle that I keep burning in the window just in case.

There is a sound that might be a tree branch banging against the door. But it's a knock. I open the door, and the professor is standing there, his hair and beard spangled with rain.

'I knew I'd find you here, boy,' he says.

I remind him I am thirty-six. Then I show him around the cottage, warning him to mind his head on the beams. He smiles when he sees the antique optometrist's charts he gave me all those years ago. He inspects my dictionary collection and applauds my shelving system, noting what's arranged on it, and in what configuration. And I show him the hermit crab.

'It's nearly finished,' I tell him. He admires the intricacy of the legs and eye-stalks. The way they emerge so neatly from the shiny concertinaed shell. I explain some of Lang's origami principles. 'When I complete it, it's for you. A gift. I wish I could have done it when you were still alive. But I wasn't ready. I'm sorry about that. I'm sorry I was the last person on earth to understand. You were right. About the new paradigm.'

'I know. I'm glad you saw it. I didn't think you would.'

'Freddy showed me.'

'We make a good threesome.'

'He's gone.'

'But he'll be back. When they've finished what they came to do. When mankind has changed enough. When the new course is set. You know that, Hesketh.'

'Do I?'

'You tell me.'

'Hoping and believing aren't the same.'

He smiles. 'No. But you can make them be. So when will you finish this famous hermit crab of yours?'

'When I've got past hoping. And seen beyond.'

More and more, I think about the never-ending universe of things that man does not know.

If the old Freddy were here, he would say, 'Yet'.

But there is no Freddy any more. He is off with the fairies.

And what does 'yet' mean, now that time has a whole new meaning?

I love him, no matter what. I know that. But what does a man do with such a love? No stories I know can tell me how this ends.

But all flow charts contain a range of possible outcomes, so I have a set of hopes. And some things are already clearly foreseeable. The process of recalibration is quietly under way on Arran. When people dare to breed here again their offspring will be fewer, and better cherished. This new generation will learn that it was children like themselves who halted the juggernaut at the brink of the abyss. That they did not come all this way to destroy us. They came as saviours, bearing the undeserved and astonishing gift of a second chance. And that it is thanks to them that we discovered a new metaphysics of being. I am not a great communicator. But in the work I plan to write, I will try to convey this. I will dedicate it to Professor Whybray, and to Freddy.

I walk on the shore, alone, listening for the cry of the black guillemot.

Lately, more rain has been falling, borne by a fresh spate of hurricanes in the mid-Atlantic. The wind picks up moisture from the ocean and hurls it far inland.

Then, one day, I see him. He's just a dot in the distance, but I know it's him, even before I lift my binoculars. I adjust the focus. All that's left of his clothing is a pair of pants and a torn vest.

'Freddy!' I shout. But he's too far away to hear me.

They all are.

Twenty or thirty of them are coming into view, shoaling by the black stone, naked or in rags, with clumps of salty bladderwrack on their heads and wet ribbons of seaweed or strings of bones around their necks. The lenses of their dark glasses flash weakly in the fading light. Their little bodies are skinny and streaked with grime. Their fingernails are black. Their dry, sunburned skin twinkles with crystals of salt. The crusted-up wings of insects and the legs of miniature sand-crabs cling to the edges of their mouths.

The hidden internal folds of an origami model in progress operate like flower buds or the folded wings of a bird. When you open them out, their intended shape, and their place in the whole and their function, become clear and true.

In that moment, when hope becomes belief, there is enlightenment.

The next morning, with the high, bright sun illuminating my desk, I complete the last fold of the hermit crab.

Outside, I turn my face to the wind and feel the salt mist on my face.

And I am filled with something I can hesitantly call joy.

ACKNOWLEDGEMENTS

No book of mine is ever completed without a huge amount of help from friends, family and colleagues who read the manuscript at different stages. *The Uninvited* is no exception. I owe a huge debt to Polly Coles, Amanda Craig, Gina de Ferrer, Humphrey Hawksley, Ide Hejlskov, Sally Holloway, Carsten Jensen, Tom Jensen, Claire Letemendia, Annette Lindegaard, Kate O'Riordan, Matthew Quick and Ian Steadman, for their sharp critical eyes and generous encouragement.

My thanks also go to Marika Cobbold, Raphaël Coleman, Adam Grydehøj, Bill Hartston and Felicity Steadman for their specialist input on matters as varied as Swedish vocabulary, action scenes, folklore, Venn diagrams and industrial relations.

And I am deeply grateful to Clare Alexander, Lesley Thorne and Sally Riley of Aitken Alexander, and to Alexandra Pringle and Erica Jarnes at Bloomsbury for their support, patience and inspiring feedback during the editing process.

A NOTE ON THE AUTHOR

Liz Jensen is the bestselling author of seven acclaimed novels, including the *Guardian* Fiction Award-shortlisted *Ark Baby*, *War Crimes for the Home*, *The Ninth Life of Louis Drax* and, most recently, *The Rapture*, shortlisted for the Brit Writers' Awards and selected as a Channel 4 TV Book Club Best Read. She has been nominated three times for the Orange Prize for Fiction and her work has been published in more than twenty countries. She lives in London.

The text of this book is set in Bembo. This type was first used in 1495 by the Venetian printer Aldus Manutius for Cardinal Bembo's *De Aetna*, and was cut for Manutius by Francesco Griffo. It was one of the types used by Claude Garamond (1480–1561) as a model for his Romain de L'Université, and so it was the fore-runner of what became standard European type for the following two centuries. Its modern form follows the original types and was designed for Monotype in 1929.